The Paraclete Conundrum

by

Emily Sutherland

HELOISE'S STORY

A storm, fiercer than any I had ever remembered woke me. Trees thrashing about by the wind, lightning forking across the dark sky; thunder, peal on peal, like the cries of the doomed. As suddenly as it began, it stopped. All was quiet except for the hoot of an owl. Our abbey creaked back into peaceful slumber, but I lay awake, inexplicably apprehensive, for who knew what the morrow would bring.

What did I fear? I was the head of a successful abbey, the Paraclete, named for the Holy Spirit. I still desperately missed Abelard but I no longer considered myself only in terms of the love I held for him. My writings were acknowledged and my advice accepted. No longer 'Abelard's whore', but a 'pious and wise' abbess. I felt more comfortable with the former title, although the latter, while undeserved, had its advantages.

Life here is peaceful, sheltered from distractions, or that is the intention. The main buildings are set back a little from the road, while a stone wall marks our boundaries. There are gates in those walls for the field workers, and a main gate for visitors. The outside world passes outside the walls, but it does not disturb our routine of prayer, study and labour. On market days the road rumbles and rattles with bustle and noise. From early morning the procession of women carrying baskets of eggs or bags of spun wool begins, then men leading livestock, and children under the feet of everybody. When they return in the afternoon it is easy to tell from their voices if they have had a good day or not. Musicians come by, beating drums, playing flutes or singing. Travellers ring the bell that hangs outside the main gate, asking for a night's shelter. Families bring sick children to our infirmary. Women who are barren beg for herbs to help them conceive. Men need our healing for different complaints: pains in their limbs, ulcers or fever, the inability to satisfy a woman.

At the time my story begins there were others on that road, men returning from fighting in the holy lands. A few fortunate ones rode by on horses, leading mules laden with booty. The others were ragged and destitute. These would ask for food and prayers. Some of my sisters had fathers or brothers or husbands who had died on that ill-fated pilgrimage. They wept when they saw these men, broken in body and spirit. If God had been on the side of the Christians it was not evident in these remnants of a once mighty force.

The gatehouse, a long narrow room with a double window in the centre, built over the main entrance gate, allows the sister on duty to see whose hand has rung our bell. If you stand at either side of the windows you can see the road from different directions. One side gives a good distance but the other is restricted because of the curve in the road. A minor problem, for it takes only a few seconds to hurry down the stairs and open the gate. Sister Christine normally attended the gate but her hurrying days were long past, so at times I took her place, to allow her to rest. This was a pleasure, not a penance, as it gave me a chance to write letters or read. It also allowed me a glimpse of my old life. Not that farming and markets were of my world. My childhood years had been spent in the abbey at Argenteuil and, as a young woman, my life centred on my uncle's house in Paris. It might be more accurate to say that by then my world centred on Abelard. Over twenty years ago it was, and yesterday.

On the day after the storm I sat there, too distracted to read the book in front of me. Sun was now shining through the window, shaded by oak trees that flanked the road. The light through the trees created a dappled effect on the small table, moving as the wind stirred the leaves of the trees. Watching it I thought of Astralabe, as a small baby, reaching out to try to catch a sunbeam. Abelard laughed and said that our son was a seeker after light. That was on the day he had come from Paris to his family estate, where our baby had been born, to tell me we had to be married. I did not wish to be married, and told him so, but he persisted and insisted. These memories from my turbulent past came, intemperate and unwelcome. The sound of the bell recalled me to the present. Wiping my eyes quickly I looked out to see three people at the gate. A woman, sitting on a mule, so stooped and hunched over that I thought she might be very ill or wounded, a young nun standing on one side of her and a monk on the other as though, without their support, she would fall. The older woman then dismounted with some help. She did not collapse in a heap on the ground, as I half expected her to do, but shook herself a little, stretched and with an effort straightened, smiling her thanks. I saw then that she, too, was a nun.

As I opened the gate and greeted them the older woman came forward.

'I am Mother Hildegard from the monastery of St Disibodenberg, near Bingen, in Germany. This is Sister Elizabeth, and Brother Volmar. We've come to seek the advice of your abbess.'

Then she looked at me intently. 'I see you are Abbess Heloise.'

At the time I wondered how she had known. Later I realised that Hildegard saw and knew many things that others did not.

'Abbess, I hope that we may stay with you for some days. We have come, guided by the living Light, to speak to you about the letter Bernard of Clairvaux has written. He is a good and holy man. This I know for certain. But the words he has written in this letter, if all I hear is true, are not. This troubles me, as it must trouble you. I've travelled through mountain passes, down rivers, along dangerous paths, to seek your help and to offer mine. Together we can plan what should we do.'

I could see that she was exhausted, but I felt that her distress went beyond the rigours of travel. Later I found that I was correct. My own difficulty was that, far from having any plan, I had no idea what she was talking about. I glanced at Volmar, who seemed to understand my problem, for he indicated that he would explain everything to me later.

'We *will* speak of all this in good time, Mother Hildegard. Now you and your companions need to rest. Your journey has been a long, and I can well imagine, an arduous one,' I said.

Although St Benedict writes that we must take all visitors first to the chapel to pray I thought that this woman, rigid with exhaustion, needed only to place her head upon a pillow. In truth she hesitated at the foot of the steps that lead up to the abbey, and might have stumbled had not Sister Elizabeth caught her arm. I decided to take Hildegard to our best room, the one that Abelard had used when he stayed here. Prayers could come later.

We had kept Abelard's room exactly as he had
arranged it, as though he might rise from his tomb and
be found sitting near the window, a book resting on his
knees. His special chair, donated by a duchess, had
comfortable cushions and ornate carved arms. Abelard
declared it too grand for a humble monk, but sat there
all the same. The bed, placed against the opposite wall,
was larger than most, again to suit the frame of my
'humble monk'. One of the sisters had woven a cover
for him from the wool of our sheep. The pillow smelt of
lavender. Scent from the roses, still in bloom,
gladdened the room. Hildegard, as she entered, turned
to me with a smile, gesturing her gratitude with a vague
movement of her hands.

No sooner were they settled and I had returned to the
gatehouse when I heard a great commotion. Trumpets
blared, horses galloped and wheeled in front of the gate
raising stones and dust as they halted, then moved back.
More horses followed, at a trot. Men's voices shouted
orders. Then what sounded like baskets, dozens of
them, being placed on the ground. A goose honked. A
goose? These were no ordinary visitors, but the group
had finally stopped just out of my line of sight, no
matter where I positioned myself, so I waited.

A young woman came to the gate, escorted by two men.
Again I hurried down the stairs and just as she rang the
bell I opened the gate.

'Sister,' she said, 'I've come to demand shelter for my
lady and for myself and for as many of her servants as
are necessary,'

'Request!' called a voice. 'Respectfully request. And I
need to speak urgently to the Abbess.'

The young woman, quite pretty except that one eye seemed to be slightly smaller than the other, blushed and sighed.

'I beg you to forgive me. We respectfully request that my lady may spend some time within the walls of your abbey. She desires to consult with the Abbess. About the letter.'

'Don't bother the simple sister who looks after the gate, you ninny. I'll speak to the Abbess about this letter at the appropriate time. All we want is to be given entrance. And to stretch my legs after being on this wretched horse.' That voice again. An impatient exclamation followed, and then I saw a woman, dressed in a cloth of gold over a cream underskirt, striding towards me.

'I do not choose to be announced except to say that I am here to speak with Abbess Heloise,' she said.

My first thought was that she was one of the most impressive women I had ever seen. Taller than I am, but no slimmer and about twenty years younger, elegant in every way except for the small golden red curls which refused to be hidden by her head covering. It wasn't just her beauty. Women can be beautiful but boring. It was the aura of energy, a slight arrogance but also humour which appealed. It was a face and presence that once encountered would not be forgotten and I remembered that had seen her before, many years ago. As a young bride she and her husband, the King of France she had ridden past our monastery on their way to Troyes.

'Your majesty is most welcome. We are honoured by your presence,' I said, giving a small bob. Did one bow or curtsey? 'I am Abbess Heloise.'

Who would have expected Eleanor of Aquitaine, then Queen of France, now Queen of England, and Hildegard of Bingen, visionary and musician, accepted as a prophetic writer by the Pope, to visit the Paraclete? And at the same time.

Unlike Hildegard the Queen showed no signs of fatigue. When I had introduced myself she replied, almost abruptly.

'You recognize me dressed like this?'

'The Queen of France is not unknown, even in these parts,' I replied.

'I did not think my messengers could have arrived so far ahead of me. You are most gracious to be waiting to greet me.'

I bowed my head, not wishing to explain further.

'You must be aware, esteemed Abbess, of the threat to our liberty, yours and mine,' the Queen continued. 'I decided to come to you, as a humble pilgrim, incognito, because of Bernard of Clairvaux. I entreat your discretion and your assistance. I'm quite desperate.'

Rather than desperation, Eleanor exuded authority and confidence. Echoing the words of Mother Hildegard, the Queen had said, 'because of Bernard' also clearly thinking that I knew what she meant.

'In deference to your vow of poverty I have travelled with the minimum,' she announced, as what seemed to be a small army, bearing not weapons but bags of fruit, wine and bulky hunks of salted meat wrapped in hessian, and one live goose struggling as a young boy, hardly bigger than the bird, tried to control it, stood in a line behind her stretching beyond the curve of the wall.

'But, being aware of that vow, I have provided some few provisions, not wishing to cause you or your good sisters any inconvenience.'

That this ensured that the Queen suffered no deprivation was understood.

I was appalled. How long did she wish to stay? Were we equipped to offer hospitality to royalty? And what was Bernard planning? Nothing that would please me, I imagined. The gateway was not the place to admit ignorance, especially not to so illustrious a visitor, but I resolved to find out everything as soon as I could. Without waiting for my response Eleanor strode towards the abbey. Her maid, taking two steps to Eleanor's one, kept up with difficulty. Despite her repeated insistence that she wished to 'be nothing but a humble visitor', the Queen could not hide her dismay when she saw her room. This guest room was smaller and even more simply furnished than the one where Hildegard now rested, but I was loath to dislodge one sent by the living Light.

'I knew that nuns were supposed to live simply,' said Eleanor with a slight sniff. 'You call this room a cell I believe. Apt.' Then she turned towards me and smiled, her face softening. 'No matter, I'm grateful to you for allowing me a few days retreat.'

Eleanor, Queen of France, Duchess of Aquitaine. In looks she most certainly did not rank lowest. I wondered about the extent of her learning.

*　　　*　　　*

It was Brother Volmar who, that evening, told me what Bernard planned for me and all other women in religious houses. At first I felt that sinking sick feeling one experiences on hearing very bad news. My next emotions were despair, then anger. I was more than ready to confer immediately with my two visitors if such a meeting would help, but I did not meet with Eleanor or Hildegard until the following morning. Even

then we did not refer to Bernard's letter. Was it
because its contents were so terrible that no one wanted
to actually put it into words?

Eleanor obviously resented Hildegard's presence and
Hildegard gave no indication that she was pleased to
see the Queen. I could understand Eleanor feeling
disgruntled at not having my exclusive attention. As
was made clear in the politest possible way, Hildegard
was not happy that we were three, rather than two. Her
attitude displeased me. All visitors must be greeted with
charity and respect, but a royal visitor demands this in
abundance. Would Hildegard have reacted more
graciously if it were her abbey being so honoured?
During that first simple meal, eaten in a room separate
from the nun's refectory, we spoke to each other quite
formally. I felt restricted, physically and emotionally.
Abelard had used this room for his meals, and as a big
man he had fitted quite neatly behind the table in a
large chair against the far wall. He was only one person.
With three of us it felt crowded, but it was not possible
to invite Eleanor to eat in the larger refectory with our
community if she were to remain, as she wished,
incognito.

A tense atmosphere. Hildegard said little and Eleanor
said a great deal, mostly about the holy lands from
where she had very recently returned. Stories of travels
to such exciting places are fascinating and at any other
time I would have asked her many questions. More
immediate concerns blunted my curiosity.

Hildegard looked restored after her night's sleep, and
she said as much, claiming that she had drifted off to
the sound of the breezes through the rushes, and
awakened to the songs of birds. She had missed the bell
calling her to prayer, and the sounds of my sisters

singing during Lauds but she would join us
tomorrow morning. She made no mention of missing
Matins, and who could blame her? Who wants to be
dragged from a deep sleep in the middle of the night,
after a tiring journey, to kneel in a draughty chapel? As
though reading my thoughts, she added, 'I did sit in that
very comfortable chair by the window and made my
prayers to God'.

Eleanor lifted her head sharply. 'The chair in my cell
does not invite one to pray, or even sit. You are indeed
fortunate, Mother Hildegard. But no matter. I enjoy
enough comfort at the palace. A little austerity will not
harm me.'

'Indeed not, your majesty,' agreed Hildegard, with an
alacrity that bordered on the ungracious. I moved about
in my chair, knocking my elbow on the wall. We were
beginning very badly. Hildegard's expression indicated
both mischief and sympathy, but she broke the ensuing
silence.

'I'm looking forward to hearing your sisters sing,
especially those chants Abbot Peter Abelard composed.
I have also composed some music, which your sisters
will like to try if there is time to teach them one or two
hymns.'

It was strange to hear Abelard referred to as 'Abbot',
although strictly speaking he had never ceased to be the
Abbot of St Gildas. Did he go to Brittany to be near our
son? These considerations had been part of our
conversations in later years, and the thoughts were not
new to me. Neither did they take me anywhere I wished
to go. I returned my attention to my guests.

'I may attend the chapel sometimes, as well,' Eleanor
announced as though conferring a boon on both the

Almighty and the Paraclete. 'My husband is more inclined to prayer than I am. Strange that, in a man.'
'I have no husband to rival me in piety. My parents gave me to God at an early age,' said Hildegard.
'And that should be consort enough for any woman, Mother Hildegard,' replied Eleanor. 'My father gave me in marriage when I was still quite young, to Louis, who is, as you know, now the King. Next time, if there ever is a next time, the choice will be mine.'
I said, with more passion than I intended, 'I didn't choose Abelard as a husband. But when I was forced to marry him it ended in disaster. I knew it would.'
There was a pause in the conversation. The sunlight shone through the small high window behind me. Its rays formed a circle, almost like a halo, behind Hildegard. Unaware of her saintly appearance she broke the silence.
'And both of you are mothers.'
'A blessing, you might say.'
As both Eleanor and I responded at the same time it would have been hard for Hildegard to tell if this last remark was made sincerely or ironically. She just smiled serenely.
'As God wills.' Hildegard shifted slightly, giving her full attention to Eleanor. "Your majesty,' she said gently, 'it is a daughter you are carrying now.'
'Am I with child?' asked Eleanor, looking quite concerned. 'I suspected so but I wasn't positive. And a girl! You're sure it's a girl? Whatever was Eugenius thinking about?'
Whatever indeed? I was beginning to think the woman somewhat lacking equilibrium, having observed that she passed from excited to despondent, barely pausing on the gradient. Was she suggesting that Pope Eugenius

was the father of her child? Hildegard knew to what
she referred, however, as she nodded sympathetically.
'The Holy Father meant well, but there are some things
which men don't fully understand. Providing the bed is
not enough.'
'Providing a bed was more than enough. Decorated
with ribbons and holy pictures. He led us to the room,
prancing along like a madam in a bordello; Louis
grinning and capering behind him, reassured that this
time our coupling could not be called sinful as the Pope
himself had ordered it.'
'You conceived that night?' I asked.
'Not then, but it started a trend. Another daughter, you
say. No chance of error? A boy would wipe a few smug
sneers from sanctimonious faces, including Bernard's.
How can you be so sure?'
Hildegard answered that she just knew. The 'living
Light' told her, I supposed. There was more to it than
prophecy, I discovered, as she explained her theory.
'Conception is not a random thing. It depends on the
seasons and where the moon is in her cycle, so that
every single day of the year is different and significant.
God has ordained it so. I can explain it further if you
wish.'
The halo of sunlight had shifted slightly to one side,
reminding me that time was also moving.
'Perhaps later. We are facing a terrible threat to our
way of life, and this must be the subject of our
conversation,' I said, but I might have been speaking to
the small cherub sculpted near the doorway. The Queen
was avid for further details, and Hildegard was happy to
oblige her.
'Tell me,' Eleanor said, 'tell me at once, all you can.
Had I met you years ago my life may have turned out

very differently. You know I once spoke to Bernard
of Clairvaux about my distress at not bearing a child.'
'Yes, Bernard of Clairvaux,' I said. 'Perhaps you could
tell us all you know about this letter of his.'
An opening Eleanor chose to ignore.
'All Bernard could tell me was to stop meddling in
men's business and to pray more. Mind you, I did have
a baby after I took his advice, but only a daughter. That
man cheerfully prophesises death and destruction. Was
foretelling the right time to conceive a male heir
beyond him?' Eleanor's demeanour had changed from
regal to beguiling, inviting us to share her exasperation.
Hildegard resisted. 'Brother Bernard was right up to a
point. Sincere prayer is always good. So is penance and
self-denial, in moderation.' I became resigned to
making little progress as she began to explain her
theories on conception. Then there was a tentative
knock at the door, Adele entered, curtsied and
whispered something to Eleanor. The Queen's response
was loud and clear.
'The goose was a gift. I have no concern as to when it is
cooked. You're a goose to worry me with such things.
Never interrupt us again, unless it is with a message
from the King. Get out of my sight!' She raised her
hand as though to strike the girl. Hildegard lifted hers in
a placatory gesture. I would never have spoken to the
lowliest of our lay sisters in that tone, and searched for
some way to soften the reprimand. Adele stammered
and bobbed her way out of the room, near to tears, face
red. I was horrified when with a smile Eleanor turned
back to Hildegard, her eyes pinpoints of concentration,
and as thought there had been no interruption said,
'You were telling me how to bear a son.'

Hildegard smiled sympathetically at me, before responding. 'When a man in the emission of his strong seed and in proper kindly love for a woman goes to her and the woman also bears a proper love of the man at the same time, a male child is conceived. It cannot be otherwise than a male child for Adam was formed from clay, which is stronger material than flesh. And the male will be prudent and virtuous, since he was conceived in strong seed and in the proper kindly love which they both had for each other.'

'What if the man loves the woman more than she loves him?' Eleanor asked.

'Well, if this love is lacking in the woman toward the man, but the man has, in that hour, proper kindly love for the woman, and if the seed is strong, a male will still be conceived, because the kindly love of the man will prevail.'

'So why have I not borne a male child?' asked Eleanor. 'Louis loves me as dearly and properly as he is capable.'

'All Christian people know that,' agreed Hildegard.

'Doesn't that mean then that this child is a male? Even if I don't love Louis as much as he loves me?' challenged Eleanor, her full attention focused on the small figure dressed in the black Benedictine robe. It was Hildegard who now looked, suddenly, very majestic.

'Was his seed strong? There, I think, you will find is the problem.'

Eleanor clapped her hands together. 'And they blamed me! Said I was frivolous and worldly, too beautiful even, not devoted enough to my religious duties. It was his fault all along.' She stood up then as though to stride about the room. The smallness of the room

prevented her taking more than a step and she
abruptly sat down again.

God is in his heaven, I thought, but where in Benedict's
Holy Rule are there words to tell me how do deal with
these two women?

'If the woman loves the man and that love is proper
kindly love, even then, if the man's seed is weak, she
will bear a daughter. Better that than to have neither
parent feel love for each other, for then the seed is bitter
and there will be born a child of bitter temperament,'
Hildegard continued to explain.

'So I have told the King. We would be better parted. No
good has come from our marriage,' announced Eleanor,
now glaring at us as though we were responsible.

So I had told Peter Abelard. No good could come from
our marriage, despite our love for each other being so
strong. That love did not need to be ruled and regulated.
God blessed it through its strength.

'I can tell you one more thing,' said Hildegard. 'Your
daughter will resemble her father, as you are slender by
nature.'

'That, at least, will quieten tongues,' said Eleanor, with
her beautiful smile. Hildegard, leaning back in her
chair, smiled in return, and I found myself smiling at
both of them.

Who did my son Astralabe resemble? There was
something of both of us, as I remembered him, but I
had seen him so seldom that I could not be sure.

Abelard had been absolutely delighted that our child
was a boy. Not long after he was born we had sat, all
three of us, under an evening sky, still streaked with
rosy and silver clouds. The first star appeared, the sky
deepening from magenta to deep blue. A soft breeze
refreshed us. A star appeared, another star and then

another, until the whole sky twinkled and scintillated. I leaned against Abelard who had one arm about my shoulders and another cradling our son. It was one of those rare perfect moments. Then I asked Abelard to tell me what life held for Astralabe.

'He will be hot, well braced in limbs, heavy, spirited, strong to think and act. My son.'

'He is my son as well,' I reminded him.

'Not in the same way, not if we are to believe the great Aristotle,' he replied, teasing, with that triumphant expression on his face that he knew made me furious. He reminded me how Aristotle had taught that women are simply the receptacle of the seed of life that the man provides. It was then he told me we were to be married. Later, after my uncle's servants had cut him, he made no further reference to virility, but he always spoke of Astralabe with pride and affection, as is the way with fathers.

I once wrote to Abelard that an evil beginning must come to a bad end. Our son could never be thought of as a 'bad end', so did this not mean that his beginning was not evil?

These women had come to me for guidance. Did they know that long after I had taken my religious vows, long after I became famed as a wise and holy abbess, I yearned for all that I had lost?

* * *

Although we did not speak of the letter that day we made three decisions. First, the room we were in was too small for comfort, so I took them to the one that had been our first chapel. This room was now used for special meetings of the community. It was a peaceful room, with its arched ceiling and white walls reflecting both the morning and afternoon sun, having windows at either end. Sunlight always makes life seem more hopeful. One end opened on to the garden, so when the weather was kind we could open the doors and enjoy the scent of the flowers and the birdsong.

Second, we would try to meet each morning, between Terce and Sext, and each afternoon between None and Vespers. There would be some days when I would not be free but I suggested they might like to confer together without me. Eleanor suggested the third decision. Our first time together had been difficult. We had never met before, so this was to be expected, but neither Hildegard nor I had spent any time at Court and Eleanor had passed her life with little regard for the Rule of St Benedict. She was incapable of maintaining silence, and we wondered if were expected to curtsy whenever we saw her, or never turn our back on her. After Hildegard had stumbled over 'your majesty' once too often Eleanor snorted with impatience.

'For goodness sake, call me Eleanor, and I'll call you Heloise and Hildegard. Only between these four walls, mind you. We must insist upon that.'

She continued to insist upon it during the next hour to make her point with excessive clarity. Where did she imagine that I would see her again except between these four walls? And as for Hildegard, after she had conversed directly with God, other discourse must seem an anticlimax. But we both held our counsel and agreed, time and again, that simple names and courteous informality would be the order only for the present situation. Nevertheless I found I liked Eleanor the better for that begrudged informality.

*   *   *

I believed that my sisters would not be curious about our visitors, which reveals how little I know about human nature. I was surprised that Sister Agatha, for one, quivered with impatience to find out who they were, for normally she is morose and withdrawn. Travellers often came to the Paraclete, and stayed overnight. But these latest arrivals, she commented, were unlike any of the others. Nuns, she reminded me, were not supposed to travel at all, and certainly not far enough to get dirty.

'Then,' she had said, 'there is the second group. Why have they brought so much food, candles, and flasks of rosewater? Rosewater, not holy water! Are they from some exotic land?'

Agatha was Abelard's niece and for this reason felt that she could talk to me quite freely. It appeared that she felt able to talk to the visitors just as freely. Their conversation must have been conducted in a variety of languages and dialects. Agatha was from Brittany, but spoke French and some Latin. Elizabeth, from Germany, did her best in Latin. Adele, lady-in-waiting to the Queen, spoke both French and Latin with surprising proficiency and had, according to Agatha, no little pride in her linguistic abilities.

'I wonder why they are here,' Agatha had whispered as we went into chapel, obviously expecting me to tell her. After our prayers she sidled up to me again, ignoring my frowned reminder that she should talk only when absolutely necessary.

'I did ask one of them, but all she would say was, "I'm called Adele. I dare not tell you who my lady is. It's worth more than my life. I can tell you she holds a high position, and we're from Paris. We brought lots of food, and a goose, so you needn't worry we'll leave you hungry." '

'We have poultry enough, here,' Agatha had said, then, realising that sounded rather ungracious, she added, 'It was kind of you to bring a bird. We do not eat goose very often.'

That was the part of the conversation she reported to me that day. She didn't feel it necessary to mention the rest, or not until long after our visitors had gone, and she had learned whom the grand lady was.

'Why did your lady come here?' Agatha had asked Adele.

'That is what I have asked myself, ever since we arrived. Why here, of all places? It's to do with a letter. I know that much. Sadly, it was sealed, so I couldn't read it. But after my lady read it she was very agitated. She didn't tell her husband about the letter, of course. She said that she was coming for a retreat. He fussed and carried on and said that there were better abbeys and wiser spiritual advisers nearer Paris. They had a noisy row about it. She said that she wanted to consult a wise and pious woman. He said that your abbess, Heloise, had a very dubious past, and that Abelard, who founded the Paraclete, was a heretic.'

This had made Agatha understandably angry, so she had replied, 'That's not true. He died as a member of the Church. I should know. He was my uncle. My aunt raised their son, Astralabe, so he's my cousin. You are discourteous and ignorant to accuse Abelard of heresy. He had a brilliant mind and was the best philosopher and teacher in the world. Anyone who knows anything knows that. And they were married,' Agatha had reminded her. 'Then she became a nun and he became a monk.'

'Only because they cut off his balls,' Adele had replied.

'That shows the sort of woman Adele really is,' Agatha commented, before she continued.

'The marriage being secret was the problem,' I told Adele. 'All our family was affected by it. No one said anything to our faces. But there were whispers, and mockery. It was a terrible time. Astralabe was taunted as well, but eventually they forgot the story and left him alone.'

Had Agatha also forgotten, when she told me this, that I was Astralabe's mother?

Such conversations had no place in an abbey. Such events had no place in our lives, which did not stop them occurring.

*   *   *

The life of the Paraclete had to go on despite distinguished visitors. As I went about my duties I tried to calm the feeling of panic whenever I thought of Bernard's plan. While we now knew about it, what could we do to prevent it? If we didn't prevent it, how could I bear to go on?

Hildegard fitted in easily to our way of life, as I expected. She and Sister Elizabeth attended chapel with the other sisters to sing the Office. It was the period after Pentecost and before Advent so we were full of music. Hildegard said that she was impressed by our antiphons and hymns, composed especially for our community. Then she decided to teach the sisters some of her own music, although I had to remind her to request permission from our choir mistress, who did not accept any interference in her domain. Hildegard is very brave, or a good musician, I thought. After hearing my sisters sing *O Virtus Sapientiae* I realised it was the latter.

O moving force of Wisdom, encircling the wheel of
the cosmos
Encompassing all that is, all that has life
in one vast circle
You have three wings: The first unfurls aloft
in the highest heights.
The second dips its way dripping sweat on the Earth.
Over, under, and through all things whirls the third.
Praise to you, O Wisdom, worthy of praise!

Abelard would have appreciated Hildegard's music,
although he would have wanted to tease out the
significance of the words. What was the relationship
between Wisdom and the Blessed Trinity? The idea of
the Spirit dipping and dripping through the cosmos
evoked wonderful images. And sweat? Yet nothing is
achieved without the sweat of our bodies or our brow,
even if it is only symbolic sweat.
How to physically sweat and struggle was the first
lesson we learned at the Paraclete. It was very hard
work, even though we were grateful to have a refuge,
the further away from Abbot Suger, who had expelled
us from our abbey at Argenteuil, the better. Did
Abelard have any idea of the deterioration of this place
when he offered it to us? We were grateful all the same,
as we had not even a foxhole to shelter us. Had Queen
Eleanor arrived then she would have ridden straight
home again, back to her comfortable palace. Hildegard
might not have minded. She talked of also moving with
her sisters to a place where they would have to build an
abbey out of ruins. What concerned her was not their
initial discomfort but the fact that the monks of
Disibodenberg would not let her leave. She was
'directed' to go. Hildegard made much of this

'direction'. At the time I wondered how she could be so sure this direction came from God and not from her own desires.

I assured her that local people would help her as they had helped us in those first miserable months while we went into the fields to weed, hoe and plant. We rebuilt the shelters, first with the reeds and wood that we found lying about, and then, later, thanks to the endowments we received, into a more habitable abode, this time with stone. Finally we constructed the abbey and its other buildings in its present form. After the first few years I would look at our progress, give thanks to God and the generosity of so many, and feel a sense of achievement at all we had done. The main abbey was completed, with room for all the nuns, a fine chapel, a courtyard, a library, infirmary, a herb and vegetable garden, grape vines, fruit trees and bee hives. There was still enough space to grow flowers, whose beauty was greater than Solomon in all his glory. Roses of every colour and perfume, irises, bluebells, blue cornflowers and the white starred jasmine whose scent filled the summer evenings. The rest of our surrounding land was farmed. There was a boundary wall, but it offered protection, not imprisonment.

Abelard had tried to hide his amazement at all we had done. I had achieved more in a year than he could have in three, he eventually told me but then added that it was because I am a woman and thus inspired pity. I laughed. What we achieved came from our own hard work as much as the generosity of others. Abelard had always been too quick to take offence, too ready to argue, too proud to accept help, even when he first began to set up the Paraclete as his refuge. However

much I loved him I had wished, so often, that he
would curb the vigour and expression of his words.

*   *   *

The third time we met, one misty morning, Eleanor
seemed quieter. Her hair hung over one shoulder, neatly
plaited, no doubt the work of Adele, and she did not
bother with a veil. Hildegard had remarked to me
earlier, that Eleanor seemed to be shedding the chains
of the protocol and strict requirements demanded in the
royal palace; I could see this was so. Adele, by contrast,
became more nun-like by the hour. This, Hildegard told
me, was due to her becoming so attached to Elizabeth.
Hildegard hoped that Elizabeth was the good influence,
rather than being led by her into worldly ways.
Eleanor sat apart from us, near the window, twisting her
plait with her fingers, constantly looking out as though
she was searching for something or someone. Hildegard
was sitting with her back to the window waiting for the
first rays of sunlight to break through the mist. She
always sought out the sunlight, I noticed. And surmised
that she loved to feel the warmth on her back. I sat
nearer the door, closed for the moment against the cool
wind.
Hildegard broke the silence, after we had said the
prayer for guidance, by talking about her childhood.
She needed to make us understand the reason for her
dread and horror when she had heard of Bernard's plan.
Eleanor replied that she did not think it affected us as
much as it affected her, and she had always believed
that nuns were very happy behind their walls.
'Except for those who are forced to be there,' she
added.
'We do spend most of our time inside the abbey,' I said.
'There are times when we need to go out to attend to

legal matters, for administration or to attend religious festivals. Our produce is sold at the local markets, where we buy livestock as needed. We form part of the wider community, and local people, including the noble families, look to us for spiritual guidance and prayers. We are far from living in a cocoon, ready to emerge as butterflies only when we reach heaven.'

'My experience of monastic life is much as Heloise describes, although I would like to have greater control over the way my sisters and I form our days. At present we're under the rule of the abbot and his monks,' said Hildegard. 'But if I tell you something of my early experience you'll understand why I can never return to total enclosure. I was the tenth and last child, not loved the less for that. Our family was well enough endowed – not enough to be tempted into worldliness and intrigue for power, but neither so poor that we succumbed to misery or envy. God blessed me with spiritual gifts from an early age. The first time I saw the living Light I was just five.

Eleanor suddenly flicked her plait to one side and turned to look intently at Hildegard. She begged Hildegard to explain how the Light manifested itself. 'In my innocence I believed that this was something every person experienced. Slowly I came to realise that I could see things hidden from others: the unborn baby in the womb, even an unborn animal, people's thoughts and desires that they masked with friendly faces. I foretold the future. These disclosures were not always welcome. I digress, however. At the age of eight my parents decided that I was to be sent away. My mother told me that there was no greater gift that parents could give to God than a beloved daughter. My father

explained that this was also a gift to me, that I would
live a holy life and be assured of my heavenly reward.
'The plan was that I enter a monastery and be enclosed
in a small adjunct to the chapel, completely cut off from
the world, and with no way of leaving that confined
space. My being so stringently enclosed was to
symbolise the tomb to ensure that when I did finally die
I would wake in Paradise.'

I could imagine just how frightening that must have
been for her. As a child she would have revelled in
sunlight and loved to run outside in the garden, playing
with her brothers and sisters. It was not, however, quite
as bad as it seemed at first telling, as Hildegard went on
to explain.

'Being only a young child I was terrified at the thought
of such a life. Nor was this God's plan for me. The
monastery was being rebuilt. It was not a double
monastery, and the Abbot said they were not ready for
young girls or women to live there. So I was sent as a
companion to Jutta, who had renounced all ideas of
marriage and wished to do something heroic for God.
She lived with her mother, Sophia and a pious widow
Uda. I was sent to join them. There we waited,
preparing for a life of discipline and prayer. Jutta was
restless and wanted to run away on a pilgrimage. One
of my tasks was to make sure she did not. I missed my
family but was happy not to be totally shut away from
the world. Uda was sensible, gentle and learned
enough to teach us. When Jutta was twenty and I
fourteen we were professed at Disibodenberg, and it
was then that we went to live in those two small rooms.
To Jutta, who was noted for her sanctity, it was heaven
almost attained.

Eleanor turned from watching a butterfly do the
rounds of the rosemary bushes, and demanded to know
how they attended Mass, or were able to eat, wash and
attend to natural functions.

'There was a small grille that allowed us to look into
the chapel, but the monks could not see us. Food was
passed in through a small revolving window, and any
rubbish or waste was passed out through a lower
aperture. These rooms were very small, dark and cold.'
She paused, seeming to be transported back to that
miserable existence.

'That was a hard thing, to be separated from family and
home forever. It sounds like a prison. I should have
hated it,' broke in Eleanor.

'So did I, at first. I certainly do not think children
should enter religious life at a young age. It did become
easier. We became less secluded, as more young
women wished to join us and we had to enlarge and
open up our extension. My own situation improved
when Jutta came to know about my visions and
arranged for Brother Volmar to help me.'

This time it was Hildegard who moved restlessly,
pacing about, hands clenched, face pale and strained.
Before we could think what to say to her she continued.
'I cannot be confined within those four walls again,
without even a window to let in the sun and the fresh
air. How can I cleanse my face in the rain when it never
falls upon me? My health is not robust. The headaches
and pain, which I still suffer, are God's way of
anchoring me to my humanity. I do not need to seek
further suffering.'

She looked at us in turn then, seeking what?
Understanding, or approval? I could not read her face. I
knew of anchorites, of course. To retreat entirely from

the world and other people – this was the path to true sanctity. Hell on earth guarantees heaven? Or is it, as the hermits would have us believe, heaven on earth? But dear God, how cold must a parent be to consider putting a child in such a place.

Hildegard's childhood resembled mine in that I spent much of my early years in an abbey. My mother had important work to do at Fontevraud Abbey, so she sent me away to be educated. Not that was I locked away from the rest of the community in a stone prison. I had the benefit of a good education, and the sisters were kind to me, probably kinder than Jutta was to Hildegard.

How much had Hildegard been affected? She seemed comfortable with herself. In fact she made me think of the small round dumplings which people from the north love to eat. I surmised that Jutta's severe fasting was not a part of Hildegard's regime. This observation was confirmed when I later heard her giving advice to some of the young nuns at the Paraclete.

'Eat moderately, but sensibly,' she said. 'You are of no value to the Lord if you are fainting in the fields.'

Like most people from the northern countries Hildegard enjoyed her bread, advising us to bake ours with spelt flour. Eleanor, who ate daintily, preferred softer food or fruit. Now, however, she was more concerned with Hildegard's account of her childhood, and her response came without hesitation.

'I would never give up any of my children unless I was forced. Children from royal families may have to be sent away, but only for the good of the kingdom. No doubt your parents had similar motives, and benefits would have been directed towards a family who made such a sacrifice.'

Hildegard was still vigorously contradicting this as they walked out into the garden. Finally I could no longer hear their voices but I guessed that they were not in dispute as I could see them sitting side by side under one of the trees. Worldly and holy; secular and sacred; they made an interesting combination.

*   *

*

By the afternoon I was ready to cry with impatience. We were in danger but fearful of confronting it. Since Volmar had told me about the contents of Bernard's letter I was tempted to dispense myself from the Benedictine way of life for a few days, and devote my time and energies to fight for my freedom. My intention, namely to prevent Bernard's letter being delivered to the Pope, was good. Failing to honour my religious obligations was not, so I continued to work and pray as I had done for years.

There was another consideration. Eleanor may have hardly been aware that I was neglecting my duties as abbess, but Hildegard would have known and probably been scandalised enough to write to our Bishop and denounce me. Even worse, Eleanor may have indeed noticed and informed her husband the King, who would feel it necessary to report it to Bernard of Clairvaux, who would take it further.

I resolved that the next time we met together we must discuss the letter. No more worrying about how we would address each other. No more about Hildegard's scientific theories or her childhood. No more stories about the holy lands from Eleanor. At any other time I would have found either discussion of great interest. Hildegard's hypothesis about the degree of love between parents, and the time of the lunar month affecting conception was quite different to the representation of reproduction taught by Greek and Arab scholars. Perhaps she was right, and maybe Eleanor later followed her ideas, for she gave her second husband, Henry, many children, sons among them.

As soon as we were seated in our meeting room I spoke.

'We must begin to plan what we can do about this letter that Bernard is said to have written. We have a good idea of its contents and...'

'He intends to bury women in the bowels of the earth,' interrupted Eleanor.

'Surely that's not his intention,' said Hildegard. 'If only we could see a copy of the letter to know exactly what he wrote. Rumours can grow from shadows to storm clouds.'

Eleanor suddenly stood up and flourished a parchment, which she had been hiding from our view. 'We do have a copy of the letter. Here it is.'

If she had wished to gain our full attention she succeeded. Hildegard let out a gasp, and I reached forward to take the letter from her, before remembering that one does not take such liberties with a queen, even one addressed by her Christian name. Then Hildegard asked how Eleanor had obtained such a copy, for Bernard would not have wanted it known outside a small circle of his disciples.

'Don't ask how I obtained it, but be sure, dear sisters. I've had to learn to protect myself within the palace from malice and lies. I have my contacts. Just rest assured that it is genuine. It makes me feel ill every time I think about it.'

Hildegard then asked if Eleanor would allow me to read out the letter, and Eleanor reluctantly handed it over, for she was enjoying being the focus of our full attention.

I settled on the chair, cleared my throat, and began hoping that the sense of Bernard's arrogance would not overwhelm me as well. The letter began with the subservient greeting that Bernard favoured.

To his most loving father and lord the Supreme Pontiff Eugenius, my humble devotion.
It is not my habit, as it is of many, to preface anything I want to say to you, or to approach it in a roundabout way. Let others fear your Majesty, so that with trembling lips and finger and by devious circumlocutions they can hardly come to the point of what they want to say. I have regard only for your honour and advantage and say what I want to say openly and at once.

Eleanor snorted. 'He calls that coming to the point? That's so typical of his style.'

'Hush,' said Hildegard. 'Failing in charity will not help our cause. We want to combat this plan in the spirit of crusaders fighting evil.'

'If you'd been on the crusade, you wouldn't say that,' replied Eleanor. 'There was even more evil on our side than in the Muslim camp, as I observed.' She took a deep breath.

Fearing that she was about to embark on another story, I said, 'With respect, Eleanor, let us keep to the point,' then returned to the letter that I had burned with curiosity to see.

Therefore I do not hesitate to tell you that the situation and position of women within the Church must be regularised. To neglect to do so immediately risks grave scandal and the downfall of many. Just as the Devil once used Eve to bring sin into the world he is again whispering in the ears of women, inciting them to rebel against God's law.

'I have no desire to rebel,' insisted Hildegard. 'My only desire is to do as God directs me. But, forgive me, it is now I who interrupt,' as Eleanor glared at her.
I continued.

Mary was raised by God to be a model for all women. During her life she remained as a quiet figure in the shadows, supporting her Son and the apostles. She lived her life without sin, never wishing to assert authority. In this she is truly blessed.

'If I remember my scripture correctly, Mary spoke up when she felt inclined,' muttered Eleanor.
'Shush,' hissed Hildegard.

While we rejoice that a number of women are choosing a life of prayer and dedication to the religious life we are disturbed at the behaviour of too many of them. Some wish to rule over not only other women but also men, taking precedence over the Abbot in a combined abbey. Others desire a greater voice within the Church, to preach in God's holy house or to dispense advice to princes and leaders. This is not God's purpose for women.

'And he'd know God's purpose for women?' said
Eleanor angrily. 'He shuns our presence as though we
carry a contagious disease.'
'He is a good and holy man, Eleanor,' insisted
Hildegard. 'You would do well to heed his preaching.'
'May I continue?' I asked.

*St Paul tells us that 'man is the image and reflection of
God, but woman is the reflection of man. Neither was
man created for the sake of woman but woman for the
sake of man'. It is thus clear that a woman should never
hold a position of authority over men. Women should
never be permitted to preach. Women should never be
permitted to write books, letters, hymns or chants for
the liturgy. They will benefit more by reading words
and singing hymns that are produced by men.*

I had to stop for a moment to collect my thoughts.
Would I be forbidden to write poetry and chants? How
could they prevent me from doing so? How could I
administer my abbey and priories without ever writing a
letter? A mediocre monk, foisted on me by a distrustful
hierarchy, would write the letter for me. Prison walls
were enclosing not only my body but also my mind. I
could not bear it.
'Go on,' said Hildegard. 'We need to know all that he's
written.'

*Give firm guidance to these women. Ensure by papal
decree that all religious houses in which women serve
God are totally enclosed and completely surrounded by
a high wall which removes them from the sight of the
world, and preserves them from the temptations of the
flesh. Women may gain knowledge but never wisdom,*

*and must therefore be protected from the world. Thus
shielded, such women will no longer be a source of
temptation to men.*

'Do all priests and monks really believe that? Women
are nothing but a source of trouble and temptation? I'd
like to see how men would fare if all women suddenly
refused to have anything to do with them. They'd go
hungry for a start, to say nothing of other deprivations,'
interrupted Eleanor with a quick look at Hildegard, as if
defying her to disagree.
'I agree with you that women have a valuable place in
God's world,' I said, amazed at my calm, 'but shall I
finish the letter before we discuss the ramifications.'

*No woman is to hold the highest position of authority
over these religious houses. This must lie in the hands
of an abbot or bishop. All business with the outside
world, when and if necessary, is to be conducted by
men. It is unseemly that women conduct lawsuits and
solicit favours and endowments from noble families. A
wise woman may be appointed as abbess but her care
will be for spiritual rather than material matters. Once
she has taken her vows a nun must not leave her priory
or abbey for any reason. Should she do so she must
undergo a fitting penance. Any nun who continues to
rebel is to be excommunicated and banished from the
society of all Christian people, even if this means she
must be placed in prison. It is desirable that women
only spend their days in prayer and singing to the glory
of God, in suitable manual labour and with sufficient
education to enable them to read the Scriptures, recite
the Office and copy manuscripts. Further education or*

intellectual activity for women leads to over-stimulation, temptation to pride and false ideas.

I paused there. Hildegard sat, her lips pursed, obviously deep in thought. Eleanor gave no indication of having any doubts at all. She rushed over and took the letter from me. Snatched, would be a better description. 'I cannot sit still when I'm angry, and believe me, dear sisters, I'm very angry. Please allow me to read the rest of the letter for this is the part that affects me.' She paced about, her skirt swirling each time she turned to face us.

I write also of those women who choose to remain in the world. Marriage is necessary if children are to be born and may be pleasing to God if it is not for lustful purposes. Sometimes marriages are annulled. In these cases the woman should be forbidden to enter into any other marriage. A union, even one which is contracted in good faith, if annulled, must be considered as sinful and unchaste. Any children of such a union must remain with their father. The woman, not a wife nor virgin nor widow, should enter religious life and spend the rest of her days in prayerful contemplation. This would take away any taint or reproach from her so that she may go finally to sing with the angels in heaven. It is for you, successor to St. Peter to give firm guidance. Restrain the vixens in the vineyard while they are yet young, lest they grow and multiply to bring about ultimate destruction.

After she had finished reading we remained silent. Then Hildegard said, 'Can that letter really have been written by Bernard of Clairvaux? Even as I came here to

consult with Heloise, I wondered if Volmar had been misinformed. Why should he now forbid me to write what he and the Pope approved before? Perhaps there's some mistake. Where did you obtain it, Eleanor?'
She still refused to tell us, but was adamant it was authentic.

Hildegard, still obviously troubled, frowned and then said, 'It's exceedingly strange. Are not abbeys and convents always surrounded by a wall? Is this not for our protection? Need it mean that we should be totally isolated from the outside world?'

'The difference would be,' I replied, ' that the gates in these walls would have no handle on the inside.'

'And once you were inside you'd never be allowed to leave. Never!' added Eleanor. 'Nor could you write letters, or hymns, or compose music. Unless I remain with Louis, I will have to join you. My dear ladies, we might all just as well be dead.

There was a sense of chill in the room. Within myself, I felt a dark anger against a man who sought to silence us all; a renewed disgust at the assumption that all women were weak and incapable of intellectual vigour or integrity. This changed to despair that I still had so little control over my own life. Anger again, initially cold, flaring to a white heat. I'd made a sacrifice of my life when I was married, and when I entered Argenteuil. Both times it was out of love for Abelard. I felt no such love for Bernard.

What real freedom had I known? Only those three wonderful and painful years in Paris when I knew Abelard. Before that I had lived within monastery walls. Even so when I was sent as a child to Argenteuil, it was not as an oblate but a pupil.

My uncle gave me a new life when I came to be with him in Paris. While I refused to admit that Abelard and I had sinned in loving each other I had to accept that I had wronged my uncle.

'I trusted in your integrity, your sense of honour and, if I may suggest it, your affection for me,' he had reproached. That was after he found us, lost in our love, unaware that he was watching us. I have never seen him so angry as he was that day. Abelard was ordered to leave the house immediately, and never to seek me out nor speak to me again. I was ordered to kneel at my uncle's feet and beg his forgiveness. There I should have wept tears of contrition because I had betrayed his trust by yielding to the blandishments of an evil seducer. Instead I ran from the room, outraged that he should seek to separate me from Abelard and later, when I was calmer, numbed, feeling that joy had left my life forever, I could not bring myself to even talk to him.

After the punishment my Uncle Fulbert inflicted on Abelard, turning him from a man to a eunuch, I made my religious vows at Argenteuil. Then I became a prisoner of my own misery and despondency. The few times that Abelard found his way along the river from St Denis made my state worse, not better. There was no longer openness between us. He spoke of our need to love God and I spoke of my enduring love for him. He looked to his future in the Church, and I felt fettered by my religious vows. Each time we met he distanced himself further from me until it came to be almost a relief when he said that he would not be able to visit again for some considerable time.

The Paraclete had saved me, saved us. I built it from a few rough shelters to a well-endowed abbey, with priories. In this I fulfilled Abelard's dream, although he claimed much of the credit. I didn't mind. We spoke to each other through letters again. He visited the abbey and together we composed hymns and shared our thoughts as we sat under our tree in the garden. He was the Spiritual Director, and I was the Abbess. Sometimes we spoke of our son, and I was content at the thought that he had grown tall, comely, intelligent, serious and that he had not forgotten his mother.

Bernard of Clairvaux approved of the progress I had made at the Paraclete. He had visited here and told me so, more than once. Why did he now want to silence and imprison me? Were I to be placed behind even higher walls and separated from all company but my sisters, dear as many of them are, I would go insane.

Hildegard, no doubt, was recalling her time locked away from the daylight, the changing of the seasons and any contact with her family. Without the feel of the earth, water, trees, the wind, the sun and shadows – in which she found the divine Spirit – without this grounding, she would be diminished.

Added to this was her fear that it would become impossible to found her own monastery even though she was directed to do so by God. She (and God) had such plans for that abbey, she told me. How could Bernard, whom she thought to be a holy man, prevent this?

Eleanor, who had been sitting unusually silent, moved her chair nearer to Hildegard then spoke, 'Tell me about your Divine Light.'

She had a reason for that question. It was clear that Hildegard did not want to respond, but perhaps she decided that, if we were to achieve anything, we needed to be open with each other.

'From my early childhood, before my bones, nerves and veins were fully strengthened,' she told us, 'I have always seen this vision in my soul, even to the present time. The light that I see is not spatial, but it is far, far brighter than a cloud that carries the sun. When this reflection of living Light is at its brightest I see, hear, and know all at once, and as if in an instant I learn what I know. I hate to talk of this Light, which is a gift from God. Can you understand it at all, Eleanor?'

'Certainly. Before I went to Jerusalem, I might have doubted. Much of what I saw there made me realise that my knowledge of the mind of God is very limited. Your Light may well be possible.'

Eleanor said no more then, but looked into the distance again, her expression now one of distress. I knew that while she was looking at the fruit trees and rosemary hedge, visible through the window, her mind was filled with twisted, bloodied men and horses, cries of pain and the stench of battle. This knowledge I came to by myself. There was no need for Hildegard's living Light to reveal it.

Eleanor also had good reason to be troubled by the letter. I suspected that she did not grieve for what she had lost, nor doubt the wisdom of her own decisions, so much as rage against the frustrations of her life, and the dread of being thwarted in plans for her future that she had already set in place. To attempt to curb her could have dangerous consequences. Eleanor would not be a placid prisoner.

Bernard's voice seemed to ring through that letter, reminding me why I mistrusted the man, even as I appreciated so much about him. In his presence I was beguiled, but I always had the good sense not to cross him, for I could never forget his campaign against

Abelard. There was nothing to suggest that the Pope would not be swayed by his arguments, or to suggest that our pleas would sway Bernard.

In those times when I wish to feel especially close to Abelard I go and kneel by his tomb built inside the chapel. This is where I will also be buried, so we will be united again in death. This thought comforts me. As I knelt there I realised that he might not have been of much help. When I had needed to hold Abelard to me, in those last years, I asked him to set down a Rule suitable for women. St Benedict's Rule was devised for men. Women have different needs, I explained to him, in case he no longer remembered. I was disappointed, but not completely surprised that Abelard had tapped the same drum as Bernard was now beating loudly, stating that the highest authority should always remain in the hands of men.

This angered me, and I told him so. Had I not proved a worthy abbess? He had looked at me with one eyebrow raised, as he used to do when I disagreed with him. 'Why did you ask me for direction then?' he said. 'If you are not prepared to accept my direction remember the decision of the Council of Seville.'

We commit the nuns to their charge in the sense that one man, the best proved of the monks, shall be chosen to take over the management of their lands in the country, or town, and also the erection of buildings, or provision of whatever else is needed by the convent, so that the handmaids of Christ may be concerned only with the welfare of their souls, may live only for divine worship and performance of their own works.

He went on to remind me that the Council had written:

God forbid the unmentionable – that we would wish
the monks to be familiar with the virgins of Christ; they
must be kept separate and far apart, as the statutes of
the Rule and the canons allow.

Then, to deflect further objections, he changed the
subject. Inviting me to sit beside him again as he had
done in the old days, he showed me some music he had
written for our liturgy, humming the chant for me. But
it was not the old days, and I was no longer prepared to
always accept everything that he said. For example,
why did he not consider the example of the abbey at
Fontevraud? There, the Abbess had ruled over the
monks, with wisdom and good administration. My
mother, Hersinde, had been Prioress there. Abelard
knew that. It suits men too well to claim that women are
a lesser species, whose purpose in life is to seduce men.
As I had seduced him?

Abelard was no longer here to either advise or accuse,
and no other man, not even Bernard, was going to
reduce my life to interminable confinement. The past
was no help to our present problem.

'This is extreme self-sacrifice!' I said, breaking the
silence. 'Men would deal with the design, planning and
building of abbeys, buying of animals and poultry,
directing the servants, selling of extra produce at the
markets and the collection of monies, and the
dispensation of alms. Women in religion would become
praying mushrooms, kept in the dark in case they
should be plucked and carried away, or grow too strong
in the sunlight. There is no impiety intended but I can
not fill my entire day singing God's praises.'

'Bernard gave me his support at the Synod of Trier.'
said Hildegard. 'He wrote urging me to rejoice in the

grace of God with all humility, and to pray for his sinful self. This feels like a betrayal.'

'He admitted that he was sinful and accepted you as a visionary?' asked Eleanor.

'He did. "We rejoice with you over the grace of God that is in you," he wrote and asked me to pray for him. Even the Pope directed me to continue writing as God dictates.'

'There, that's our answer,' said Eleanor, beaming. 'It's so simple. You should have told us all this before. Bernard and the Pope accept that God speaks to you in a special way, Hildegard. Tell him that God has directed you that women are not to be treated differently to men. Those who have abilities are to take their rightful places of authority. Women whose marriages are annulled must be free to marry again, and retain all their property. Perhaps you could refer to my situation in particular, without naming names, of course. Just say a royal marriage.'

She was mightily pleased with herself. Problem solved. Time to return to the Palace. She had her future restored. Then she looked at Hildegard and her smile faded. The nun began to speak.

'You neither acknowledge God nor respect me. Do you not realize that I have been commanded to transmit, for the benefit of humanity, an accurate account of what I see with the inner eye and what I hear with the inner ear of my soul. I have seen great miracles, which my tongue could not describe had not the Spirit of God taught me that I might believe. I am a humble woman striving to serve God. I will never be a cypher for your unworthy and worldly ambitions.'

'But God must see that Bernard is wrong.' Eleanor persisted. 'Can't you at least ask God next time he appears to you?'

Hildegard stood before us, hand raised, claiming our full and undivided attention.

'Listen! Once I heard a voice from heaven say: " Since God is Reason, how could it be that God, who causes all divine actions to come to fruition through human beings, is not active! God created men and women in the divine image and likeness. I am life that remains ever the same, without beginning and without end. All life lights up out of me. For this life is God, who is always in motion and constantly in action." God speaks to me of the cosmos, not your marriage plans.'

'But what I'm suggesting is God's divine actions coming into fruition through human beings,' Eleanor insisted. Then, matching Hildegard's authority, 'I order you to do as I ask.'

'Do not pursue that path,' I pleaded as Hildegard, hesitated, then looking smaller and as strained as she had the day she arrived, left the room and turned in the direction of the chapel. Eleanor, tall and clothed in dignity, made no attempt to stop her but followed straight after turning towards her own room.

While I had to agree with Hildegard that Eleanor's idea was outrageous, I could not help thinking that it might have been an easy way out of our dilemma.

*   *   *

Eleanor was no doubt ordering Adele to make preparations to leave next morning. Hildegard would also leave as soon as Brother Volmar returned from Cluny, where he was visiting Abbot Peter, a man we called 'the Venerable'. Bernard would be preparing to leave for Rome, his letter to the Pope carried close to

his heart to protect it from all opposition until the
Pope read it and approved. There was nothing I could
do to stop any of them.

As I walked despondently down the passageway I heard
something most unusual, laughter, and companionable
female chatter. Sister Agatha, and two others whose
voices I did not immediately recognize, were working
in the kitchen as though it were any farmhouse. Agatha
supervised the preparation of meals with barely
disguised reluctance, so I had expected her to abandon
her duty of obedience altogether when she found herself
faced with important guests and the extra food that
Eleanor had provided. It was only to enlighten myself
that I waited just outside the door and listened to their
conversation.

'A goose can be very tasty but it must be cooked
correctly,' announced Agatha. 'Our cook at home
always stuffed it with herbs and spread honey on the
skin, and roasted it slowly. The skin would crisp,
golden brown and crunchy.'

'How do you cook it in your country?' said someone.

'That I couldn't tell you.' Elizabeth. I recognized her
voice. The other voice must belong to Adele.

'I knew nothing of what went on in our kitchen when I
was small, only what came out of it,' continued
Elizabeth. 'In our abbey we eat bread, fruit and
vegetables, as well as fish from the river. Mother
Hildegard insists that we eat enough to be healthy. She
says our bodies are a gift from God, not to be abused.
Some of the sisters want to rigorously fast and do
severe penance, but she won't allow it.'

'Our Abbess sees learning as the way to know God. So
did Abelard,' said Agatha.

I could picture her deftly plucking the last of the
goose feathers, just as her mother used to do.
'She's had enough suffering in her own life not to go
seeking for more,' Agatha added.
'My mistress has a great love of music and poetry.
Refining influences, she calls them. Courtesy and
manners are important. She can't stand to see men
eating like pigs at the trough.'
I should have stepped in then, and stopped such idle
chatter.
'What's it like to live in your household?' asked
Elizabeth. 'It must be very different to living in an
abbey.'
'It is different, but also the same.'
'How could it be? You talk such nonsense. We are
women devoted to the service of God. People of the
world pursue their own pleasure.' Agatha's face would
have been creased and pinched as she spoke. I knew
that look so well.
'You still have to eat, and sleep and pass the day. We
do the same, only we do it differently. And we have
more excitement.'
'Conflict and lustful congress is what you have. I've
heard a few stories, I can tell you. That's the sort of
thing that goes on in the palace. Why was King Louis
excommunicated?'
Where would Agatha have heard about that?
Adele giggled. 'Elizabeth, do you also think all noble
houses are ungodly?'
'Why was the king excommunicated?' Agatha
persisted, not giving Elizabeth a chance to reply.
'That was to do with the Queen's younger sister,
Petronilla. She could have made a brilliant marriage but
she fell in love with Duke Ralph of Vermandois. Old

enough to be her father, but she didn't care about that. Trouble was he was married already, so they had to find three bishops to annul the marriage. Then the first wife's brother became angry and arranged for the Pope to cancel the annulment. Petronilla and the Duke Ralph refused to be parted, especially as she was pregnant by then. The Pope became angry with the king for supporting his sister-in-law, and Abbot Bernard of Clairvaux came to the palace to tell him he was not doing the right thing, and he should behave more like a king. That made the king furious and he ordered Brother Bernard to leave. Then the Pope excommunicated the Duke and his new wife. Later on...'

'We're meant to be doing our work silently and prayerfully, not indulging in gossip,' interrupted Agatha. 'Sister Elizabeth and I are not interested in such stories.'

'You were the one who rushed up to us before, wanting to know who we were. Wasn't she, Elizabeth? Now it's Sister Silent Saint. What are you doing to the goose?

'Basting it in mead,' Agatha said abruptly.

'I'll prepare these vegetables,' offered Elizabeth. 'A pity that chestnuts are not yet in season, but we can use the walnuts.'

They didn't even notice me enter the kitchen. Agatha's face was rosy from her exertions, she who usually seemed sallow and sullen. Adele, with no idea that nuns are required to maintain silence, was still chattering away. She had settled on a stool away from the heat of the fire, content as a cat. Agatha and Elizabeth, who should have known better, only then signalled her to silence.

Abelard would have been completely mortified at
such levity, and Bernard totally vindicated if he ever
came to hear about it. What is it these men say about
speaking: As venom destroys life, so idle talk means the
complete destruction of religion. St Antony taught:
Whoever sits in solitude and is at peace is rescued from
three wars, that is wars of hearing, speech and sight; he
shall have only one thing to fight against, the heart.
That is a fight I have not won, even now with Abelard
dead. Neither am I convinced that communication with
other people, our 'neighbours' whom we must love as
ourselves, is so sinful. As I had listened to the three
young women I wondered how Hildegard would have
regarded it. She was such a strange mixture of
knowledge and innocence that I couldn't be sure.
Eleanor might have forgotten her royal status just long
enough to join in.

Was my kitchen becoming a place of desecration? I
thought not. There was a feeling of enthusiasm and
good cheer. Agatha, when she noticed me, smiled and
said, 'It's such a pleasure to cook for our guests,
Mother. Boiled vegetables are no challenge. If the good
Lord put this wonderful food on the earth for us, is it so
sinful to enjoy it?'

'Make sure there's enough for all the sisters,' was my
reply. 'We can all enjoy the fruits of the earth during
this season.'

*   *   *

Early next morning Hildegard was in the chapel for
Matins, Lauds and Terce. Later, Eleanor was in our
small guest refectory for breakfast. They greeted each
other with a smile, Eleanor's a little distant, and
Hildegard's tolerant. Their truce, even such a

precarious one, was welcome, and my disturbed night unnecessary.

Before we went into have our breakfast Hildegard and I walked together in the garden, around past the well along the path to the gatehouse. From there we were able to turn towards the back of the infirmary and then return to the main abbey building. I wanted to show Hildegard where I planned to have some drains dug, as she had suggested, to see if she approved. We were going to dig drains running from the abbey building and from the infirmary, and these two would join to make one and then run off towards a stream.

'You must divert the waste water well away from the stream,' said Hildegard. 'The water will become unclean otherwise. Isn't that the water you use in the baking of your bread?' I felt foolish not to have thought of that. Even diverting the wastewater further down stream was not possible, for there were priories and villagers who relied on it. Eventually Hildegard, talking with one of the lay brothers, devised a system that meant that the water went through a series of reed beds until it eventually drained away into the forest. Those who had to do all the digging grumbled at first. After they realised the benefits I noticed some of the villages set up their own drainage system, simple but effective. Hildegard would have been delighted had she known about it.

In her piety, when she arrived Hildegard had some idea of trying to keep to our Rule of Silence. How were we supposed to communicate? By sign language? As we returned from our inspection of the drains I reminded her that St Benedict had written that *whenever weighty matters have to be transacted in the monastery let the abbot call together all the community and himself*

propose the matter for discussion. Obviously
Benedict saw the need to talk some of the time. I did
not wish to call the full community together at that time
to discuss the way drains should run. But I felt that our
small group of three met the spirit of the Rule, even if
one of us was not, strictly speaking, part of our
religious community. We were meeting to discuss a
matter that affected us all. I also reminded Hildegard
that St Benedict had ordained that the Lord often
reveals to a younger member what is best, and that we
should listen to all advice rather than stiffly defend our
own opinions. She turned to me, just as we were about
to return to the abbey, her expression disapproving.
'Does that mean you agree with Eleanor's suggestion?
You also wish me to have a convenient vision?' she
asked.
'Of course not.' I was becoming impatient with the pair
of them. Maybe I would be better left alone to deal with
Bernard. 'What I mean is Eleanor might still make a
valuable, if longwinded contribution. Neither can we
realistically expect her to remain silent for hours at a
time.'
It was a joy to have conversations in Latin, as I had
with Abelard. I had been surprised to discover that
Eleanor's Latin was quite fluent. Her father had insisted
on his children receiving an adequate education.
Hildegard, while professing insufficient education, also
spoke the language well enough.
'If I do speak acceptable Latin, you can thank Volmar
and Richardis,' she told us. 'Both of them have toiled
with me over *Scivias* smoothing any awkwardness.
Not,' she added firmly, 'that they have changed any of
the meaning. The words come from the living Light,
not my feeble mind.'

Scivias, we learned, was a book containing her account of the visions that God had commanded her to write down. I could not help but wonder why the Almighty bothered to dictate in indifferent Latin. Eleanor was more interested to know where Volmar came from, having ascertained that Richardis was another nun. Volmar, Hildegard said, was one of the monks at St Disibodenberg. He had travelled with her. But more than a travelling companion and protector on the road he was her secretary, spiritual confidant and a wise friend.

'You're very busy in this abbey of yours,' Eleanor then remarked to me. 'You grow grapes, make wine, raise poultry, bees...'

'And produce the best honey in the district,' I added, wondering if that was being boastful.

'That may be so, but your wine is good as well. I may take some home with me,' she replied. 'And pay for it, of course,' she assured. 'Then there are all those sick people coming to be treated, and the travellers, and others wanting prayers. When you find time to pray is a puzzle, except for the fact that you never sleep.'

An exaggeration. I was taught that the rule of St Benedict insists on a balance of prayer, work and rest. However nothing was to be put before the saying of the Divine Office and as soon as the bell signalled us we were obliged to put away whatever work we were engaged upon and hasten to the chapel. I explained all this to Eleanor so that she would appreciate our way of life more fully. Matins was, correctly, if inconveniently, sung in the dead of the night after which we returned to sleep until dawn, when we sang Lauds. Prime was sung at six, Terce at nine, Sext at noon, None at three in the afternoon, Vespers in the evening, at the time of the lighting of the lamps, and Compline at the hour of retiring. Fortunately these times were adjusted in summer otherwise we would be permanently sleepwalking in those long hours of daylight.

There was a certain comfort in the monastic routine. The Divine Office cradled our day, and interrupted our nights. Our prayers were interspersed with work, study and simple meals. We also shared the cares and concerns of the outside community, whether Bernard approved or not. Were we to hide our light under the bushel basket?

'Why do you have to pray in the middle of the night?' asked Eleanor. 'Is not prayer just as efficacious at a more convenient time?'

I had often had that same thought. To rest through an entire night was to ensure a fruitful day. But, in the rule it was written: 'The prophet says, *Seven times I have sung Thy praises*, and for the night watches, *at midnight I arose to confess to Thee*'. So we rose from our beds finding our way through the chilled corridors, minds still fogged in dreams, to confess to the Lord.

*   *   *

At our first meeting Eleanor had worried that she would not be able move freely outside the Paraclete. I assured her that the people who lived near us would never harm her, but that was not her fear. On the second morning Adele came to the door of our meeting room, flurried and panting.

'My lady, there is a servant from the Royal Court. He has a message for you,' she said to Eleanor.

'What exactly did he say? Speak up child, don't witter.'

'His majesty, King Louis of France, requests that the lady within your walls return to the royal court in Paris.'

Hildegard and I looked at each other with dismay. Eleanor laughed.

'Go and tell him that the lady in question is praying in the chapel and cannot be disturbed. She will return in God's good time.' As Adele left, Eleanor then smiled at us. 'That'll be that. Louis can never argue with prayer.' After Eleanor left us Hildegard wanted to talk about Richardis. To Hildegard the young nun represented all beauty of form and spirit, music and friendship.

'Is she a greater support to you than Volmar?' I asked, expecting her to reject such an idea.

'Volmar is without peer, a man who has made my work possible, but he is not beautiful. He is a craggy firm rock; Richardis is an exquisite flower. I am blessed to have them both by my side.

*   *   *

'He seems very devoted,' said Eleanor as we walked in the garden and noticed Volmar and Hildegard at the further end, deep in conversation. 'Do you think…'

'No,' I replied before she could complete her sentence. 'It is possible for a man and a woman to have a close spiritual relationship. There are many such monastic friendships. Volmar and Hildegard allow no ambiguity.'

Abelard had wished such a relationship for us in those final years. Our earlier passion was by then a shameful memory to him. For me this was not possible. I remembered every moment, lying together, content in our unity. There was no coating such feelings now with religious intent. I had once written to him: 'Just how intimately dear you are to me, the hand of this writer is in no way able to fully reveal, because a feeling of inner sweetness urges me to make you my special beloved above everyone else.'

I still have our letters. I made copies of them as
though I had divined that they would one day be all I
possessed of him. From time to time, when I am feeling
particularly sad, I read them, even though I hold each
word in my heart.

Abelard had replied: 'Most truly my love for you grows
from day to day and is not diminished by the passing of
time. On the contrary, just as the sun is new every day,
so your most delightful sweetness flourishes in its
newness, sprouts and grows vigorously. Farewell. Be as
mindful of me as I am of you.'

He grew less mindful of me, and I diminished as the
sun set each day; yet, despite everything, he never
ceased to be my special beloved. Once he had been my
bright star, golden constellation, jewel of virtues, and
sweet medicine for my body.

There was nothing to be gained, dwelling on these old
stories. Instead I had to look to my future, and I still had
no idea how I could convince Bernard that nuns did not
need to be shut away for their own and the world's
protection.

*   *   *

Hildegard and Eleanor arrived at our next meeting with
firm resolves. Each had decided to take control.
Hildegard began by calling our meeting a synod,
'without wishing to sound too grand'. Eleanor
immediately disagreed, insisting that it was a council of
war and no need to pretend otherwise. Hildegard,
ignoring her, began with a prayer to the Spirit of
Wisdom. Eleanor took over again, before the last Amen
had ceased to resonate, saying we needed to draw up a
battle plan. By this time I was feeling very irritated.
Eleanor might be the Queen of France, and Hildegard a

prophet in her own country but the Paraclete was my abbey.

Hildegard noticed my attempts to control my chagrin and smiled sympathetically as though she was not at fault. I had to smile in return. There was something encouraging and reassuring about her expression. She would never have been beautiful, even as a young woman, yet her eyes and mouth revealed confidence and serenity. I hadn't noticed this when I first saw her, for then her forehead had been creased with lines and her face pallid.

Hildegard won the battle to be the first to put her plan before us.

'I have been thinking about the power of music to touch men's hearts. The angels sing their praises of God in celestial harmonies. On earth we join tongue with them raising our voices to reach the Trinity. Music speaks to the spirit of every man and woman who loves God, as Bernard surely does.'

'What form of music?' I asked. 'It would need more than a hymn or chant.'

'With God's help I will compose a musical drama. The theme will be the triumph of virtue over evil. The devil, in the form of a man, will represent all that is seductive and dangerous in the world. The Soul, or Anima, will struggle with temptation, until she yields to the blandishments of the devil. Women, who represent all good women, will bring the soul back to the path of virtue. Thus Bernard will understand that we are not all like Eve.'

'He will believe that we are more like Mary?' I suggested.

'Mary, ever virgin and the mother of our Saviour, is our model, yes,' replied Hildegard serenely.

'A wonderful idea, brilliant!' said Eleanor. 'Dear
Hildegard, such a musical drama would be an
inspiration to all people. We will begin learning it
tomorrow.' 'Tomorrow! With respect, Eleanor, you
overestimate my powers to compose, even with divine
help. Such a musical drama would take weeks rather
than days.'

'Weeks! We may not even have days,' said Eleanor.
'You do not know that,' I said.

'Maybe not, but never underestimate the enemy. Who
would sing the part of the devil? Volmar is not here at
present. Bernard, when he arrives? Or would he feel
that there was a hidden message in placing him in that
role?' continued Eleanor.

Hildegard shook her head slowly.

Eleanor responded. 'No to Bernard singing, or no to his
feeling aggrieved? We will find someone. Perhaps I
should sing the role of the Soul for they tell me I have a
fine voice. Adele plays both the harp and flute. Perhaps
some instrumental music as an interlude? But you could
not have it ready in time, you say. That's the tragedy of
it.'

I'm not a violent woman but at that moment I could
have hit Eleanor, sitting so smug, superior and sure of
herself.

'With God's help all difficulties can be overcome,' said
Hildegard 'But you may have a better plan,' she said,
looking directly at me. Before I had even drawn breath
Eleanor spoke.

'Of course I have a plan. Hildegard and Heloise, we are
here to discuss something that threatens to make us
prisoners, when we have committed no crime except
being born female. The men of the church condemn us
to a living death, and we have the right to defend

ourselves. The Pope and his cronies will receive
Bernard's abominable letter only too gratefully. There's
no need for me to tell you that men are greedy to
accumulate power, and exceedingly reluctant to
relinquish it. We'll need strong weapons, and we must
have absolute trust in each other. Heloise, you say that
Bernard is going to travel to Rome. He will come here,
or at least pass on this road?'

'He may even stop here. In any case he'll use the road
which goes past,' I replied.

'I rode from Paris with soldiers to protect me. They're
still quartered nearby, waiting to escort me back. We
have a small army at our disposal.'

Hildegard turned slowly, looking directly at Eleanor.
'What would we three do with an army, large or small?'
she finally said.

'Remove our enemy. This is how it is done in the real
world. We use more permanent methods than letters,
prayers or pious music. Once Bernard is out of the way
no one else will bother with his cruel campaign against
women.'

'You mean we should kidnap Bernard?' I asked.

'Kidnap? Of course not. Where would be the value in
that? I said, out of the way.' Eleanor replied.

'Do you mean, kill him?' whispered Hildegard.

'Killing, murder, these are words that start unsavoury
rumours. We wish him no harm. Bernard has often said
he yearns to go to his eternal rest in heaven. We would
enable him to attain all that he desires.'

I could feel my own face stiff with horror, until I
realised that the idea of killing Bernard was so
preposterous I almost laughed. Hildegard looked at me
with no sign of seeing any humour. The Queen could
well carry out her plan without our approval, but we

would be implicated. She was staying at the
Paraclete, meeting with us and we all had reason to
reject Bernard's plan.

'Eleanor,' I said, 'we will gain nothing by breaking
God's law.'

'God allows us to kill in self-defence or in a just war.
How more just can it be than defending ourselves
against a total threat to our freedom,' she answered.

'There is a way to defend ourselves,' said Hildegard,
'but not as you suggest; not slaying a good and holy
man. Such a deed would remain with you until the end
of your days. I trust in our abilities and divine guidance
to find a solution without miring our hearts and souls in
evil.'

Eleanor countered our attack.

'I said we needed to trust each other. Trust is not
quickly won, and while we do not lack good will we do
lack time. Let us tell each other something of our lives,
and in what specific ways these edicts will affect us.
This will firm our resolve and permit you both to see
sense. Then we can draw on our strengths and attack
effectively. Attack, not defence, is the key to victory,
and you may even come to appreciate the wisdom of
my suggestion.'

What did we need to learn about each other that we
didn't already know? Nor could merely talking
engender this trust she extolled. We would only tell
what we wanted the others to hear. I felt a great
uneasiness at that moment. Why had they both sought
me out? Eleanor spoke of trust. Could I trust a woman
whose husband was guided by Abbot Suger? He was
the man who had expelled me and the other nuns from
the abbey at Argenteuil. Eleanor's concern was that if
her marriage to Louis were annulled she would be

forced to enter religious life. She had, she told me, other plans, hinted at another consort. But royal families have a way of arranging things in a way not available to ordinary people. She could apply for a dispensation.

And Hildegard? Could I trust this German nun, fresh from the approval of Bernard and the Pope? Realistically, what did she have to fear? So far she had attained all she wanted. Her writings were sanctioned, her role as a prophet recognized. No suggestion that her books should be thrown into a fire, or that she should be branded as a heretic. What if she were here now as the eyes and ears of Bernard? From the little I knew of Hildegard if a high wall were to be erected around her she would create an opening somehow and still come and go as she pleased.

My doubts grew. Was I allowing Bernard to trap me as he had Abelard? Despite his friendly smiles and expressions of support he might still think of me as a lustful and sinful woman, unworthy to be the spiritual mother and guide of innocent virgins and modest widows.

I tried to calm my thoughts. Bernard would never have sent the Queen to entrap me. That would be like using an avalanche to bury an acorn. She spent her free time walking about the garden, usually alone, occasionally with Adele, not snooping. I think she often sang to herself and once I saw her dancing a few steps. We kept a careful watch for any more messengers from the king. The first sign of a cloud of dust on the horizon and Eleanor planned to hurry to the chapel to bury her head in her hands in an attitude of fervent prayer. Any messenger returning to the king with such an account could expect only royal gratitude. These did not seem the actions of a spy.

On the other hand Hildegard had been all over the Paraclete, teaching hymns to my nuns, who had been perfectly content to sing those already written for them by Abelard and myself, talking to the gardeners, conferring with our workmen and women, poking about in the herb garden, suggesting schemes for better drainage and removal of waste; even wandering into the kitchen, according to Sister Agatha, advising on the need for more balance in our diet. A meddler. A spy? Can I trust either of these women? Do they trust me? I turned my attention back to the 'council of war' to hear Hildegard emphatically declaring that she had no desire to talk any more about herself.

'I have told you of my childhood. I have mentioned my visions and the living Light, which stays with me. You've heard my music. That is enough,' she said, 'For people in religious life talking about our strengths is not considered conducive to spiritual advancement. We prefer to correct our weaknesses.'

'You must have strengths, however, for you say you see God,' said Eleanor. 'I would love to hear more about that. When you talk with God, what do you say? And does he talk back, like you and I talk to each other? You could ask all manner of questions.'

Had she forgotten how angry Hildegard had been, only the day before, when the subject of her visions was mentioned? Eleanor aptly called this meeting a council of war. Now we, in this small room, threatened a war of our own.

'I also have little to say about myself,' I said, before Hildegard could reply. 'I am Abbess here; was Prioress at the Abbey of Argenteuil; was married to Peter

Abelard who died seven years ago, and is now buried here at the Paraclete; have a son whom I rarely see; and live out my life in obedience to my vows.' I didn't say which particular vows upheld me.

'Perhaps you're right,' said Eleanor. 'There's too much to speak about in such a short a time. But if we are to succeed we must find ourselves standing in the same part of the forest. Let's try something different. This is what my ladies sometimes do in the evenings when the conversation becomes desultory. They only talk about knights or troubadours and love, for their lives are limited. To establish harmony amongst them I suggest that they tell each other the memory that stands out most clearly in their minds. What moment in your life would you have back again, if only you could recall time?'

What moment would I take back and relive? The time when I first held my son? Every moment I was with Abelard from the first time I saw him until the day he came to watch as I took the veil? Not on that day which marked our parting, but so many of the others. If I could have only one of those moments back I would die happy.

'I have to attend to something. I forgot to tell the sacristan.' My words were scrambled and unclear, my eyes misted over as I rushed from that room and those women who wished to intrude into my private heaven and hell. In seeking for my strengths Eleanor had probed my weakness.

It wasn't to the chapel but to the garden that I hurried, to the bench under the tree where Abelard and I used to sit in those last years when we were comfortable together. Just being there made me feel calmer. For one extraordinary moment I thought that I could hear his footsteps, feel his presence, but the person who approached was not my only love, but Hildegard. She sat near me, without intruding.

'Eleanor told me something of your story. About you and Abbot Peter Abelard. Less than she wanted, as too much detail is her wont.'

'Is it so long ago that people need to be reminded?' I asked her. 'It was the talk of Paris for a long time.'

'Paris perhaps, I live a long way from Paris. We heard something of the condemnation of Abelard's writings at Soissons and then the further trouble at the Council of Sens. He seems to have been a person who attracted controversy, yet his hymns and writings reveal a man who thought deeply and was close to God. I can understand that you loved him.'

Could she understand how I loved him? The only other person who had room in my heart was our son and he was part of both of us.

'Come with me,' I said to Hildegard, standing up and beginning to return to the abbey. She arose more slowly as though her knees were stiff. Not surprising given the amount of time she spent on them. 'If you doubt Abelard's faith you need to see this.'

She followed, still protesting that she had no doubts. We came to my small room, and while Hildegard sat on the chair near the window I reached up to the shelf over the table and took down a small leather satchel. From this I carefully selected one letter. There were others, which no one would see until after my death, if then.

'Here, read this,' I commanded.

The letter is too long to reproduce here. It was Abelard's 'Confession of Faith', sent to me after his condemnation at the Council of Sens. He addresses me as *Heloise, my sister, once dear to me in the world, now dearest to me in Christ.*

The part I wanted Hildegard to read concerned the Trinity:

I believe in the Father, the Son and the Holy Spirit; the true God who is one in nature; who comprises the trinity of persons in such a way as always to preserve Unity in substance.

He wrote more about the nature of God and said that this was the faith in which he drew his strength in hope. The letter meant everything to me, even though I had never doubted his integrity or faith. How would Hildegard react?

She read it slowly, almost as though she were sounding out the words to herself, although I do not think it was difficulty with the Latin that impeded her. Eventually she looked at me, her brown eyes revealing both compassion and understanding.

'He was misjudged. He may not have known how to make friends with men, but he was close to God. Those gifts, which God gave to him, were also his burdens. Am I not right?'

It was then that I knew that I could trust Hildegard. Her divine Light and my intelligence would guide us. I watched her returning to the garden. The round, busy figure walked briskly under the canopy of trees. Slender branches bearing wine red and amber leaves extended over the path, creating a colourful symmetry. I saw her stop to talk to one of the sisters. Hildegard reached out to pick a leaf, smell it and then talked some more as she passed the leaf over. I felt no anxiety.

Before I returned the letters to their usual place I reread some of them. Abelard and I had written to each other when we first met, even when we lived in the same household. It was a joy and a challenge then, each trying to outdo the other in our expressions of love. Years later we wrote to each other again but these letters contained less about the nature of our love and more about our monastic lives, scripture and philosophy. It was the earlier letters that I now read.

It was while I was placing the letters back on the shelf that the idea came to me. I knew how we should appeal to Bernard.

*   *   *

People often ask me about Abelard, but few mention my son, Astralabe. It is a never ceasing sorrow that I was denied the joy of seeing him grow from a baby to manhood. I had hardly time to realise that I had both a son and a husband when Abelard commanded me to relinquish our baby and enter religious life.

'Command, my lord?' I was disconcerted. This was not as I had planned our conversation. I had come to tell him that after all that had happened, the evil done to him, and the wound he had suffered I would return to live in the abbey at Argenteuil. When I pictured myself there, it was always with my baby beside me. Thus I would spend my days reading and writing, praying for Abelard, rejoicing as I heard of each new triumph, or enjoying the books that he could now write. He would be free, as a philosopher must be. Even as I began to tell him all this he roughly bade me be quiet and hear what he had to say.

'Am I not, although maimed and useless, still your husband?'

Marriage and commands from husbands to wives go together, one reason why I had strongly resisted the idea of marrying. He continued, 'I will enter St Denis as a monk. I have spoken to the abbot. All is agreed. But

first you will enter Argenteuil and make your vows
in religion. In this way there can be no reproach against
me, or against you.'
I had envisaged myself rushing into his arms,
reassuring him, comforting him, assuring him that I
would sacrifice everything for his future. That was to be
my redeeming gift. His punishment was not only
robbing me of my joy in giving, but in demanding even
more.
Anger came much later. Then, as I watched him, sitting
with his head bowed and heard his voice, now
uncharacteristically soft, issue his order once again; I
could not wound him further. Later he told me that he
feared our marriage might be declared invalid and my
uncle would seek another husband for me.
'I could learn to live without your presence, your wit,
your *joie de vivre*, even your teasing. I could not live
with the thought that these would be enjoyed by any
other man,' he explained. As if, after I had possessed
Abelard, I could ever have accepted any other man.
Those who know me know that I can be determined –
stubborn some call it. They tried to prevent me taking
my vows.
'Wait for a year,' they said, 'take time for the sorrow to
heal.'
I would not wait.
'Think of your son. You may never see him again.'
Then I hesitated. Chubby, dimpled, sweet smelling,
mouth greedy for my milk, fingers uncurling as he
drank. Learning to walk, learning to talk, to love music
and poetry, all without my guidance.
'Promise you will care for our son?' I pleaded, the last
time I saw Abelard alone before I entered Argenteuil.

He frowned. 'Astralabe is safe with my sister. She
will raise him with affection.' Then, becoming aware of
my distress, he promised that he would see him as often
as was possible, and always send me news.
Finally my sense of loss overwhelmed me and I put my
head in my hands to try to hide the tears. Abelard came
and held me close. His tears fell on my head, a baptism
of sorrow, and I felt his loss too.
'God will provide for us. Trust in his goodness.'
Abelard had never spoken of God in quite this way
before.
I, instead, had found a barrier between God and myself,
an impediment which would take many years to
dissolve.
Thinking back on that day of decision I realised that I
had sacrificed my life out of love. As I now walked
about the courtyard, noting the orderly green hedges
and the shadows from the cloisters I understood that my
life was contained but not confined. If my liberty were
further threatened I would not surrender. This would
not be a call to prove my loyalty and fidelity, but an
attempt to restrict and enclose me even more
stringently, for a reason that I could never accept.
Sometimes mothers are permitted to enter a monastery
with their young children, but by the time I returned to
Argenteuil their rules had changed and it was forbidden
to have a male child there, even one so appealing as my
tiny boy. It may not have been the best place for him, in
any case. After all, at the age of eight Hildegard was
destined to be enclosed in a stone cell. She had told the
story without rancour. I wondered if that was how she
really felt. The next time we sat beneath the tree I
thought of as mine and Abelard's I asked her if she had

been happy to leave her home and family while still quite young.

'You're right,' she had said, 'I did not reveal the whole story. Eleanor would have misunderstood my sense of vocation. At the time when my mother told me that she and my father were sending me away, giving me to God, I was totally crushed. Only eight years old! Why be forced to leave my family and my home? Telling me that I was a gift to God was small consolation. My mother cried, and hugged me so hard that I couldn't breathe. She might have sent me to God sooner than she had planned.

'That day I walked about our home, the farm yard and orchard, the vineyards and the vegetable garden, placing each image in my mind so that I would always remember the greenness, the changing colour of the light through the branches of the trees and the clouds racing each other across the sky. Winter, just upon us, matched my emotions. The grey light seemed further distanced by my sadness. My only support was God, who is a loving God, but who seemed a long way away from me. Still, I clung to him in hope.'

She stopped talking for so long that I thought she had come to the end of all she wished to tell me. Then she gave a deep sigh, putting her hand to her forehead. She suffered greatly from headaches, I knew, brought about by tension and determination to get her own way, according to Eleanor, who recommended bathing her temples in rosewater. Hildegard's reply was that her pain was a necessary suffering, and she had her own remedies, but thanked her for her concern. Suffering and sanctity are reputed to be inseparable. Or rather, sanctity cannot exist without suffering, but not all who suffer became saintly. My life has provided me with turmoil and grief, but I have no pretensions to holiness. Hildegard looked at me then, and smiled. 'Do not doubt that you are pleasing to God,' and continued as though unaware she had responded to my unspoken thoughts. 'Talking to you has brought back so many memories. I remember the day my parents gave me away. It was a cold day. I was dressed in a lovely blue robe, one I had not seen before. Then they put jewels around my neck and bracelets on my arm. My hair was brushed and brushed, and pinned back so that it fell down my back. "Such glorious curls," my mother said and sighed. "The pity of it."

'At the church I was presented to the Abbot, my ornate dress was exchanged for a plain robe and my jewels placed in a small box together with other gifts that made up my dowry.'

'How did you feel at that moment? Knowing you would never see your mother again?'

Hildegard closed her eyes for a moment, as though reliving the day she was separated from her parents, her nurse, and her brothers and sisters.

'More desolate than I can describe. It was such a struggle not to cry. I kept hoping my mother would hold out her hand and say that it was a mistake and they would bring me back when I was older, but she just kissed my cheek, and asked me to pray for her. I had no choice but to go with Jutta. When I tried to hold Jutta's hand she shook it free.

'Jutta longed for the life of an anchoress. When I first met her she announced that we would live in a stone cell from the beginning, and never emerge to the outside until we died. My nurse had also told me that this was how it would be, adding that she thought it a

cruelty to expect a child of eight to live like that. So
for weeks I had believed that I would soon be enclosed
in a small area attached to the abbey, three small rooms,
with openings so that we could see into the church and
take part in the liturgy. Thinking about it each night
brought on terrible nightmares. I dreamed that I was
being held under water so that I could not breathe, or
that there was a tight band around my chest, restricting
me. I was powerless to move. Then I would wake up
screaming, and my mother or my nurse would hurry to
my room, and hold me until my sobs subsided and I
could breathe freely again. My mother would tell me
that God was always there to look after me, but she then
started to cry herself, and I did not feel convinced. I
told her I would like to be a nun, but not for a few
years. I loved my family.'

'The Church does many harsh things in the name of
God,' I said.

'My parents' intentions were well meaning, but it
would have been so cruel, as you say. To be deprived at
that age of family love, sunshine, the changing seasons
in nature, the joy of making a free offering of myself to
God when I was old enough. My foreboding was great,
yet proved unnecessary. I like to think it was through
my parents' intervention, but it may only have been
what suited the abbot or bishop that Jutta and I returned
to live for a time at Jutta's home, being taught by Uda
instead. She prepared us for our future lives at the
abbey. Not that Jutta needed much preparing. I was
satisfied that I had the chance to experience something
of the world, the way people lived and thought, before I
renounced it. Thus I could be more open to God who is
in all Creation. The contemplation of its wonder and
beauty brings us as close to the knowledge of God as

would hours spent kneeling in a chapel watching shadows against a wall. But I have never lost that terrible fear of being buried alive. Isn't this what Bernard is planning for us?'

'Perhaps he does not see it quite like that,' I replied. 'Tell me about Jutta. Did she become like a mother to you?' As I asked I wondered how good a mother Denise had been to Astralabe. No doubt she saw to his bodily needs, but did she show him love, feed his mind as well as his body, teach him about the stars and the planets, find him books to read, and help him to write poetry? Hildegard's answer to my question did not reassure me.

'Such a strong one, Jutta. As though she were afraid that to show affection, or even to feel any for a living creature would rob from her love for God. When I cried at night, missing my mother and my nurse, she admonished me to think of Jesus in the Garden of Gethsemane, when his disciples slept. Then she told me to be quiet. Instead I thought of Jesus as a child, with Mary and Joseph, growing in knowledge and wisdom. I will grow in wisdom and knowledge, I thought, although how this was to be I wasn't sure because Jutta wanted to teach me only what Latin was necessary for the saying of prayers and singing hymns. Her own education was limited and her thoughts and ambitions were only towards growing closer to God. She couldn't see that learning about God's world, studying the intricacies and wonder of his creation is another path to holiness.'

I wondered why this Jutta ever agreed to take an acolyte unless it was thought by her family that Hildegard would be of some practical help to her. The other reason may have been that it would have caused scandal to have a young woman, alone, in an abbey full of monks. Didn't Bernard claim that it was impossible for men to be near women without thinking about sexual activities?

'God provided for me,' said Hildegard. 'I learned to love the Holy Office, the psalms and the liturgy. I wrote my own music. When we were freed from our stone cell, after it became too small for all the young women who joined us, I discovered the abbey library. I escaped there as often as I could to read and study. The books about the way nature is arranged were the most interesting for they were like a map of the mind of God. His creation is too vast for anyone, even the most brilliant person, to begin to understand fully, but what is provided for us on earth leads us to appreciate the power, the love, and the force of God.

'I did not mourn for Jutta deeply when she died. She had left us long before she was called to her home with God. Her "children" had had to learn to fend for themselves. After she died – a holy death, I might add, and at a time she had foreseen – I was put in charge of all the young women who had joined us at Disibondenberg. By then Volmar was with me, because after I had finally told Jutta of my visions she understood better and arranged for me to have a monk to assist in writing down what I learned through the living Light. Volmar became my closest friend and spiritual adviser. If I had ever thought of marrying and bearing children it would have been to someone like Volmar, a stalwart, wise and good man. It is possible that he may have thought of me a little, in that way, in the beginning of our association, but he put all such desires from him in order to concentrate on the Lord's work. I suspected he talked to Jutta about his feelings.

He never did, or not directly, to me. Instead he concentrated on my poor Latin, encouraging and supporting me. My other, dearest helper is Richardis von Stade, a soul who has joined herself to me in loving friendship in everything and comforts me in all my trials. Were she my daughter in the flesh I could not love her more.'

I took her hand in both of mine, and then kissed her gently on her cheek. She responded by placing her other hand over mine. We sat there, in silence for a few moments, until the bell, that ubiquitous bell which controls us, indicated it was time to go to chapel.

*   *   *

Life in an abbey is meant to be uncluttered, freeing the mind and soul from earthly concerns so that one may give full attention to the Divine. This was what Bernard would claim he wished for women. Of course it is impossible. If we didn't have to eat, sleep, spend hours on divers activities, in other words if we were disembodied spirits, then we could spend our day in holy contemplation.

Being in charge of an abbey is similar to administrating any estate, a province, or even a kingdom. I realised this as I heard Eleanor talk about the concerns of her grandfather and father, and then her husband. Many women would think that being married to a king would be the fulfilment of all their desires. Eleanor is not among them. I never desired marriage, and once told Abelard that I would rather be his mistress than the wife of an emperor. At the time he saw nothing strange in that. Later he chided me for having had such sentiments.

A mistress greets her lover as an equal. A wife is a possession. The Church, gracing marriage as a sacrament, quotes from scripture that a man and wife become as one flesh. In reality marriage is a contract that has nothing to do with love. The troubadours, those experts of the heart, would have it that marriage and true love can never cohabit.

Eleanor married Louis because their fathers arranged it. He was from a royal family and she, also nobly born, had rich lands to endow. They hadn't even met when it was decided. No one asked them if they wanted to spend the rest of their lives together, and it appears that she, at least, does not. She gave us the impression that Louis was malleable, but I think she may have underestimated his tenacity. Neither was he one to accept a refusal. A second messenger arrived this morning ordering Eleanor to return. There were, the King pointed out, enough chapels in the palace where she could pray. This messenger also left our abbey without having accomplished his mission. Eleanor had given him a letter to take to her husband.

To my dearest husband, from your loving wife. Forgive me but I must ask your indulgence to allow me to remain a little longer. Here, in this abbey, I have prayed and I have seen a Light, which bathes me in the knowledge of goodness. This Light has revealed to me that should I travel now the baby in my womb may suffer. Allow me a few more days, for it may be the longed for heir that I am bearing.

We were not troubled further by messengers from Paris. I learned about that letter from Agatha who knew of it from Adele. I hoped that if Elizabeth knew she would keep her counsel.

'Being in love and being in the married state are quite incompatible,' Eleanor had said to me once. The matter of marriage and conjugal love had been far from my mind. I had done no more than greet her as I entered the room, finding her sitting in our only comfortable chair, feet tucked under her, with the toe of one embroidered shoe just showing under her skirt. With her face half in shadow, she looked very young, vulnerable. It was hard to believe that only the day before she had suggested that we kill Bernard.

'Look at Petronilla. Sisters can cause such trouble,' she had continued. 'A beautiful young woman, with her own wealth, sought after by so many suitable men, and she would have no other than Ralph, who already had a wife. Such a fuss when that marriage was annulled.'

'And your sister?' I asked, 'Is she happy now?'

'Contented enough. She has a son and two daughters. Bernard, naturally, has predicted that no lasting good will come of their union because it was not God's will. Do you think he actively wishes evil upon them? She's my only sister, my closest friend.'

We talk so often of God's will. Was castration really God's plan for Abelard? For what purpose was he brought so low in the view of so many people, if not in his own self-regard? It served little for my uncle. He was never the same again, either, but I can reconcile that to being the will of God more easily. Fulbert was to be pitied, ending his life as a sad lonely little man; he who had set so much store on family honour and the opinion of his peers. Yet I fear we were sinful, Abelard and I, in deceiving Fulbert.

When Eleanor first arrived she quickly grew impatient because we could not spend all day on her concerns. I assured her that they were our concerns as well, and that we would find the time we needed. Within a short time she seemed more relaxed, bending to the rhythm of the Benedictine day, sometimes coming to the chapel, keeping well hidden in the shadows. As we sang the Office she closed her eyes as the music echoed and resonated against the stone walls.

She was there the day we sang the responsory for St Ursula, which Hildegard had composed and taught to the ablest singers. The others contented themselves with listening, and maybe theirs was the better part as they could concentrate on both the words and the beautiful sounds.

A dripping honey comb was the virgin Ursula
who longed to embrace the lamb of God,
milk and honey under her tongue:
because like a fruit laden garden and splendour of
flowers,
she gathered a throng of virgins about her.
Therefore rejoice, daughter of Zion, in the noblest
dawn.
Glory to the father and to the son and to the holy spirit,
Benedicamus domino. Deo gratias!
Let us bless the Lord. Thanks be to God.

Hildegard's music is entrancing, as the higher voices rise and fall, always supported by a lower tone, like a heaven that is grounded in earth. As happens so often in the chapel my thoughts returned to Abelard. He would have approved her imagery, taken from the Song of Songs, but he may have thought her music extravagant. His religious music is more austere. Hildegard sees such beauty in virginity, but she has never experienced earthly love between man and woman. Could she love God more than I love Abelard?

So many said that he had used me for lustful
pleasures and then abandoned me. The manner in which
he distanced himself from me made it hard to deny their
accusations, and doubts became torment. In those last
few years, when we shared our work, I felt consoled.
His sufferings tamed him, but beneath it all his spirit
and intellect still shone; enough to enrage Bernard and
his supporters; enough to make them fear that the lion
might stir, or like Samson, bring the temple down
around them all. Now Abelard is dead, but I feel that
loss less keenly than when he turned his back on me at
Argenteuil, to walk his solitary path.

*   *   *

The nostalgia induced by Hildegard's music had abated
by the time we met that afternoon. Autumn had won the
battle over summer. Winter waited to collect the spoils.
Our room, although sunny, was chilly. Hildegard
rubbed her hands together; I sat with mine inside the
sleeves of my habit. The only one who looked really
warm was Eleanor, wrapped in a fur-lined cloak, more
than ever determined to march us to victory. Letters and
hymns did not convince her. She stirred impatiently as
Hildegard once more invoked the Spirit of Wisdom to
enlighten us. Scarcely was the prayer finished when the
younger woman once again urged us to action. Would it
help, she wondered, if we invited Bernard to meet with
me at the Paraclete, so that I could dissuade him from
sending his letter to the Pope.

'Hasn't he left already?' I asked, wondering if I issued
such an invitation while Eleanor was here with her
'small army' would Bernard ever arrive.

'I believe not,' said Hildegard. 'According to Volmar
he wished to take it personally, and he plans to visit
other abbots, to gain support.'

'There you are then. He covers all approaches,' said Eleanor, who refused to abandon the concept of this being a military campaign.

'Brother Volmar will be back from Cluny soon, and then Sister Elisabeth and I must return with him to our abbey at Mount Disibodenberg. We're running out of time and have achieved very little,' said Hildegard.

'We have achieved nothing,' Eleanor accused.

It was then I told them that I now knew what we had to do. We would write a long letter to Bernard, putting our arguments about the value of women both in the Church and in the world, in a respectful but positive way. I could then ask his opinion and advice about what I had written, as I had often asked Abelard. Bernard would not connect my letter with the one he had written, because he was unaware that we had obtained a copy.

Following this I would ask if it were possible for him to come to the Paraclete. If he had time to read and reread my letter before he confronted us it was less likely that he would explode in anger, interpreting our ideas simply as examples of women puffed up with pride. Eleanor looked less than impressed. Hildegard solemnly agreed that a letter was a good first step, but the power of music should not be discounted.

'Your words, and my music, those are our weapons,' she said.

'And my weapons?' asked Eleanor.

' Certainly not a sword. Your role will not be insignificant. Of that I am certain,' said Hildegard. 'It is just that for now we are not sure what it will be.'

Thus we decided on a two-pronged attack. I would write a letter to inform his mind. After he had read it and considered its contents he would come to the

Paraclete to talk to us. Hildegard's music would then soothe and calm his spirit. He would understand that we could do much good in the world.

'He is a saintly man,' said Hildegard. 'God will guide him.'

'You've never met him,' Eleanor, perhaps angry because her abilities were not appreciated, retaliated. 'I've seen him, this saintly Bernard. It was from a distance at Sens. Only later, at the consecration of the abbey church at St Denis did he deign to speak to me, and that was four years later. He has little time for women, although I'm told he honoured his mother, and has great devotion to the Mother of God.'

'You were at the Council of Sens?' I stuttered. 'You were there at his trial?'

'Whose trial?' she asked – stupid woman. 'We were there to honour relics being displayed in the new cathedral.'

She paused as though trying to recall an event that was etched on my soul.

'Ah, you mean the trial for heresy of your beloved Abelard. Yes I was there. Louis said that he was too proud and had to be humbled. Abelard appealed to the Pope in the end.' Eleanor smiled reassuringly, as though her final remark expunged all the suffering Abelard had endured.

'That is so, and much good it did him. Had it not been for Abbot Peter of Cluny he might have died discredited and disgraced. It's too long and sad a story to tell you now,' I replied, feeling suddenly tired and dispirited.

'Of course it's disgraceful. I never believed that he was a heretic.' Eleanor spoke quickly and again smiled at me. Immediately I warmed to her. She was so quick to understand an issue and to form an opinion. I could imagine her leading armies into victory, given the opportunity.

'Forgive my asking, but are you a competent judge of what is heresy?' asked Hildegard.

Eleanor's face hardened, but it was I who replied. 'We don't need the Church Fathers for everything. If one cannot discover the truth through one's own endeavours, then God has failed us.'

'Which is what the heretic Cathars believe. We must accept the guidance of the Church or fall to error. God's truth should not be trifled with,' rejoined Hildegard.

'Years before, I went to hear Abelard in Paris. Such a wonderful teacher, a fascinating man, and I'm sure, once an exciting lover,' said Eleanor, who had perfected never being deflected from her subject. She looked at me, quizzically. How did she expect me to respond? What would I want to say to her? What would Hildegard want to hear? In the ensuing silence I became aware of buzzing just outside the window. Walking across I stood for a few moments looking out on the sunlit garden, then turned back to them, my face calm. 'Last summer was fruitful,' I said. 'Listen to the bees. We had excellent honey this year.'

'You have goldenrod growing, so you should have good honey even now,' added Hildegard.

'I heard him speak when the Royal Garden was open to the schools,' continued Eleanor. 'A brilliant teacher, but I knew that life had disappointed him; beneath his animation there was an undercurrent of sorrow. Something I could understand, and share.'

Having brought the topic of conversation back to Abelard she then brought the subject back to herself. These were the times when she exasperated me. Even if

Hildegard did not, I wanted to hear all Eleanor could
tell me about Abelard, not her own minuscule suffering.
Hildegard intervened, 'A great soul, searching for truth.
You were privileged to have heard him teach. But
maybe we should now think of what Heloise may write
in her letter. And I must look for inspiration to write a
beautiful hymn. If we fail it will not because we did not
strive our utmost.'

'If we fail, it doesn't matter why. We will spend the rest
of our lives regretting the fact that you rejected the most
obvious solution.' Eleanor, with the last word.

*   *   *

Before our next meeting I took time to think. The letter,
I had told them, was not going to be difficult as I had
one from Abelard to guide me. Eleanor wondered if
using Abelard's letter as a guide was wise. He had
never convinced Bernard before.

'In truth, I doubt that anything written by a man would
serve our cause,' she concluded.

Hildegard told her not to be so prejudiced. Not all men,
she assured the Queen, fail to appreciate women's
particular abilities and gifts. That, I added, is precisely
the point that Abelard had made in his letter to me.
Years ago I had written to him, asking him to set out
the justification for the existence of nuns. His reply
described the favoured position of the women who
followed Christ, the heroines of the Old Testament, and
the women who had positions of authority in the early
Church. All I had to do was draw Bernard's attention to
these examples to convince him that women still had an
important role to play in the world.

'How many of those women were married, and needed
to have their marriage annulled?' asked Eleanor.

'Ah! The most important point,' said Hildegard.

Eleanor, impervious, continued. 'What about Ruth?
She was married, twice, and Sarah who forced
Abraham to send away his concubine Hagar and her
son once Isaac was born. Then there was Rachel, whom
Jacob married after he had married Leah.'

I thanked her for her suggestions. I could imagine
Bernard's reaction to Ruth, who had lain down at the
feet of her kinsman in the middle of the night, and who
knows what went on after that; Sarah, who had laughed
in the face of God's messenger, and Rachel who stole
household goods from her father.

'Choose the humble ones,' Hildegard advised.

'You're right,' said Eleanor. 'Forthright, confident
women will not advance our cause. Bernard, especially,
cannot abide women who speak their minds. But what
about Mary Magdalene?'

'What about her?' asked Hildegard, showing rare
impatience. 'She was a great sinner, a prostitute who
repented through the loving intervention of our Saviour.
What has she to do with the virgins and holy women
who give their lives to God in religion?'

Not being a virgin, in fact being closer to this accepted
view of Mary Magdalene than I was to the other Mary,
I felt moved to defend her.

'I have studied the Scriptures very carefully and have
come to the conclusion that Pope Gregory was wrong
when he declared Mary Magdalene to be the same
woman as the one Luke called the sinful woman. Nor is
she the one that John calls Mary of Bethany. I'll admit
there are a number of women called Mary in the New
Testament, but it is careless or lazy scholarship to
combine them into the one female figure, or two if you
count Mary the mother of Jesus.

'Perhaps Pope Gregory wished to discredit her, and make her an example for other sinful women,' suggested Eleanor.

'Abelard certainly would not have agreed with any Pope that Mary Magdalene was a sinful woman. He always said that of all the disciples she was the one whom loved Christ above all others. In the same way nuns are women who are devoted to Jesus,' I replied.

'I agree with Abelard, not Pope Gregory,' said Eleanor. 'In my land we honour Mary Magdalene. We believe that she came to Aix and was buried there, after living in a cave for thirty years, praying and fasting.'

'Others say that she lived in Ephesus with John the apostle whom Jesus loved, and died there,' I replied.

'Be assured that she is united with Christ, wherever she departed this earth. She is a woman who has much to tell us. Was she not the first person to whom Jesus appeared after his Resurrection? And, I believe that there are writings attributed to her, even a gospel. I've written a drama to be performed at Easter, in which Mary Magdalene searches for the risen Christ.'

Eleanor wanted to know nothing about my drama but all about this Gospel of Mary and how she could obtain a copy. Hildegard looked outraged, but, restraining herself, remarked only that such a piece of writing, if it existed, would lack the approval of the Church. More likely it was heretical nonsense and Eleanor would be better to disregard it.

Later, when we were alone, Hildegard spoke sternly. 'Take more care when you speak to Eleanor. As the spouse of a king she has some influence. It's for us to support the Pope, help him to guide his flock as Christ intended. We mustn't seek to diminish him.'

'Which Pope should we support?' I asked. 'Over the last decades there have been a number of rivals for the position, motivated by greed and a desire for power. Eleanor must be aware of that. There have also been ignorant and worldly bishops who dared to pass judgement on good men and women, just as those bishops at Soissons and Sens did to Abelard. Just as Bernard wishes to do to us.'

'Your own judgement has been warped by all that happened to Abelard,' she snapped.

'Hildegard,' I said as gently as I could manage, for I felt a fierce anger rising within me, 'I fear that your studies have not included history. If they had you would be aware that the actions of some popes, bishops, abbots and priests have been scandalous and would not be accepted by Christ as representing his teachings. The Cathars have some justification for their concerns.'

There was such a long silence that I feared that I had expressed myself too forcefully and Hildegard would decide that my faith, more than lacking depth, was non-existent.

Then she gave a deep sigh and said, 'It's true. Many of the popes, and even cardinals and bishops have not been true shepherds. There is pride and unworthy ambition among those who wish to scale the mountain peaks. Is it any wonder that the sheep are straying?'

'Thus speaks the prophet,' I said, but she knew I meant no malice.

'I have had such visions,' she replied. 'Would there were time to share them with you. When they are all written down you will read them.'

'I will, with all my attention and interest,' I promised. Our conversation had strayed far from the subject of those women who could be regarded as an inspiration and evidence of the value of women within God's kingdom here on earth. It seemed that writing the letter was not going to be so easy after all. To gain some privacy I went to the gatehouse, hoping there would be no visitors or interruptions. If Hildegard and Eleanor approved of the letter I could send it to Bernard to read. He would visit the Paraclete, and, I hoped, then return to Clairvaux, having decided that there was no need to travel to Rome and speak with the Pope.

A vain hope, for within the first hour Brother Volmar arrived back from Cluny, with disturbing news. Brother Bernard had left Clairvaux. It was impossible to send the letter to him now. I could not decide whether the rest of the news was good or bad. Bernard planned to visit the Paraclete before he travelled on to Rome. He could be arriving in a few days.

*　　*　　*

If my mind had been acting with its usual clarity; if Sister Anne, who was chosen to read for that month, had not developed a husky voice as a result of a slight chill; if Eleanor had not looked so unusually humble instead of being imperious and demanding, I would have replied that her idea was not to be considered. Even today I wonder at her audacity and my acquiescence. Would it be possible, she had asked, for her to read to the sisters as they ate their meal? Not only to be the lector, but also to read something she had written.

'I think that a rather unwise plan. Why do you desire to read to my Sisters?' I asked.

'It would give me a sense of belonging to your community, and I could tell Louis of it when I return to Paris. He'll be pleased to know how much I had entered into the life of the abbey. Royal approval might earn benefits,' she said.

We had gone to such great lengths to keep her presence there a secret. This would not be possible if she were to stand before the entire community and read, I reminded her.

'I've thought of that,' she said. 'Do you have a habit I could wear? Dressed in that I would appear, not as the Queen of France, but as an abbess, visiting from another monastery. No one will think to doubt it.'

An abbess, no less! Heaven forbid that they mistook her for a humble nun.

My sisters now knew and accepted Mother Hildegard and Sister Elizabeth from Bingen, but did Eleanor have no idea the amount of interest there was in the other mysterious visitors? To my own amazement, however, I agreed. Having obtained my assent she announced that she would read an account of the crusade. She had felt moved to write it, something she was sure I, as a scholar, would understand. I was welcome to read it first, she said, while making it clear in every line of her stance that any censorship would be resented.

'After all,' she pointed out as I hesitated anew, 'there are sisters here who have lost brothers, fathers, husbands even, dying to defend the holy lands. To hear of their feats and endeavours may bring consolation.'

Hearing of the scheme Hildegard was sanguine, soothing my misgivings.

'Remember that she has only recently returned from the places where Our Lord lived and preached. She wishes to share an experience which made a deep impression on her soul.'

I was not convinced. 'Most of the experiences she has shared with us are not suitable for the sisters here. But I

will not retract my word. Perhaps, dear Hildegard,
you should be there as well with Elizabeth, to create a
distraction if necessary.'

How far we had come from the simple, tranquil,
prayerful life of a Benedictine abbey. Since the advent
of these women I had so often thought that Abelard
would not have approved of all, or even any, of what
was happening. Bernard, if he knew, would insist that
this more than proved his argument. Members of the
weaker sex were not fit to take positions of authority.
Suddenly I felt very tired, old and discouraged. I
returned to the task of finishing the letter with no
degree of optimism or confidence.

Women have to be regarded as equal partners in the act
of creation and the governance of their world. But to
begin I set out the opening greeting to Bernard: *Abbot,
Learned Preacher, Holder of the Flame of Truth and
Integrity and my Father in religion.* It soothed me to
prepare my letter thus, even if Eleanor and Hildegard
thought it submissive and excessive. I was the epistler.
Abelard's letter to me regarding women in religion
gave me some inspiration. However, his arguments
supported Bernard's position far more than I liked. I
needed to show that women, within or outside the
abbey's confines, should not be isolated from the rest of
society. My biggest problem, however, was that
Bernard mistrusted logic. He believed that we would
come to truth and knowledge through prayer, loving
God and following the teachings of the Church without
questioning. I would be well advised to confine my
arguments to texts from the scriptures and the teachings
of the Church Fathers.

Starting at the beginning in the book of Genesis, we
read that the first man was created from the dust and

slime of the earth. God commanded him to name all
the things on the earth. The first woman was fashioned
from the rib of that man, not from the dust of the earth.
And when the man saw her he said, 'This at last is bone
of my bone and flesh of my flesh.' If you read Genesis
in Hebrew it is clear that in the beginning he did not
call himself Adam, which means human being, but *ish,*
which means man. The woman was named *Ishshah,*
which means woman.

I had gone to the gatehouse so that I would work
without distractions or interruptions. I had not counted
on the window that drew me, even as I told myself I
must concentrate on the letter. It was a windy day, the
trees and grass moving in rhythm, the trees urgent and
the grass with a certain languor. While many of the
trees had lost most of their leaves, others still held
theirs, reluctant to give up their glory, as a vain woman
dreads her thinning hair. I wondered what colour hair
Eve had, and was she tall, short, plain or beautiful. The
Bible does not give us such detail and as she was the
only woman alive it is unlikely that Adam was
discontented. Certainly he loved, or feared her, for he
did as she asked.

It is written that the first woman succumbed to the
blandishments of the serpent, and Adam followed her
example. Should he not have admonished her for eating
the apple, and refused to follow her lead? Instead he
joined her with little reluctance and then blamed her for
the whole catastrophe. For we read that Adam said to
God: 'The woman whom you gave to be with me, she
gave me fruit from the tree and I ate.'

He did not say 'the woman whom you gave to me', but
'the woman whom you gave to be *with* me.' Doesn't
that confirm they were equal?

The first man and woman were driven from the Garden of Eden. Adam called his wife Eve, as she was to be the mother of all the living. Women were to bring forth children in the pangs of childbirth, and men were to toil and sweat to produce the food needed to sustain life. Thus they were punished equally.

I was pleased with that argument, but wondered should I make reference to another verse in Genesis, which states that the husband should rule over his wife? Did this weaken my contention that men and women were equal? Had I not obeyed Abelard who was my husband when he wished me to make my vows in religion before he entered St Denis? I accepted that bondage out of love, and in that love I found equality with him. Did Eve love Adam, I wondered, with a strong, passionate love, as I had loved Abelard? I doubted it, for I could not believe that any other woman had been so engrossed and encompassed by love, or received such love in return so that we truly became as one flesh and spirit. Once, when I was feeling very discouraged, I asked Abelard if it was the lot of women to bring total ruin on great men. If there is no intention to do wrong, can there be fault? I may have been the instrument of Abelard's downfall, but it was through no consent of mine.

Returning to my letter, I wrote of Mary. At the marriage feast at Cana, Jesus made his entry into public life at the request of his mother. When she asked him to help the young couple to save them from the embarrassment of running out of wine, his reply seems very offhand, disrespectful even. 'Woman, what concern is that to you and to me? My hour has not yet come.' Mary was not deterred and bade the servants do whatever he asked of them. Jesus, yielding to his mother's wishes, turned water into wine.

This was the beginning of his mission. He was present there, with his mother and disciples. At the crucifixion, the last act of his public life, who was still with him? His mother, his mother's sister, Mary Magdalene and the disciple whom he loved were all that remained from the thousands who welcomed him into Jerusalem the previous Sunday. Several women. One man. What of the other eleven disciples who had followed him for three years, listening to his teaching and sharing his thoughts? One was hanging from a tree. One had denied even knowing him. The rest skulked in fear.

Only the women stood silently, observing Christ's agony, comforting him with their presence. They heard him call to the Father who had abandoned him. As he breathed his last sigh they cried out, then wept for his agony and degradation. Whatever blame may be laid at the feet of Eve was wiped out by the tears of those women. Could Bernard deny the worth of women who devote their lives to God and his people? They do not lead men to evil. Rather, through charity, suffering and sacrifice, they bring men closer to God.

Nor were women lacking in intelligence or wisdom. I wrote of Paula who, with both material help and her knowledge and skill as a translator, assisted the work of Jerome in translating the Bible. There were others, more than I needed, and I resolved to spend some further time in the gatehouse to revise and finish my letter on the following day when I had ordered my thoughts effectively. Then Hildegard and Eleanor could read it and hopefully give their approval.

The next day, however, was lost to me. Sister Christine, who had resumed her role as gate-keeper that morning,

came to find me as fast as her arthritis would allow.
It took a full minute for her to catch her breath and gasp
out her news. A messenger had arrived. Bernard, Abbot
of Clairvaux, was not far behind He was planning to
arrive at the Paraclete the next day. That meant I had to
see that all was in order. There would be no reproach
against my stewardship. So busy was I that I forgot to
give the letter to Hildegard and Eleanor. So busy that I
only remembered that Eleanor was to provide the
reading during the evening meal when she appeared
before me, dressed in our habit, and asked me to check
that it looked right.

'I might be revealed as an impostor if I have something
on back-to-front,' she said. She was more cheerful than
I had ever seen her.

'You look every inch the good abbess,' I assured her,
although no proper nun would stride down the corridor
with such a confident gait, or swish her skirts about as
she rounded corners. Hildegard and Elizabeth joined me
as we watched Eleanor and Adele, also dressed as a
Benedictine sister, stepping out towards the refectory.
They followed them, looking far more decorous, and I
was about to join them when I heard the bell from the
gatehouse. Sister Christine who had just entered the
refectory hurried back out, returning a short time later
with a worried expression.

'It's the Abbot,' she said, 'Abbot Bernard, with two
other monks. They are in the chapel praying and giving
thanks for their safe journey. I told them you would
greet them there.'

*   *   *

It must have been a hazardous journey for they were
long in giving thanks for their safe arrival. How much
more fervently they would have prayed had they known

of Eleanor's suggestion. Bernard walked out of the
chapel; stiff legged, as though still tired from his long
ride. This was my enemy, the man who had hounded
Abelard, and the man who wanted to enclose me behind
high walls so that the world would forget I ever existed.
With this thought in mind I noted the warmth and
friendship in his expression, and felt unmoved.

'We are filled with pride and rejoicing, gracious father,
because you have deigned to visit us,' I said.

'For my part I rejoice to be here, where there is true and
sincere charity, which proceeds from a pure heart, a
good conscience and an unfeigned faith.'

Having paid our respects to courtesy I urged him to
follow me to the small guest room, the room that had
been used by Abelard, where a sister would prepare the
table for him and his brothers. They must be weary,
hungry and thirsty, I said. Bernard insisted that no
special arrangements be made. For that evening he and
his brothers would join the sisters in the refectory.

I did all I could to suggest that he would be more
comfortable eating separately, but how could I object
strongly without appearing to protest too much? Well, I
thought, Brother Bernard is about to hear Queen
Eleanor of France preach on the recent crusade, and I
doubted that he would be pleased with what she had to
say. Our hopes of convincing him to change his attitude
towards women were looking very bleak.

The sisters had said grace before meals and were
settled, ready to eat, and to listen, simply waiting our
arrival. As we entered the refectory I noted that the seat
next to mine was left vacant for Bernard, while his two
companions were to sit at the end of a long bench
slightly apart from the nuns, and, as I saw with relief,

on the other side of the room to where Hildegard and
Elizabeth were sitting.

Eleanor, adjusting to her new persona, looked so
humble and devout that I feared she would be
unmasked through over acting. That feeling of being
tired and old returned, and I wished that I could just
close my eyes in sleep and never wake up. Eleanor
cleared her throat.

'Many women, as you know my dear sisters, took the
Cross and rode to Jerusalem, anxious to play their part
in the fight against the infidel.'

Eleanor paused for a second and looked down at the
parchment she had in front of her. Incongruously I
pondered on the injustice that a woman who had no real
interest in writing should have access to parchment
whenever she wanted. I stared hard at her, trying to
catch her attention, but she was too engrossed in the
pleasure of the nuns' rapt attention.

'Even the Queen went forth, with the knights and
soldiers from Aquitaine. She would not allow her
husband, the King of France, to outdo her in support for
the holy lands.'

As I feared, this was to become a eulogy for Eleanor's
adventures. Had Hildegard noticed our visitors? Could
she somehow distract Eleanor? Could Elizabeth pretend
to faint? Should I? Bernard's head was bowed and his
eyes closed as he said his own private and interminable
grace before meals. Considering how little he ate such
effusive gratitude was ostentation.

'But let me tell you, my dear sisters, the true story of
the crusading army which set out three years ago.'

Then, and only then did Eleanor look in my direction,
and pause. Her eyes narrowed slightly as she looked at
the thin man sitting on my right, then she smiled. That

smile sent a chill to my heart. What was she
planning? She continued, after swiftly moving the paper
and parchment that she had placed before her. Instead
of her own words she now began to read a different
account.

'Yes, it was in the Year of the Incarnation of Our Lord,
1146, that the illustrious King of the Franks and duke of
Aquitaine, Louis, in order to be worthy of Christ,
undertook to follow the path his Saviour had trod, and
to free the holy lands for all good Christian pilgrims.
There burned and shone in the king the zeal of faith, the
scorn of pleasure and of earthly glory. But men's hearts
were hardened and it required the impassioned
preaching of the saintly Abbot of Clairvaux. He
mounted the platform accompanied by the king, who
was wearing the cross, and when heaven's instrument
poured forth the dew of the divine word, as he was
wont, with loud outcry people on every side began to
demand crosses. And when he had distributed the
parcel of crosses, which had been prepared beforehand,
he was forced to tear his own garments into crosses and
distribute them.

'Thus the army left in an aura of sanctity, and if you
have heard stories of subsequent happenings which
were less admirable, remember that men are always
subject to temptations and sinfulness. Soldiers at war
may lack the gentling hand of women, for it is women,
following the example of Mary the mother of God, who
nurture, who heal, who restrain and guide men to the
path of righteousness. Let us now pray.'

So saying she bowed her head then, giving every
indication of complete humility and self effacement,
she turned quickly from the podium and hurried out the
side door. Would Bernard think that such a scripture

reading and conclusion was too unorthodox. Perhaps
the reference to him as 'heaven's instrument' would be
sufficient compensation. I hoped so. He watched the
departing figure with keen interest, then turned to me
and said, 'I wonder, my dear Abbess Heloise, that you
do not follow the practice of having your sister read
only from Scripture or the Church Fathers. And should
the reader not then rejoin the others at the table?'
'You are correct to point this out to me,' I replied
humbly. 'Our normal practice is as you advise, but our
reader today is not from our abbey. Perhaps, where she
comes from, they follow a different procedure.'
'No doubt they do,' he replied, 'there are some
disturbing practices in places which do not faithfully
follow the Rule of St Benedict. I have never doubted
that this Rule is strictly honoured at the Paraclete.'
Having said that he indicated that he was tired and
would retire to his bed immediately after Compline and
Vigils. He wished to speak to me on a very serious
matter, he said, and hoped that I could attend him after
he had said Mass on the morrow. Even as I agreed he
grimaced involuntarily.
'You must excuse me. I suffer sometimes from great
physical discomfort, especially after I have eaten. The
Lord sends us suffering to remind us of his own.'
I doubt that God sends us suffering for that reason, but
my thoughts on God and suffering were not to be
shared with Abbot Bernard. Far more important was the
need to confer with Eleanor and Hildegard. Would it be
better to tell Bernard that they were here, and ask him
to speak with us together? He was known to be quick to
anger. Maybe the sight of all three of us in the one
room might inspire one of his famous harangues. We
would have no opportunity to explain our concerns and

arguments before he stormed from the room,
prophesying our early demise. I went to find them.
Hildegard, who was sitting forlornly in our meeting
room, said nothing about Eleanor's reading, which
surprised me, until I discovered she had far more
serious worries. Bernard had been poisoned.
'I told Elizabeth that she needed to put a small amount
of the herbs in the body of the fish before it was
poached. That way the flavours are absorbed and
digestion is improved. The leaves are not to be eaten.'
I had never seen Hildegard so distraught.
'What are you talking about? What leaves?' I asked.
'I knew that Bernard would be here to dine with us so I
selected a fish which was fresh and moist, and
instructed Elizabeth on how to prepare it. She's more
familiar with this method of cooking fish than your
Sister Agatha. I gave her some fennel and field mint to
stuff the fish. I'd also picked some betony leaves, to be
placed under Bernard's pillow. It wasn't Elizabeth's
fault, I'm sure. Adele must have done it.'
'Adele must have done what?' asked Eleanor who had
been sitting so quietly in the corner, still wearing the
nun's habit, that I had not noticed her. Earlier I had
seen her, when Bernard had gone, holding my letter in
is hand, and my mind was taken up with all that might
mean. I had failed then to praise Eleanor sufficiently for
her quick reaction when she first noticed Bernard sitting
next to me. The account of the crusade she had begun to
read then was not her own but that of Odo de Deuil,
who was a priest who had travelled with the King and
his advisers. It was extraordinarily good luck she had it
with her. Had she anticipated she might need it?
Eleanor deserved credit for being so quick-witted, but I
had been absolutely shaken by the incident. The edifice

of my life was crumbling at my feet and I could not find any way to prevent it. In all the turmoil I had failed in charity.

'What crime are you attributing to my lady in waiting?' Eleanor demanded coldly.

Hildegard snapped back 'She put the betony leaves inside the fish with the mint and fennel. They should have been put in a small cloth bag under his pillow, not eaten. I fear that Bernard will have a very restless night of it.'

Then she buried her face in her hands before looking up again, her face drained of colour. 'He may not live to see the morning.'

'You should have been there to make sure it was all done correctly. It is a poor general who blames his troops for failure in battle,' responded Eleanor. 'Our whole plan is jeopardised because of your carelessness.'

It might have seemed amusing, such a compilation of errors in the abbey kitchen, except that the result might be Bernard's death. Too often poisoning was a means of eliminating adversaries. If Bernard, whose digestive system was none too robust, died after having dined at the Paraclete, what would people say? There were three women there who wanted him dead. That is what they would whisper among themselves until the whisper became a murmur and the murmur became a shout heralding our condemnation before we faced the roar of flames.

Hildegard attempted to reassure me.

'They're not usually fatal if eaten, but they can cause very severe indigestion, fever and delirium. As we know, Bernard doesn't have a strong constitution and the effect on him might be much more serious.'

I felt short of breath.

'All we can do is pray that he's spared,' Hildegard continued.

'Pray!' hissed Eleanor.

This time I agreed with her. There had to be more that we could do. Bernard dying at the Paraclete because of our cooking did not bear thinking about. Hildegard may have known something I did not for suddenly she appeared quite calm.

'God guides and directs us. After Compline would you permit a few of your sisters to sing the hymn that I've taught them? It praises the Mother of God, a woman much loved by Abbot Bernard. They can stand in the corridor near his room and their sweet voices and loving sentiments will soothe him into a dreamless, restoring sleep. Do not let your hearts be so troubled,' she said.

'You and your eternal hymns,' muttered Eleanor.

Much as I admired Hildegard's music I again agreed with Eleanor. If he survived, music would be insufficient to turn his intentions away from enclosing all monasteries which housed women, if only to protect other travellers from such severe discomfort. Our cause was lost.

Eleanor spoke again. 'You realise that had I continued to describe the crusade as I intended it would take more than a few young nuns singing or a letter, no matter how learned, to convince Bernard. Are not thanks due?' She dragged the veil from her head and released the plait that Adele had pinned behind her head so that no hair would be visible. The plait was twirled and twisted in her hand until she quickly flicked it behind her as though ridding herself of an unwanted appendage. Hildegard watched her; decided to re-enter the fray.

'Had you chosen something more appropriate to read in the first place, then there would have been no need to change anything at all. You risked much for the sake of self-aggrandisement. When pride attacks you, so that you consider yourself wiser than others, remember that you will one day return to dust and ashes,' she said.

'And it wasn't pride that led you to concoct some recipe out of fish, herbs and leaves which is likely to cause Bernard's death?'

I could see our trinity disintegrating, just when we needed the strength of unity.

'Perhaps you have another idea,' I said to Eleanor.

'Why do you ask? You don't seriously believe that I can make a difference, but you may have a different opinion when all this is over. Do not underestimate my ability to think quickly.'

'Therein lies what you believe is your strength but which may be your weakness,' said Hildegard. 'You would be better served to think ahead to all possible consequences before you act in haste. Bear that in mind, Queen Eleanor, for there will come a time when you will be asked to support rebellion and disorder within your own family. Remember that I have warned you.'

'What would you know of royal families?' said Eleanor. 'Keep your prophecies and warnings for your sisters. They bore me.'

'Please, let us deal with each other in charity,' I pleaded. 'There's still hope. Bernard has the letter.'

'You gave him the letter! Without consulting us? Our chief weapon, yet you gave us no chance to read it properly or make any comments,' said Eleanor. 'That was wrong. And unwise.'

'I would most certainly have wished to see it first,' added Hildegard. Moving to join Eleanor. Differences were forgotten, as they stood united in their anger. My voice caught in my throat, and I said nothing to my accusers.

'But,' said Eleanor softening a little, 'we were all caught unawares and you had to grasp your opportunity. If he dies in the night make sure that you take the letter back.'

'Did he read it? How did he respond? Dare we have any hope?' asked Hildegard.

'He didn't read it while I was there. When I offered it to him I simply said that, after much prayer and reflection, I had put down some thoughts about women, and their part in God's creation. Would he, in his great wisdom, be so kind as to read it, and offer me further guidance.'

'But did he say he would read it tonight?' asked Hildegard.

'He said he would, if tiredness did not defeat him.' I looked at them. For reassurance? For forgiveness? Again I felt the sinking feeling one has before impending disaster. 'He really did look very ill.'

The bell calling us to Compline prevented further dissension. Eleanor, despite being appropriately dressed, decided against going to the chapel. Hildegard, whom Bernard had never met, felt it was quite safe for her to kneel in the shadowy corner in case Bernard joined us to recite the Holy Office.

I took my usual place at the centre, behind the choir stalls. The sisters, ignorant of all the drama, were praying. They reminded me of flowers planted in a row, bowed down with evening dew. Their shadows, enlarged by the angles and tall candles, were like an avenue of large trees , so I had a complete garden setting before me. The mosaic of the Virgin regarded us all with a benign expression that never faltered. Neither did she ever frown or break into a warm, wide smile. Hildegard looked small and hunched. Elizabeth, opposite her, had red eyes from weeping. The fish, no doubt. I looked across to Abelard's tomb, and wondered what he was thinking. I desired with all my heart to sit with him now and tell him the whole silly, sorry story. Would he agree that I was pious and wise then? At a time when I especially needed to pray I succumbed to worry and distractions. All I could hope was that my letter would speak for us all, and that Bernard would survive his night of suffering well enough to be convinced by it.

*　　　*　　　*

Our story is far from finished. There was to be heightened drama that night but Hildegard and Eleanor will wish to tell their part in all that, and I could not deny them.

HILDEGARD'S STORY

God has revealed himself to me in signs and wondrous visions. I have sat with an emperor, conversed with bishops, corresponded with popes, admonished and advised kings, queens and abbots, and consulted common folk. Among all the important, holy and wise people I have met in my long life Heloise, Eleanor and Bernard hold a special place. More importantly, they came into my life when I was eager for change, planning to establish my own monastery at Bingen, against the opposition of Abbot Kuno. The women supported and encouraged me. The man would have held me in chains.

Eleanor, wife, queen, mother: red embers, slumbering flames, waiting to blaze and burn, fire. Heloise, mother, widow, and abbess: blue-white ice, cracked and splintering, thawing, limpid water. Eleanor as air, blowing questions and demands about in a frenzy. Heloise as guiding star, integrity, wisdom, poetry. And Bernard? A scorching fire; staunch rock upon which so many leaned and others broke; an arrow aimed at the heart of God. Heloise once called him an angel.

He was the shadow that loomed across our path as the sun was setting; the black smudges made by the trees in moonlight. Bernard saw no wisdom in women. That he was able to attribute to us such potential for evil is therefore a mystery.

*   *   *

During those precious weeks at the Paraclete Heloise and I were forced to relax our vow of silence. Eleanor made no effort to respect it so we talked freely, shared our thoughts, revealed what was dearest to us, discussed

our hopes for the future, came close to quarrelling,
but grew closer as we reconciled. Our union was born
out of intense fear. It grew to be a time on which to
look back with intense gratitude.

After Bernard had visited us, after it was all over,
Heloise suggested that we three women each write a
record of our time together. Women should not be
allowed to forget what we did, she said. Nor should
men be allowed to tell it, misrepresent or misunderstand
our collaboration. Eleanor and I solemnly promised that
we would do as she asked. Heloise, being a scholar,
said she would write her account almost immediately. I
have had to wait some twenty years before beginning
mine. Eleanor, active in intrigues, does not think of us
now, but there will come the time when she, too
remembers her promise.

The task seemed a simple one at first. It has, however,
been accomplished with no small difficulty, needing to
be left aside for more important work, so that it has
grown piecemeal over time. I cannot claim Heloise's
trained and orderly mind. She, now gone to her eternal
rest, will never read my story, although one day I may
find some means to read hers. Nothing will alter the
fact that while we were together we became a potent
and united force. Within the cosmos, how small our
unity of wisdom may seem, but how important it was to
us at that time.

*   *   *

We are all God's creatures, blessed to be part of his
creation. For me his world is light and shade, water and
wind, trees and the greening of the earth; all things that
God created. Light shows us truth. Light is the sun, an
orb, red as apples, yellow as sunflowers; at dawn rising
over the hills, at dusk dipping beyond the grape vines.

Light is the moon, daughter to the sun. From the golden sphere she receives nourishing power, just as the soul gives life force to our fleshly body. The light in my cell is from a small candle. Firelight warms and comforts. There is another light, a living Light, which cannot be extinguished even by the strongest wind. This Light has led me, step by often painful step, through the journey of my life.

How did I come to be so favoured by God? I was born into a good family, yet not so elevated that we succumbed to worldliness. I loved my parents and my brothers and sisters. Especially I loved my nurse who was tender and gentle unless I crossed her. None of them could accept that God had singled me out for his own purpose. When I spoke about visions and prophecies, they angrily warned me to be silent. My brothers spoke about witches and burnings. My sisters teased me and said that no man would ever want to marry me My parents decided to give me to God. It may be that they felt only God would know how to deal with me. I grew silent and remained so for many years. When I entered the abbey of St Disibodenberg I finally found I could no longer hold the gift of the living light to myself. I told Jutta, my spiritual mentor, that God spoke directly to me. I expected her to doubt, to accuse me of lying or pride, maybe to suggest that I was being tempted by the devil. Instead Jutta, through her wisdom and patient guidance, became another light, banishing darkness. Thanks to her intervention Volmar came into my life. Each day he was there, sitting at a desk in the corner of my cell, ready to write down the words God had spoken to me. He corrected my poor Latin as I dictated. He calmed my anxieties and offered me sage advice. Even now, if I close my eyes I can see Volmar as he appeared on that first day, standing at the door of my cell, holding out both hands in a gesture both of humility and support; a tall man, sinewy and strong in body and spirit. I trusted him immediately and felt no sense of restraint as I talked about my Light and visions. Fresh autumn winds invigorate us. Volmar was such a wind, sending my thoughts swirling about, until they settled where they belonged.

St Disibodenberg is not one of the great abbeys, but neither is it insignificant. A scholarly monk named Disibod had travelled from Ireland hundreds of years ago, finally choosing this place for his monastery. Built on a mound, surrounded by apple orchards and fields where sheep grazed, the abbey buildings are pressed into a confined area, crammed together. There is little enough room for all the monks. Jutta and I, when we entered and took our vows, were kept strictly segregated. We began our religious life in two cramped, confined cells and would have remained so if Jutta had had her way. All she needed was standing room, bare feet on the cold stone floor as she prayed, and a glimpse of the chapel through a small grilled aperture. I hated the cold, dark space and found the walls tightened like a band of ice around my forehead. My head throbbed so persistently that I had to fight the urge to beat the sides of my tiny cell in rhythm. Where was the sunlight? Would I never again hold a buttercup to reflect the colour under my chin? Must I always pray without the joy of singing the Office in community with others? Each day I grew more desperate until we were suddenly set free. After a few years other young women wished to join us, although if they had known of the conditions under which we lived they might have wished otherwise. We were given a larger space with the

freedom to move about out in the fresh air and
daylight. Jutta mourned the loss of her deprivations. I
rejoiced that I could breathe again.

Volmar often said how fortunate we were to have a
good supply of sheepskins to make into vellum, and
goose feathers for quills. He was practical as well as
learned, a solid stone the gave me support. At times I
grew very weary because of the intensity of our work,
and my head ached and pounded, my limbs grew heavy
and I yearned to close my eyes and relax my body next
to the warm fire or outside in the freshness of the day.
Volmar knew then to allow me time to withdraw into
myself and regain my energies. He was the perfect
companion, guide and amanuensis.

A short time later Richardis joined us. Richardis, flesh-
pink as a lily, gentle as the spring rain, fresh water
quenching my thirst. Without water there could be no
life. Without Richardis I would have been barren.

I saw that her soul was noble and had guided her to a
great knowledge and love of God. Even today my love
for Richardis remains. So does the memory of the pain I
felt when she left us to become an abbess elsewhere.
She would never have thought to leave me of her own
accord. However, she was lured away by a family who
wished to take pride in her status and position.

Who could have needed her more than I did? She had
been with me from the beginning of my work on
Scivias, through the turbulent first year when we left
Disibodenberg to establish the new monastery, until we
had finally triumphed. Some weaker, softer sisters
grumbled about the lack of comfort, then left for other
monasteries. Richardis tried to shame them into
remaining, reminding them that in just such difficult
circumstances Brother Bernard and his small group of

young men had founded Clairvaux, and the Abbess
Heloise had rebuilt the Paraclete. To share in the glory
of Easter they must suffer their Calvary. Never, not for
one moment, did I think that Richardis would ever
desert me as those other daughters had done. I loved her
too much.

I did not let her go lightly. Instead I fought like a wild
animal protecting her young cub. I called out to
whomsoever might listen and heed my pain. To her
family I wrote that they should take care lest by their
will, their advice and their connivance, Richardis would
lose her soul. For the position of abbess that you desire
for her, I wrote, is surely, surely, surely not compatible
with God.

They did not heed me, nor regard my anguish.

Pleading, I then wrote to Hartwig, Richardis's brother,
believing him to be a man of intellect and integrity.

*Now hear me, cast down as I am, miserably weeping at
your feet. My spirit is exceedingly sad, because a
certain horrible man has trampled underfoot my desire
and will (and not mine alone, but also my sisters' and
friends') and has rashly dragged our beloved daughter
Richardis out of her cloister. Since God knows all
things, He knows where pastoral care is useful, and so
let no person of faith canvass for such an office.*

Bishop Hartwig's reply delivered only disappointment
and despair.

The day Richardis rode away was bereft of light and
warmth. The others stood at the gate to farewell her. I
remained at my cell window, listening to the horses'
hooves on the hard ground growing ever fainter, the
wind howling and prowling about the cloisters, the cry

of a raven. I listened longer, hoping to hear the sound of horses returning, but there was silence, until my ears could strain no more and my eyes could not hold back their tears. So long ago, yet the hurt of betrayal remains, tempered by understanding and forgiveness. I wrote my sorrow to Richardis in another letter after she had gone.

Daughter, listen to me, your mother, speaking to you in the spirit: my grief flies up to heaven. My sorrow is destroying the great confidence and consolation that I once had in mankind.
Now let all who have grief like mine mourn with me, all who, in the love of God, have had such great love in their hearts and minds for a person – as I have had for you – but who was snatched away from them in an instant, as you were from me. But all the same, may the angel of God go before you, may the Son of God protect you, and may his mother watch over you. Be mindful of your poor desolate mother, Hildegard, so that your happiness may not fade.

Two years later she was dead. Her brother, Bishop Hartwig, wrote to tell me that on her deathbed Richardis had shed tears of longing for our cloister. Would that she had remained with us and been spared those tears.

Never say that because I have not given birth I have not suffered the loss of a beloved child. She was my spiritual daughter. I had bestowed a mother's concern on her; had shared my life's work, my plans and aspirations with her. To me she was exquisite, rising like a flower in the beauty and glory of the world. When I accepted that God took her to him because he

loved her even more than I, only then did my pain
ease a little.

Throughout all that time Volmar remained, faithful,
steadfast, loyal and indispensable.

*   *   *

At times my living Light resembles the sun. At others it
is like the softer light of the moon, a candle, or even the
dim glow from embers. So wonderful is God's creation.
I am the breeze that nurtures all things green
I encourage blossoms to flourish with ripening fruits.
I am the rain coming from the dew
that causes the grasses to laugh
with the joy of life.

*   *   *

It is sixteen years ago that Eleanor, Heloise and I sat
together in the white room overlooking the garden of
the Paraclete. Since that time Eleanor has been crowned
Queen of England. I doubt this suits her much better
than being Queen of France. She belongs in Aquitaine,
sun drenched in music with her own people around her.
Frederick, known as Barbarossa, has been crowned
Emperor. Alexander is Pope, while Victor claims the
chair of Peter for himself. There is grave disquiet within
the Church because of it. These matters disturb me, as
they must all who desire God's kingdom.

Other events are closer to my immediate concerns.
Fifteen years have passed since my sisters and I left
Disibodenberg to establish our monastery at
Rupertsberg, near Bingen. We have established another
at Eibingen, which shows that God has blessed our
work. It is twelve years since Richardis died. These
years have taxed my strength, but my life has never run
smoothly. Even as I had overcome my fears and begun

to write my book, *Scivias*; even as I was granted
permission from the abbot and bishop to do so; even as
I had gained the gift of Volmar to work by my side, I
was sorely troubled. Without the approval of the Pope
and all the Church I could be condemned as a heretic.
Such condemnation meant excommunication or being
burned to death. So I wrote to Bernard of Clairvaux,
and opened my heart to him. He responded, not as a
loving father but as a careful cleric. Consequently my
writings were to be examined by the pope and cardinals
at the synod of Trier. Volmar attended the synod on
behalf of the abbey, and I yearned for his return, finding
each day longer than the one before.

While I waited I tried to work in the garden, pulling at
the weeds with an urgent energy. On other days I
slipped into the abbey library, hoping that no one would
notice me as I read the books on medicine. The way our
bodies work, and the methods of healing – all this held
my interest until I remembered, with that sick feeling
that feels like a lurch in your stomach, that my future
was being decided hundreds of miles away by a group
of men who had never even met me. How could they
judge fairly? At the time I told myself that God would
not ask me to write down what he told to me in a vision,
and then permit me to be accused of heresy or, worse,
witchcraft. Unless, I considered, he wished to send me
trials and further suffering? Each new day I prayed for
strength, and continued to wait.

They were long weeks where my anxieties gnawed at
my faith, so that, on the day they told me that Volmar
had returned from Trier, I felt a sudden, unwelcome
fear. As it was already early evening I doubted he
would come to see me before the following morning,
and anticipated a long night. Such was his compassion

that he ignored his fatigue and came after Vespers
had been sung. I looked at him closely, noting his face
creased like a walnut shell, his eyes full of weariness,
but serene. I felt hope.

'Sit down, Brother Volmar. Such a long tiring journey
you've had,' I said, congratulating myself on my
restraint. 'Did the synod achieve all you expected?'
Thanking me for my courtesy he settled on the chair
opposite mine, by the fire, and began to tell me the
general news, delaying reference to what I wanted so
desperately to hear.

'We didn't meet at the main Cathedral of Trier or the
Church of Our Lady, as I thought we would. Instead the
Council was held at the abbey of St Eucharius, south of
the city. The apostle Matthew is buried there, as are the
bishops Valerius and Eucharius. We had an illustrious
audience.' He looked at me with a sly smile.

'Tell me what happened about *Scivias*. I don't want to
hear about dead bishops or apostles, no matter how
saintly,' I begged. 'Had Abbot Bernard shown the Pope
my writings?'

'Your writing is more important than you might think.
It was the Pope who brought it to the attention of the
assembly.'

'Surely all those bishops and priests must have
wondered why they should waste their time on the
scribblings of a very ordinary, unlearned nun. Did you
see their faces? Did they look receptive?'

Volmar leant forward to stoke the fire. Sparks sprang
free from the glowing logs and flames leapt about like
playful cherubim.

'Now there you can thank Brother Bernard. He made
sure they listened, saying that there were no heresies in
Scivias but only words of inspiration. Pope Eugenius

indicated his agreement. Then they all stopped looking as though they were anxious for their dinner and settled to attention. The Holy Father himself read passages from your work. The Holy Spirit was with us and there was no hesitation about granting approval to your work after that, no voice of dissent. We can begin in earnest now.'

Volmar stood up and moved to his usual chair, as though ready for dictation.

'It's not my words that they heard, but God's,' I reminded him. 'God uses me as a humble instrument, for his greater glory.'

'Yes, yes,' said Volmar almost impatiently.

'Come back and sit longer by the fire and warm yourself my dear Brother, before you go to your rest. Tomorrow is time enough to recommence the work,' I suggested.

'I am tired,' he agreed, 'but happy to know that those who are our shepherds recognize their sheep.'

'And who are the goats?' I laughed and I felt a rush of relief as the news began to sink in. Had I really doubted that the Church would approve the words of God? There are many prophets and it is not always obvious which are false and which are true.

*   *   *

My last years on earth should be spent in quiet prayer and peaceful contemplation, moving sedately from my cell to the chapel, between visits to the garden and refectory. Instead I am continually invited to visit and preach in cities up and down the Rhine. These journeys are tiring but how can I resist? Twenty years after the synod of Trier I also went to that city, at the invitation of the Bishop. By then I was in my seventies, and my knees, gnarled like an old tree trunk, had counted every

year. My reputation had grown since I made that
first trip to the Paraclete. Even then I was in my late
forties, well past my youth. It is rare, no it is
unprecedented, for a woman to be invited to preach in a
church but on the feast of Pentecost I stood in a church
at Trier before the bishops, the prelates and the doctors.
Was I standing in the elaborately carved pulpit in the
church that had once been Emperor Constantine's
palace? Certainly I visited the cathedral, for I remember
looking around the magnificent building and being
reminded of Bernard of Clairvaux's call for plain,
unadorned buildings in which to worship God. Perhaps
he was right. These churches are as ornate and grand as
many a ruler's castle and the ordinary people may have
difficulty in telling the difference between their
spiritual and their secular leaders.

Volmar, inured to the rigours of travel, was delighted
to revisit the Roman ruins and to see some of the
treasures which were kept in Trier's churches and
abbeys. I had heard talk of a very special relic, so
precious that it was never displayed, but kept carefully
hidden. It should not be hidden from me, I decided.
'You have an object which is greatly venerated I've
been told. Would you allow me the privilege of seeing
it?' I asked.

There was no immediate response from the Bishop.
Firstly he pondered as to what we knew. That much
was written all over his face. Then initial suspicion was
chased away by the thought that we could be trusted. I
was eminent enough to preach in front of him; surely I
deserved to be shown their greatest treasure. Maybe he
was remembering my admonitions from the pulpit the
day before. Not wishing to appear prideful I had begun
by affirming that I was nothing but a poor female

figure, lacking health, strength, courage and
learning. Then I issued a warning.

'The four corners of the earth have grown cold. We see
no longer in the east the dawn of good works; in the
south the warmth of virtue grows chill; in the west the
twilight of mercy has given way to the blackness of
midnight; and from the north Satan blows his noisy
wind of pride, faithlessness and indifference to God.'

They had to understand that evil would come to the
earth if they did not listen to God's words and obey
them.

Perhaps the Bishop's hesitation to show us the holy
relic was inspired by pique. No bishop likes to hear that
he is neglecting his flock, and he had grimaced and
frowned, squirmed about and cracked his fingers in a
most irritating way as I was speaking. We waited, as he
conferred with two other priests and returned, agreeing
to show us Christ's tunic, brought back by St Helena
from the holy lands. Volmar's lined face creased into a
broad smile when he heard their decision.

The robe lay in a carved wooden box lined with purple
and golden cloth. A simple brown robe, faded in places,
with tucks, like small pleats at the neck, and wide
sleeves. I knelt in reverence for a few moments, before
reaching out my hand to touch the precious tunic,
ignoring the Bishop's intake of breath and raised hand.
I felt nothing except the sensation of dried cloth; no
sense of the Spirit nor the presence of Christ. Still
kneeling I thanked God for the gift of his Son who had
won for us all the entry to Paradise. As I got to my feet
one of the priests placed the cover back over the box,
and quickly carried it away to who knows what safe
hiding place. Volmar, who had knelt in respect, made

no attempt to touch the holy robe. He remained
silent, only gesturing his thanks to the Bishop.
Was it really the robe which Jesus wore, and for which
the soldiers cast lots at the foot of the cross? Could we
ever be sure? St Helena believed that it was, and how
wonderful were it truly so.
We stayed at the abbey of St Eucharius where I had
been granted permission to follow God's direction
twelve years before. The large white church dominated
the grounds of the abbey whose lands reached as far as
the river. Walls marked the boundaries. There was a
sense, within those walls, of peace and quiet, away
from the bustle of commerce and people going about
their daily business. Walls make prisons, but they also
provide shelter and safety.
Within the church itself there was the beautiful
Weihekreuz, a sacramental cross of ochre red stone
against a white circular background, as though it was
marked on a host. Simplicity houses beauty. Elaborate
tombs held the remains of St Eucharius and St Matthias.
St Eucharius became somewhat a favourite of mine. I
wrote a hymn for him, which I still love to sing.

O Eucharius! You were blessed
When the Word of God seized you.
In the dove's fire,
When, brilliant as the dawn
You established your church.

I like to think that the Word of God has also seized me.
Not to puff myself up with pride, but to believe that all
that I do is to ensure that his kingdom comes on earth as
it is in heaven.

*　　　*　　　*

The first journey I undertook, to the Paraclete, was
not in answer to any invitation but was born out of fear
and anger, undertaken with great trepidation tempered
by excitement. Volmar told me of a letter which
Bernard of Clairvaux had written, a letter which would
mean the end of all my plans. Bernard claimed that
what he proposed was based on the teachings of Christ,
expounded by the apostle Paul, supported by St
Augustine, and therefore it should be the practice of the
Church. I accepted that Paul, Augustine and others may
have espoused such a view, but nowhere could I find
that Christ had taught it.

'How have you learned of this letter?' I asked Volmar
after he brought it to my attention. 'Surely you have not
been speaking to Abbot Bernard?'

'I was informed by a cardinal's secretary. He said that
Bernard has written a letter to the Pope recommending
changes in the rule for religious women, to be put in
place as soon as possible. Nuns are to be very strictly
confined, forbidden to leave their monastery once they
have taken their vows, be forbidden to write anything,
or compose music. They will confine their daily
activities to servile work and prayer and have no
contact with the world outside the walls which surround
the monastery buildings,' replied Volmar. 'I have no
need to explain how this affects you.'

The effect was immediate: tension in the nape of my
neck, spreading down to my shoulders, stiffening the
small of my back. Should the Pope agree, and why
would he not follow Bernard's advice, my own plans to
establish a monastery with my sisters would never be
realised. I had chosen the site, on the junction of the
Nahe and Rhine rivers, closer to Mainz, yet still
accessible to Disibodenberg; a position where we could

be detached from the world, yet feel its pulse; well placed to poke a stick into any nest of vice or indifference, to stir men and women to respond to God's commands.

Abbot Kuno grew red with outrage when I told him that God was directing me to establish my own monastery. 'You must all remain at Disibodenberg,' he insisted. 'You and your sisters are part of our monastery. St. Benedict would not have approved. The God I understand would never direct you to leave and I forbid you to even think of such an idea.'

That was the Abbot's position. On the other hand I believed that we would have the moral and, as important, the material support of the widowed Richardis von Stade, mother of my beloved Richardis. Once that was secured we could then count on the help of Heinrich, the Archbishop of Mainz, and others. That should counter any attempt by the Abbot to stand in our way.

If we were granted permission my sisters and I would have to work, for a time, as hard as peasants in the field, or as carpenters or builders even. Tender hands would become roughened and soft bodies become strong. Local people might help us, but our community would be tested. I trusted we would not be found wanting. While anticipating many serious problems, I had not counted on Bernard advising the Pope to forbid the project even before it had begun.

'My plans?' I asked Volmar.

'Abandon them,' he replied.

'But if God commands me? Am I to be given permission in Trier to follow God's directive, and have it denied in Rome?'

What can a condemned prisoner say? What comfort can the person who conveys the sentence offer? Volmar put his face in his hands. All I could do was look through the window at the blue sky, marbled in clouds, and remember my first years at Disibodenberg when I was forbidden sunlight, moonlight or any glimpse of the stars.

Volmar suddenly straightened and said: 'Nothing is settled as yet. Pope Eugenius has the final decision, although he is receptive to advice from Bernard. The Abbot of Clairvaux sees himself as a broom sweeping out all the dusty corners. That man has a way with words; you can be persuaded as you hear him in the heat of the afternoon, yet wonder about it in the cooler evening light. We must not just ignore this letter.'

'What can I do except pray?' I asked.

'We can both pray in loving faith, but has not God also given us wisdom?'

Men can be expected to side with men. What wisdom I had led me to seek help, not from a man but a woman. Whom could I trust? I had heard of one; Heloise who was widely reputed to be a great scholar and a prudent abbess. Were I to suggest her would Volmar accept the idea?

'Is there some person who could advise us? You have met with some of the great minds of the Church, Volmar. Is there someone who might join us in fighting this directive?' I said.

'There is one man who might help you. The Abbot of Cluny is an obvious choice, for he and Bernard are often opposed.'

'I've heard that he is a learned man, but very occupied with serious matters, often away from his abbey. Could you think of any other head of an abbey who is noted for scholarship, who may have suffered some time earlier because of some problem with the Church, and yet who now has an exemplary reputation?' I then asked, gently.

'Is it possible, and you will not have considered this, that you could talk to a learned and respected woman?' replied Volmar.

Arranging my face appropriately I gestured to him to continue.

'Some still talk of her liaison with Abelard, but that was been many years ago, and they did finally marry. I am thinking of the Abbess Heloise at the Paraclete. Unfortunately her abbey is in France.' Volmar continued. 'It's a long way,' he continued, 'but not impossible as we could travel much of the way by river.'

'It is impossible,' I told him, not allowing myself to smile.

'It is an extraordinary idea,' I repeated.

'Could it be possible?' I asked.

Then, 'Leave me pray about it. The living Light will guide me. If God wishes us to go, no man will prevent us.'

It was simple to choose a woman whom I hoped would join me in opposing Bernard's idea. Gaining permission to travel such a distance was be far more difficult. Nuns do not climb over mountain passes, ride mules along long roads and sail down rivers in order to visit other nuns. But once I was determined to go nothing deterred me. Volmar understood that. Perhaps he could read the signs of suffering on my face and body and realised that I would soon become ill, incapacitated by pain if I were refused permission. Certainly he approved my choice, believing it to be his own.

Abbot Kuno was very reluctant to grant the necessary permission. It was true, he said, that the approval given to me at Trier gave me some authority but this was no reason to allow me to travel across the country into foreign terrains just to speak with the Abbess Heloise on spiritual matters. Abbot Kuno always spoke slowly and deliberately, ruminating over each phrase. That day he was so ponderous that he stood for some minutes not speaking at all, stretching my tolerance to its last sticking point, until he finally offered his own solution.

'There are good and holy women in Germany. Elizabeth of Schönau, for example, who though younger than you, dear Mother Hildegard, is noted for her piety and visions. Had you thought to speak with her?'

I had not, nor would I.

'Is it by God's direction', he then asked, 'that you plan to make such an unorthodox and dangerous journey? Have you searched your conscience? Might I warn that you are becoming proud, thinking yourself above the Rule and the wishes of your abbot. Is your conscience totally clear?'

Of course, when he questioned me, he believed only that I wished to consult on matters that pertained to my spiritual writings. Had he had any idea of the real situation he would have sent me to my cell and firmly shut the door. God was on my side, and through my tears of humility, and Volmar's tacitly agreeing with the abbot that by permitting me to make this journey I would certainly lose any desire to establish my own monastery, Abbot Kuno reluctantly gave his permission.

'How did he come to such an idea?' I asked Volmar.

'He may have misunderstood something that I said
about you realising how difficult it could be, but I did
not wish to contradict my superior, who is a learned
man,' Volmar replied, with not even the hint of a smile.
 So it was agreed that I should travel with Volmar to the
Paraclete, which was near Clairvaux and Cluny. We left
in early September, the days still holding strong
memories of summer; then returned in November when
the autumn chill had changed to winter. In all I stayed
away for seventy days, not fasting as did Jesus in the
desert, but feasting on ideas and shared experiences.
How difficult and illuminating that first journey turned
out to be. It is easy to say I will travel to France, to the
Paraclete, to confer with Abbess Heloise. It is not so
easy to persuade the abbot of your monastery to agree
to such an idea. The whole idea comes to seem almost
impossible when you begin to prepare for a journey
which will take you to unfamiliar places, into danger
from robbers and the uncertainty of where to lay one's
head each night. My own fears, growing by the minute,
might have put a stop to the trip before it even began. I
was reassured by Volmar, who had recently travelled to
Trier and back. My dearest Richardis prepared a special
bag to carry all that I would need, with a small pocket
sewn into one side so that I could find my prayer book
easily. That completed she had arranged for the baker to
prepare special loaves for us, and found me a warm
woollen shawl to wrap around my shoulders as
protection whenever the cold winds blew from the
mountains. I wished with all my heart that Richardis
was coming with me, but she was needed to take my
place while I was away. Whom to choose then? Volmar
and I certainly could not travel alone. I sat with
Richardis on the seat outside the chapel, the warm sun

on our faces and the sounds of the birds quarrelling
in the trees. She, happy and relaxed, me nervous and
querulous, we went through all the possibilities.
'Sister Elizabeth,' she declared, after I had dismissed
the suitability of several others. 'I'll tell her all she
needs to do to ensure that you are healthy and
comfortable, for I could not bear it if you did not return
safely to us. Don't stay away too long,' she added.
Elizabeth had cheeks like apples, rosy and freckled. A
cheerful if timid soul, she shrieked at shadows,
complained of the mud and rain, said her bed was
lumpy and uncomfortable, yet rose each morning newly
full of joy.
We left the next day. A strange procession, moving
down the steep slope, through the trees, past the sheep
that looked at us without curiosity, along a narrow path
to the river where the boat was moored. Volmar went
first with Abbot Kuno who had insisted on coming to
give us his blessing and admonitions. Sister Elizabeth,
blushing with importance, led the mule which carried
such luggage as we had, for we were travelling with as
little as possible. Richardis and I walked behind, and
she reached out a steadying hand as I slipped on some
loose stones, almost sitting down in an undignified
heap.
'Hardly the best beginning,' I said.
'Believe that the worst is over, and there will be no
more stumbles,' she answered. Of course there would
be much worse to come. Even Richardis recognised
that. I looked up and saw that she had tears in her eyes.
Mine then became misty so I abruptly wiped my hand
across my face and forced myself to smile. Did any of
them know how close I was at that moment to deciding
that we would all be better remaining at Disibodenberg?

I was spurred to continue by the knowledge that
Bernard's letter could only be defeated with delicacy
and wisdom, which I could not do alone. I had not even
read the letter, but knew enough of its contents to be
very alarmed. No doubt Heloise had received a copy,
for these letters seem to multiply and disseminate
between monasteries. I had to have faith that she would
know what to do, which may seem strange because I
had never met her. How often do we find ourselves at
important times in our lives stepping towards the
unknown in the hope that this will be our salvation?
Abbot Kuno had arranged for us to travel on a boat
which was collecting some wool from our monastery.
The boat, of medium length, looked fragile. Only
planks of wood lay between us and the muddy bottom
of the river. The boatman gestured to us to hurry for
there was a fair wind and he wanted to take full
advantage of it. Volmar stepped in confidently. The
boat rocked in a most alarming way until he had sat
himself down. Elizabeth stepped across then, looking
less secure, but making only slight disturbance, which
did not prevent her from letting out a shriek. Abbot
Kuno frowned, as if to say that if this was the way we
were going to conduct ourselves we were better not to
go. The boatman and the young boy who sailed with
him loaded our bags. With Volmar holding one hand,
and Richardis steadying the other I stepped over the
gunwale and sat next to Elizabeth. It took a few seconds
for the boat to stop rocking, a minute for the boatman's
young helper to release the boat from its mooring, the
boatman to set the sail, and then we pulled away from
the river bank. I looked back until the figure of the
Abbot, arms raised in blessing, and Richardis, clutching

her hands to her chest as though supplicating heaven were tiny figures.

'We're away,' said Volmar with a smile.

I saw then that the regimented life of the monastery was not always to his liking. Elizabeth also seemed to be released in some way, as though she were preparing herself to be open to new experiences, and shed her apprehension and timidity. I felt a surge of excitement as well. What lay around the bend of the river? What lay beyond our own part of the world? What would this journey accomplish? Would this be the last time I was free to move beyond the walls of our abbey? The sun came from behind the clouds, just as that last thought niggled at my peace of mind. I took it as an omen.

As the wind picked up the boat heeled to one side. I grasped the bench and prepared myself for a watery immersion but Klaus, the boatman laughed and assured us that with the load of wool and sheep hides that he was carrying the boat would be stable and steady. Gerard, the young boy, moved about the deck as though he had been born on a boat. Perhaps he was, for there was enough room on board for a small family. We were quite comfortable, sheltered from the breezes. Once I grew accustomed to the smell of lanoline and greasy wool, I was delighted just to be there, skimming over the water, between the banks of reeds and water plants.

I encouraged Sister Elizabeth to be prayerful and modest, yet to observe the beauties of the rivers and the mountains, the trees coming into their final bloom before the leaves changed to golden, red, scarlet and bronze, and the flowers folded against the cold winds and rain.

At Mainz, our boatman, Klaus, guided the boat to
the jetty. Gerard, the young boy, stepped across to the
wharf, even before the boat had come to a stop. He tied
a rope to a post of the wharf. Elizabeth, with
uncharacteristic courage, stepped on to the wharf
unaided. Volmar helped me to disembark, then asked
us not to stray too far from the wharf area. He was to
take some letters to the Bishop, and could move faster
without us. There was plenty to see in that small area.
Shops displayed signs advertising their wares: a mortar
and pestle, keys, a bullock and a fish. Men pushed hand
carts loaded with wine barrels, cloth and leather goods.
Women strode by, their arms wrapped around large
cloth bags. Merchants riding horses supervised the
loading and unloading of their merchandise. One
dismounted, handed the reins of this horse to some
urchin or other, and hurried forward to reiterate and
repeat, in loud angry voice instructions he had already
given. More people than I had ever seen in one place
rushed about with care-frowned faces. Elizabeth and I
would have loved to visit the cathedral, as I had heard
so much about its splendour, but there was not enough
time. Instead we went to the shop of the apothecary, to
see what I could learn about his potions and remedies.
Klaus organised the unloading of the wool, and took on
some barrels of wine. He sent Gerard to the weaver's
shop, which was next to the apothecary, to bid us back
on board. Then we were ready to set off again. Volmar
arriving, short of breath, and with new letters in his
leather pouch, had been in danger of being left behind.
What would Elizabeth and I have done then?
For the next stage of the journey we were joined by a
Jewish merchant, carrying a strangely shaped parcel
wrapped in cloth. At first we looked at each other with

some reserve, but on a boat that heels and tacks from side to side it is hard to stay aloof. Within a short time he had nodded and smiled in our direction. By the time we had sailed around the bend of the river he was unwrapping a set of candlesticks for us to admire, and Elizabeth was telling him about the lamps and lamp holders that her great grandfather made. For me it was a chance to talk to one who belonged to a religion which was even older than Christianity and whose Old Testament we shared.

Gerard, lively and adroit, moved about the boat like a seasoned boatman. I called him over, when he had a free moment.

'Tell me,' I said 'is this how you wish to spend your life, on the river, working the boats?'

Thrilled to have my undivided attention he told me about his wish to one day own his own boat, to become a great trader and to provide cloth for his mother and sisters to make themselves dresses. 'My brother is a lay monk at your abbey,' he said. 'He works as hard as I do, especially when the sheep are dropping their lambs or the fields are being prepared for sowing.'

'What do you do when the wind drops? What makes the boat go then?' It was something which had concerned me from the time we came on board.

'We use the oars. That's hard work. In the canals sometimes people on the paths alongside pull the boats, with ropes around their shoulders. That's hard work too. When they use horses, then it's easier.'

For the first week of our journey we travelled by boat, if not always the same boat or on the same river. There were stops along the way, to unload and load goods, to pay the taxes and tolls which caused so many complaints from boatmen and merchants. At night we slept on board, wrapped in warm blankets and soothed by the movement until the light and chill of dawn woke us. During the day I would often sit away from the others, watching the ripples, swirls and eddies. Swans and water birds swam placidly about. Little grey ducks hid in the rushes. Trees shaded the riverbanks. Now they were a glory of colour: golden, brown, russet, green. Soon they would hold out bare branches in mute supplication to the grey winter sky.

Sometimes we passed small farms, where black-faced sheep grazed and the trees stood green-leafed, displaying little red apples for the world and his wife to admire. Elizabeth would come to sit beside me, exclaiming at all she saw until I would suggest that we recite a psalm.

Hildegard: *I lift my eyes to the hills-*
             from where will my help come?
             My help comes from the Lord,
             who made heaven and earth.
Elizabeth: *The Lord is your keeper;*
             the Lord is your shade at your right
hand
             The sun shall not strike you by day
             nor the moon by night.
Together: *The Lord will keep your going out*
             and your coming in
             from this time on and for evermore.

Thus we recalled that God was with us at all times, and we were in the palm of his hand. With true faith, we feared no danger.

*   *   *

Volmar caught a fish. This was incredibly exciting.
The boatman showed him how to put a line with a
spinner over the side. The spinner attracts the fish and,
with luck, it is then caught in the fishing hook.
Volmar's fish was large and shiny as he pulled it from
the water. He looked more surprised than the fish,
which fought for its life valiantly, flapping about in the
boat until the boatman dealt it a death-blow. Elizabeth
tried to control her shrieks but the horror at such
violence overcame her self-control. That day we pulled
into the bank and made a fire. So good to eat fish, after
a few days of eating almost nothing but fruit, nuts,
bread and cheese. Volmar led the grace before meals
with a proud smile, so we added our thanks to him for
his skill. After the meal Elizabeth shuffled and hopped
about until I had to tell her to go across to the bushes,
be quick about it, and stop making such a fuss. Even the
highest born in the land needs to pass water or empty
her bowels each day. Nature can be quite inconvenient
when one is travelling, especially with knees as stiff as
mine.

We passed castles bricked against the sky, and towns
where we exchanged cargo. There were other
passengers from time to time, men and women bent on
trade or returning home. Each one had a story, and each
story had to be told. That itself was a journey.

Once we left the waterways behind Volmar said that we
would need to travel by horse, as walking would be too
slow and tiring. Abbot Kuno had given him enough
money to buy three horses on the way, and arrange to
sell them on our return. That was far easier than trying
to take horses from the abbey by boat. I had never
thought of Abbot Kuno being a man who knew about
such things, but of course as the head of a monastery he

would have dealt with such practicalities more than once. Once I had my own monastery I would be faced with many different situations. I looked forward to that. Every problem has a solution.

So many horses; which to choose? I was immediately drawn to a grey horse, not too large, with a beautiful face and bright eye. 'This will be my horse,' I announced firmly. Volmar shook his head. 'It would take all our money just to buy that one. Besides, it's a stallion, which means he'll be headstrong and wilful. Look around, Mother Hildegard, for something more suitable.'

So we chose more sensibly. Mine was a small bay, with an evil eye. Elizabeth selected an even smaller black mare that picked her way among the stones like a dancer and Volmar chose a solid chestnut. As we rode away I took one last, regretful look at the grey. Such a horse could have taken me to the ends of the earth. Even mounted we were not safe on the roads from thieves and robbers. Though we had no treasure it would have been worth killing us for the horses. For safety, whenever we could we became part of the groups of traders or pilgrims who were going in the same direction. There were nights when we had to sleep in the open. Mostly we found a monastery for food and shelter.

Each morning we would set out again. If we stayed at a monastery we heard mass before leaving. Monks or nuns would gather at the gate, to wish us 'God-speed' and a safe journey. Still chilly, the morning mists wrapped us in a grey veil until the sun, at first shining through the clouds and finally, winning the battle, came into its full glory and warmed us.

You can discover a great deal from people if you
just listen to their conversations. I learned, for example,
of the disquiet over the recent crusade. The great army
that had marched away proudly to free the holy lands
was defeated. The stragglers returning had no stories of
glorious victory to relate. There were complaints about
the increasing taxes which people had paid to support
this failure. Bernard of Clairvaux had encouraged the
men to go, one man said, then spat upon the ground.
'I didn't notice him taking the cross and joining them,'
he added.
'It was not the men, but the women who brought about
our ruin,' another replied. 'Women have no place in the
battlefield.'
Such talk puzzled and saddened me. I had believed, as
had all our community, that the armies had gone to free
the holy lands so that the sacred sites would be returned
to Christian hands, and made safe for pilgrims. Surely
God would have favoured these soldiers against the
Muslims? We learned even more at a small monastery,
sheltered among pine trees, where we stayed the
following night. The abbess made much of us, for they
did not receive many travellers there. We were told to
sit near the fire in the refectory, a comfort not normally
allowed, but welcome for all that. The soup was rich in
meat and vegetables, the spelt bread tasted grainy and
excellent with the beer for which this monastery was
becoming justly famous. But the mood of the sisters
was sombre. The abbess had just heard that same day
that her brother had died at Mt Cadmos, where the
Turks had massacred the French army.
'Henri would have fought so bravely,' she said. 'I
prayed night and day for his safe return. Now I must
pray for the repose of his soul. They blame the Queen,

with her baggage and her fine dresses. What army
takes women to war? The King tried to forbid her, but
she knows how to get her own way with him.'
What could I say in comfort except to assure her that
we would also pray for Henri. Should a queen and
noble ladies go to war? I suggested to the abbess that
these women were filled with zeal to see the lands
where Jesus had lived and been crucified, and their
piety overcame their good sense. She replied with a
scornful grunt. Later, Eleanor's stories of the crusade
put it all in a very different light.

The following day we had to travel alone. No one else
was going our way. Even more frightening, we had to
pass through a forest, a place where robbers love to
hide in wait. God protected us. As the morning passed
we ceased to move in fear, finding only peace and
quiet. Our horses made no sound, walking on the soft
pine needles beneath trees higher than any cathedral.
Sunlight filtered down; a sudden flash of a bird, then
the call of a raven. Elizabeth, quiet, naive Elizabeth,
told me more about the crusade.

'They say that Queen Eleanor wanted to stay with her
uncle at Antioch, and not travel on to Jerusalem. The
poor man is dead now, may he rest in peace, but they
say that he was a very handsome man and she is a
beautiful woman. Many people think that their feelings
for each other went beyond that of family. It was a
scandal.'

Where had Elizabeth heard such things? From a trader's
wife, no doubt, for I cannot imagine any nun or even a
pilgrim passing on such scurrilous gossip. I talked to
her seriously about the need for charity, respect and
discretion. Poor Elizabeth, shoulders bowed and face

puckered up to prevent her tears, rode soberly
beside me. Irritated by her sulks I moved forward to
Volmar.

'Are we doing the wise thing?' I asked him.

'It's too late now to turn back. We've travelled more
than half way,' he replied, which did not answer my
question nor quell my anxieties. A voice distracted us.
Elizabeth, some way behind us, was singing out her
sorrows in a voice as bright and clear as moonlight; a
voice that ascended like a lark to the very heavens.

'I didn't know you could sing so beautifully,' I said
when she caught up with us.

'When we sing in choir, Mother, you hear only
Richardis,' she answered with a hint of sulk still in her
voice. What she said was true. Richardis' voice was
like honey, warm and silky, resonant, rich, ravishing.
Her voice so often inspired my music. It was of
Richardis that I wrote:

O Virginity, you stand in the royal bridal chamber
O how tenderly you burn in the King's embraces
while the sun shines through you
so that your noble flower never falls.
O noble virgin, your flowers will never come
to fall in the shadow.

Here, in Elizabeth, was another treasure; silver to
complement the gold, emeralds to highlight the sheen
of pearls.

'You must thank God for your gifts,' I reminded
Elizabeth, 'but not look for praise. I'm glad to have
heard you sing as you did today.'

I learned many new things. People were free in their
criticism of the bishops and clergy. Some of the

shepherds in God's kingdom were more interested
in their own luxuries and prestige than in serving the
people. There were wise men and women, humble in
the eyes of the world, whose gifts will never be
recognized or valued. In my journey to the Paraclete I
was not only seeing new places, but my knowledge of
the world now went beyond the mountains, rivers and
villages.

Volmar guided us from monastery to monastery. Monks
greeted him as an old friend, as they exchanged news of
other, familiar names. Letters were delivered to one
monastery and collected to be taken to another. These
monks, I came to realise, had set up a system which
allowed them to know what was happening all over
Europe. Like the poets who acted as diplomats moving
from court to court, conveying messages and bringing
news, these monks travelled from city to abbey, from
cathedral to the cloister schools, spreading news of the
Church and the world over Europe, like a large spider
web. We nuns, given less chance to travel than monks,
had minimal chance to exchange ideas and reflections.
What little we had would be taken from us if Bernard
had his way.

It was at our last resting place, a priory within a day's
walk of the Paraclete, that we faced the greatest danger.
The priory set in a sheltered area surrounded by
vineyards, had an aura of serenity, but the sister who
opened the gates for us was tense and hesitant. I
discovered the reason when she took us, as was the
custom, directly to the chapel to pray. At first I thought
of nothing but the joy of kneeling in this blessed place
and thanking God that our journey was nearly
accomplished. As I prayed a sudden movement caught
my attention, something in the darker shadows, a

bundle of rags, rags that began to move. The bundle suddenly twisted about and took human form. A voice called out such profanities that I will not write them here. The bundle stood up, now clearly a woman, but so filthy and unkempt you could not tell if she was young or old, nobly born or a beggar. Volmar, kneeling beside me, stood up, ready to protect us, as the prioress came forward and whispered the sad story.

'We're at our wit's end. This woman has been prowling about the village, cursing and threatening any one who comes near her. The villagers drove her here, as though they were herding an animal. As soon as we opened the gate she ran in to the priory, urinated in a disgusting steaming puddle. Before we could restrain her she ran into the chapel. If any of us try to approach her she screams and tears at herself with those long fingernails. We sent for the priest but he refused to come, saying he is powerless to help her. Maybe you have been sent to us, Mother Hildegard, for we are truly desperate.'

Clearly the woman was possessed. I had seen Jutta exorcise devils. I had never attempted it myself.

Closing my eyes I prayed with all my strength that God would guide me. Then I approached the woman. She stood silent for a moment, wary and suspicious. I held out my hand, but as I went to touch her she bent double, writhed, moaned then fell to the ground.

All the sisters had come into the chapel by then. I told them to stand around the woman in a protective circle, hold hands and pray as they had never prayed before. As they did they felt a force – I could feel it too – and their chant lifted higher and louder, stronger, overcoming the moans and shrieks of the woman. The pathetic creature began twisting about as though in

extreme pain. Some evil being was tearing at her
soul, fighting to remain.

It was now quite dark outside. Lights from the candles
flickered in the draughty chapel; shadows smudged and
grew into grotesque shapes. The woman suddenly sat
up and pointed a grubby finger at me. For a moment the
sisters grew silent, as though resting in the eye of a
storm.

'What are you looking at, you wrinkled ugly old hag?'
the woman hissed at me, then threw back her head and
laughed. The sisters moved back a step and once more
their chant, louder and more desperate, echoed through
the chapel. At the sound of their voices the woman
howled and grunted, more like an animal than a person.
I felt drained, unsure that I had the strength to cast that
devil out. I placed all my faith in God.

'In the name of the Father, and of the Son and of the
Holy Spirit, I command you to come forth,' I cried out.
The prioress ran forward with a crucifix which I held
high above my head. For a moment I was tempted to
smash it down upon the head of the suffering creature
and put her out of her misery. Where could such a
thought have come from? No doubt the devil was
fighting.

For what seemed for ever, but could not have been
more than a minute we all waited. There was no sound
but the wind, a branch of a tree knocking, again and
again, against a window, the repressed breathing of the
sisters, the scuffing of their feet as they fought
weariness. The woman suddenly shuddered, groaned
and curled herself into a ball. We were faced with a pile
of dirty rags once more. All we could do then was pray
and hope, so we prayed on into the dawn. Just as the
sun was rising the woman sat up. An eerie sound, half

death rattle, half smothered scream came from her contorted mouth. We watched, every eye fixed on her, every energy urging her to expel the devil from her soul. She glared back at us, eyes red and feverish. Again she cried that strangled scream, and then vomited a black marsh-mud like substance that smelt so vile it must have come straight from hell. The only person who did not cry out and hold a hand to her face was the woman herself who had sunk to her side and seemed either dead or in a deep sleep. Some of the senior sisters carried her to the infirmary, washed her and covered her with a blanket. She did not move or wake, but we could see that she was still breathing.

There she stayed until her body repossessed her soul and she was herself again. I had sent the others to the front of chapel to give thanks while Volmar and I set about cleaning the mess, afraid that if any of the sisters were to be exposed to the stench the devil might find a way to take possession of them. Sister Elizabeth insisted on remaining, however, and I was glad of her help. My spirit was filled with gratitude that we had succeeded, but my body was cold, stiff and reluctant to breathe in that filth for longer than necessary.

That evening, a clean, subdued and attractive young woman joined us in the chapel to pray. She came to kneel at my feet and wept tears of gratitude. I placed my hands on her shoulders and urged her to stand up and face the crucifix. That was where she should direct her thanks, I told her, and bade her go to live her life in peace and tranquillity.

We remained at the priory for one more day, needing to rest. My horse had a swollen fetlock so we decided to leave all the horses there. They had ample stables and the nuns promised to see that they were well looked

after, ready for our return. So, on the last morning
of our journey we set out on foot. At least Volmar and
Elizabeth walked. I was still so drained of energy that
the sisters offered me a mule to ride. We had been
rained on, splattered with mud, chilled by sudden winds
and were exhausted by our journey and the fight for that
woman's soul. Our progress was slow and I wondered
how much more I could endure, until we came around a
sharp bend, and saw the walls of the Paraclete. As
Elizabeth helped me from the mule I stood and said a
silent prayer of thanks. Had I sunk to my knees I would
never have arisen again.

*   *   *

During our journey Volmar often talked to me about
Heloise, Abbess of the Paraclete. 'She is,' he said, 'a
woman who has been cleansed through suffering,
shaken off the sins of her youth and converted her life
to serve God. Having studied both secular and religious
writings she is renowned and respected for her
intelligence and learning. Finally, and this is an
important consideration, both Peter the Venerable,
Abbot of Cluny, and Bernard, Abbot of Clairvaux, have
the highest possible opinion of her. She will be a useful
ally.' How, I wondered, did Volmar come by such
knowledge? Then I wondered if she would impress me
as much as she had him. Possibly not. I have no time
for abbesses who are filled with pride, when their only
claim is that their family is wealthy enough to give vast
donations to the monastery. Heloise was not one of
those, if all I heard was true, even if her family was
quite prestigious. There was some mystery about her
father, which does not help one who wishes to be held
in high honour, but her achievements ensured that all
would respect and honour her. Heloise had suffered

great losses too. Perhaps the greatest had been
giving up her child, for what mother does not hold her
infant to herself, encompassing him with protection and
love. To have that child taken from you would be like
having part of your heart torn from your breast.

When, at last, Heloise stood in front of me, hands held
out in support and welcome, I was overwhelmed. A tall,
slim woman, with such kindness in her face that I, who
am usually reserved, found myself placing my fate in
her hands, talking of Bernard's letter before I had even
entered the abbey. Put my impulsiveness down to the
vicissitudes of the journey. Heloise assured and
reassured, that all would be well, and insisted that I rest
before we talked. Having finally met her, after all the
travails and difficulties of the journey, my heart filled
with hope that we would succeed. No sooner was my
head on the pillow than I was fast asleep.

That night I dreamt about the day Jutta died. She had no
fear of death, that one. In fact she longed and prayed for
that time when she would be dissolved in Christ. Worn
out with fasting and penance she suffered an acute
attack of fever, and as the end drew near she lay on a
hair-mat strewn with ashes, praying without ceasing,
joined by her sisters and the monks. Finally she made
the sign of the cross as she gave up her soul.

I helped to prepare her body for burial. Her skin was so
white that it was translucent and the chain that she had
worn was tightly secured, making three furrows right
around her waist. We washed her body with our tears as
well as water from the well. While I could never
emulate her in such severe penance I understood that
for Jutta this was the extreme manifestation of her total
love of God. The dream left me feeling disturbed.
While she was alive Jutta would never have approved

of my leaving Disibodenberg to visit Heloise at the
Paraclete. I hoped that she would lend us her support
from heaven.

*   *   *

Looking back I can see that both Heloise and Eleanor
had reason to feel wary of Bernard even before the
letter, whereas my gratitude towards him was immense.
He had removed barriers from my path. When I had
written to him it was in the spirit of a trusting child to
her spiritual father. Sadly, his reply did not speak
directly to my heart. I reminded myself that he could
not know me as well as I felt I knew him. I had seen
him in a vision where he looked at the sun and was not
afraid. I knew him then, although I had never met him,
as a man who would not be crushed by the falling
wooden beams in the winepress of our human nature.
Now there was another letter written by Bernard, which
was why I was visiting the Paraclete. But there were
other matters I wished to discuss with Heloise, if we
succeeded in preventing Bernard's letter reaching the
Pope. If we did not there was no point in further talk.
Had she, as I planned to do, set up a system of water
drainage for the abbey? Was it difficult to negotiate
with the local people? I had often met with them at
Disibodenberg, while tending the sick, or in giving such
counsel as they requested. Would they regard me any
differently when I was an abbess? Because of her own
experience Heloise could answer to all these concerns.
On the other hand Eleanor, Queen of France, was not a
woman I would have chosen to consult. For a start she
had a certain reputation, and it was not for piety or
wisdom. There were stories. When I saw her, an
imperious, but wonderfully beautiful woman, I believed
every one of them. Eleanor looked in my direction

before turning away with a dismissive gesture. Even after I was presented to her she nodded, took a deep breath, then tapping her foot, waited for me to withdraw. Only when I informed her that we had a common cause, did she take the trouble to really look at me.

'Bernard's letter makes reference to changes in the way all nuns must live, changes which may not please you. You do not realise that Bernard's letter affects me as well.' Eleanor spoke to us as to inferiors. In the eyes of the world this would be correct. And yet she was forced to concede power to others. I do believe that God made men and women different. I do not believe that he made one sex inferior to the other, although there are many who say otherwise. Looking at Eleanor, in her arrogance, I wondered if she could really have managed better than her husband and his advisers, or would she have stumbled on her pride. The fact that she believed she could administer a kingdom as well as any man was what really mattered, for she would never be given the opportunity to govern in her own right.

Heloise and I remained silent. Eleanor glanced at our faces, then softened her voice.

'Bernard has a reputation for great sanctity and wisdom. But so do you, Mother Hildegard. You are his equal. For a start you were both born about the same time, into minor nobility,' she stated.

I pointed out that neither Bernard nor I cared for worldly status. The treasure we sought was in heaven.

'Yes, I know all that,' she said impatiently. 'But tell me why is it that he's been given positions of authority within the Church because of his writings, and you've received less recognition? You both compose music, but I have heard it said that yours is superior.'

So she did know something of me, after all. That
made her earlier indifference to my presence even more
discourteous. Charity was being strained to the utmost.
'Are there other similarities?' asked Heloise, before I
could make any reply. 'I know that most of his family
became monk and his sister left her husband to become
a nun. Have your brothers and sisters followed you?'
'Two of my brothers and one of my sisters have given
their lives to God in religion. I claim no credit for that,'
I replied.
'Nor did you send armies on a crusade which was
bound to fail. Bernard must accept the blame for that,'
said Eleanor. 'I consider his prestige and reputation
greatly overrated.
'Must he be blamed for having an vision?' I asked. 'He
saw an external Jerusalem, which needed to be
defended. My vision is different, of a New Jerusalem
needing to be built.'
Bernard's teaching, his writing, his preaching, his love
of the poor, his manifest virtues; all these made him
admired and loved. How could he now wish so much
harm to women?
I do not mean to denigrate Eleanor. We did not begin
well but our mutual antagonism did not remain for long.
She brought another type of wisdom to our table, that of
the 'children of the world' who are wise as serpents.
Nor do I mean any disrespect in this allusion. The
brightest angel of all, Lucifer, chose the guise of a
serpent when he tempted Adam and Eve. Eleanor's
world was one of conquest. She was ambitious for her
husband to consolidate and increase his territories. As
she explained to me, he must move forward. It was not
possible for him to stand still. To do so would be to fall
further and further behind. In this she respected Abbot

Suger's role as adviser although she had little love
for the man.

'He had too strong an influence on Louis when he was
young. At first, after our marriage, Louis would listen
to me, but after the fires destroyed the village of Vitry
he shunned me and ran like a frightened child back to
Suger. I felt that I was married to a king and a monk,
and neither was prepared to listen to anything I had to
say. I can't tell you how infuriating it is to be suddenly
excluded from all discussions of important matters. If
ever I ask about anything remotely connected to state
affairs I'm advised to concentrate on my prayers and
embroidery, or, even more importantly, to produce an
heir. How do I do that with Louis praying half the
night? When he does come to my bed he wears a
hairshirt!'

'Didn't your time with him in Jerusalem change the
situation? Abbot Suger was not there,' I asked, not in
total innocence. Eleanor look at me in silence for a few
moments, then very adroitly changed the subject.

'Hildegard, you talk of the beauty of nature and the
wonderful churches which you saw on your journey
here. When I set out on the crusade I marvelled at such
things as well until I saw the opulence and splendour of
Constantinople. You could not believe it unless you
actually saw it with your own eyes. We played our part
for the honour of France, riding in to the city with as
much splendour as we could manage. I salvaged one of
my best gowns, and rode at the head of the other
women as part of the procession. My dress, I remember,
had gold embroidery all along the hem. We strove not
to feel overwhelmed by the city but it eclipsed anything
I had ever seen before. The buildings were unbelievably
magnificent, decorated with beautiful wall hangings

and marble statues. The royal party stayed in the Philopation, which, they told us, had had to be refurbished after Conrad's men had pillaged it, so the rest of our army had to remain outside the city walls. Louis was furious about that.

'"Why worry about such trifles," I said to him. "Enjoy the comfort while we can." Such a relief after the trekking and travelling and fighting, being in danger of losing our lives at every mountain pass, hearing the clash of battle or the cries of the dying. There the lush gardens were filled with the sound of cool cascading water, from fountains and rivulets. We feasted every day, each dish more sumptuous than the one before.'

'And did you pray there as well?' I asked, striving unsuccessfully to keep the sharpness from my voice.

'Pray! Rest assured that we prayed, early, late and in between times. We attended ceremonies in St Sophia. Huge! Bigger than any cathedral in Europe. There were thousands of candles and oil lamps, casting shadows almost to the top of the great dome. Hard not to be distracted.'

Hard for her not to be distracted at any time, I judged, and then accused myself again of lacking charity. She had to deal with her world, which was far removed from the serenity of a monastery. Serene it still is, despite the tensions and concerns that pervade even our sheltered communities. In rebuilding the Paraclete Heloise had created an unadorned, austere, yet sympathetic ambience. Bernard, who shunned all ostentation, had given it his wholehearted approval. Here, as well, the candles cast their shadows on the chapel walls, but these did not distract unduly. The only decoration was a mosaic of the blessed Virgin, wearing a blue dress and a white veil on her head. The artist had depicted her with a slight smile, one that a mother bestows on her wayward children. The ceiling unfolded from the altar area and down the side of the chapel. I have always liked the way ceilings of churches spread and gently curve, like angel's wings. I have been told that the cathedral at St.Denis, the pride and life's work of Abbot Suger, has a roof that soars up to heaven, and stained-glass windows, which reflect the glories therein. Let us hope that the light illuminates the souls of those who worship there.

Eleanor had only just returned from the crusade and it was still foremost in her mind. It had been, she said, an experience that changed her whole life, or, rather, which made her want to change her life. She was impatient and anxious, searching for a new purpose and position.

'Visiting the holy sites in Jerusalem would have strengthened your faith,' I said.

'Maybe I'm not of good faith,' she said. 'By the time we reached Jerusalem I was so furious with Louis I could hardly bear to raise my eyes in case he was in my line of vision. He had me kidnapped, you know, humiliating me and forcing me to travel with him. No, it was experiencing so many new things, seeing other countries, meeting other monarchs, which made me realise that there is a world beyond Poitiers and Paris.'

How sad to think that while she walked the same roads which Jesus had trod, her eyes were cast down, her face contorted with anger as she plotted, if not her revenge, then her escape.

'As if I hadn't suffered enough I was nearly drowned on the way home,' she continued. 'Our ship was blown away in a storm and we all thought that we would die.'

'You mean that France could have lost its king and queen?' asked Heloise.

And no male heir, a thought I kept to myself.

'Louis was not with me. I refused to travel on the same ship with him. Imagine being cooped up with a man you despise, and being forced to pretend to like him in front of other people.'

'But you don't feel like that about him now?' I asked.

'Can we control our feelings? He's not the man I would have chosen, not that we do have any choice, but we've been together for years. We have one child and still hope for a son. You know, I nearly died on that journey. I was ill for weeks. That changes your way of thinking. I really didn't care about life or death.'

'Didn't you want to see your daughter?' Again Heloise spoke.

'I've seen my daughter more often than you have seen your son,' said Eleanor.

She was prone to such sudden malice, which subsided as quickly as it was manifested, after which she would try to make amends through an act of kindness. She must have had an ample supply of rosewater for she sent me a bottle to ease my headaches every time we had a disagreement. After a particularly unkind comment she gave Heloise a rare book for the library. Pride was her stumbling block. Eleanor saw all women as rivals, and Heloise, although in no way assertive, had such an air of being able to cope with whatever circumstances she encountered, that while she did not rival Eleanor in beauty she certainly did in force of personality.

Heloise had made no attempt to respond to Eleanor's remark about her son. 'We've no time for talk of your travels or travails,' she said. 'A decision must be made.

It may be necessary to call on others in our community for help, if we cannot find the solution for ourselves.'

Benedict has laid out in his Rule that all the community may be called on to offer opinions about contentious matters. Surely Heloise realised that if we three could not find the answer the likes of Elizabeth, who was young and naive or Abelard's niece Sister Agatha, who presided over the Paraclete kitchen with a dour and doleful expression, would not. Oddly though, in a way they did, but through being over-zealous, not because of ingenuity or insight.

Adele, who had arrived with Eleanor as her maid, came to me with a problem of her own.

'Sister Elizabeth has told me, Mother, that you have the gift of healing. I'm much troubled by my eyes, which are not strong and need to hide from the light. I would hate not to be able to see.'

I looked into her eyes and saw that she was reaching out for God's love and healing. It could not have been helpful to spend so much of her day with Eleanor who was centred on the world rather than the spirit. Then I asked her to move closer to the window so that I could see her eyes more clearly. They were blue. This meant that they were weaker than other eyes because they are affected by air shifting through warmth, cold and humidity. Blue eyes are easily harmed by fog and moist air.

'Come with me,' I said and led her to the herb garden. Like a small child who believes that her nurse can solve all her problems she followed me. Like a small child she chattered of this and that: of her friendship with Elizabeth; of her finding the abbey, not dull as she had expected, but a place where she could find the peace to think and to play her music; of the idea that perhaps God wished her to be a nun. That, I told her, was an important decision. Our life is not easy and she should pray to hear God's voice clearly. By that time we had reached the part of the garden where fennel was growing.

'Pick some fennel seeds and parts of the plant,' I told her. As she did that I collected dew from fresh grass blades that were growing upright. Then we went to the kitchen where I asked a sister to give us a small amount of fine wheat flour.

'Now come to the infirmary and I will show you what needs to be done. In that way you will learn something which may enable you to help others,' I said, and we walked together back through the garden to the part of the abbey where sick people were treated.

In the apothecary I took the fennel plants and seeds and showed Adele how to pulverise them. For a young woman who was so adept with an embroidery needle she was clumsy with the pestle and mortar at first, but eventually she ground them down to minute particles, with some liquid as well. To this I added the dew and the wheat flour and showed her how to make it into a paste.

'At night place this over your eyes, binding it with some cloth to keep it in place and it will soothe your eyes as you sleep,' I instructed.

'Will it cure my squint?' she then asked, this being the real cure she was seeking.

'It will help, as it eases your eyes. Once they are better you should try a different remedy. Take some rue juice and twice as much liquid honey and add a little wine. Place a piece of wheat bread in this liquid and when it has absorbed the moisture place it on your eyes. You

will then see clearly, and be seen to have two
perfect eyes.'
Adele rushed away in a confusion of gratitude,
repeating my instructions to insure that she would make
no mistakes, and promising to pray hard for guidance in
case she was meant to join my monastery. My thought
was that her affection for Elizabeth was the most likely
reason for this sudden desire to take religious vows.
Eventually Adele's squint lessened, to be hardly
noticeable. Eleanor, noting the improvement, declared
that now she would have no problem finding a husband
for her, if she could ever bear to let her go.

*   *   *

We spent many hours over the following month
discussing not only the letter but also matters that
touched our own lives. Outside the times we met
together I made myself useful in the infirmary, garden
or kitchen, as Heloise attended to the administration of
her abbey. The garden at the Paraclete was similar to
that at Fontevraud, according to Eleanor. She also
began to spend a lot of time wandering about there,
time which she might have spent in the chapel, although
contemplating green grass, the clouds scudding across a
blue sky and the glorious pink, purple and red roses is a
prayer in itself. Rumours followed rumours; people in
Paris, noting the queen's absence, were beginning to
think that she had retired to an abbey. Maybe, they
conjectured, she was removing herself from public life
to allow Louis to annul their marriage and find another
wife who could bear him a son. These stories were the
usual silly tittle tattle, ignorant of the fact that she was
expecting another baby, and that the king, far from
wishing to find another wife wished to live in harmony
with the one he already had. Eleanor had brought great

wealth and land to the marriage. Even had Louis not sincerely loved his wife; even if he felt she gave too much time to music, poetry and levity, he would have been very reluctant to return her dowry. No, if the truth were known it was Eleanor who was thinking of finding a new husband, hinting to us that she had actually selected him. I could have told her that such hints were unnecessary, and warned her that she was choosing a man who would bring her some joy and many children, together with disappointment, anger and loss of liberty. She would not have believed me, or accepted that these were things I 'just knew'.

When I walk in a garden I like to be alone, to study the plants and to mark those from which I could take cuttings. These were the usual kitchen and herb gardens. Monasteries need to have condiments for the kitchen close to hand but the herb garden is used to grow medicinal plants as well, to help teach young nuns and monks how to recognize them properly before going out to pick plants in the wild areas. Otherwise those who sought to heal could do great harm.

Wisely they had placed two wells in the vegetable garden, so that the plants could be adequately watered. I noted that the green vegetables were grown separately from the root vegetables and the legumes; common sense and common practice. I asked the sisters who tended the garden if they ever rotated the beds. It seemed a new idea to them.

Flowers grew in unexpected places: in hedges, around corners, in little clumps and larger, more formal beds. The roses were in their final bloom, still painted in royal reds, gold and purple, still perfumed. Yet, it was to the herb garden that I always returned, to weed a little, to walk down the aisles between the garden beds, to meditate, and to open myself to the divine Light. My immediate problem with Bernard's letter did not always occupy my thoughts. In such a setting my mind would strive for God's wisdom in many things. Abelard had tried to explain the Holy Trinity, and through his efforts had earned the enmity of Bernard of Clairvaux. I had also, in my own small way, tried to explain it. Or rather I had been directed, for my understanding came from that which was revealed to me. This is how I picture it: the Father is brightness and this brightness has a flashing forth and in this flashing forth is fire and these three are one. You could say that the Father is the creator, the living light, the Son is the flash of light and the Spirit is the fire and the force which holds it all together. We can appreciate the unity of the Trinity if we depict it as a circle, which has no beginning and no end; although I am the first to admit that a circular triangle is nonsense. Bernard could accept my writing in this way about the Trinity, but could not accept Abelard's philosophical writings, comparing the Trinity to a seal. I cannot see that what he said was so very different. A fire and a seal have multiple functions and can both be used as a metaphor. Maybe Bernard, like Eleanor, had difficulty in accepting rivals. Such a trait would have been a thorn in the side of a man striving to attain the true humility that Benedict exhorts us to achieve.

We all have our thorns, our personal battles. Who can think that the life of a monk or a nun is easy? Virginity is a crown and a crucifixion, a struggle against that which draws us to others and which allows us to share in the act of creation. Sexual pleasure in women is like the sunlight, which mildly, gently, and continuously suffuses the earth with its warmth to make it fruitful. A man still feels this great sweetness in himself, and is like a stag thirsting for the fountain. He races swiftly to the woman and she to him – she like a threshing-floor pounded by his many strokes and brought to heat when the grains are threshed inside her. Do not ever believe it is easy to deny ourselves that pleasure. It is only in pouring out such love and passion to God that we can attain this ideal.

O dulcissime amator, o duclissime amplexator:
aduiva nos custodire virginitatem nostram.
Nos sumus orte in pulvere, heu hue, in crimine Ade;
vale durum est contradicere quod habet gustus pomi.
tu erige nos salvator Christe.
Nos desideramus ardenter te sequi.

O sweetest lover, sweetest embracer;
help us to guard our virginity!
We are born of dust, and alas, alas in Adam's sin.
How very hard to hold against whatever tastes of the
Apple.
Thou, saviour Christ, set us aright.
Ardently we long to follow you.

*   *   *

Three accomplished women, one problem which affected us all. You would think that with our combined intelligence, earnest endeavours and the guidance of the Spirit we would have found our way out of the morass, yet we seemed no closer to finding a solution in that first week. I suggested we move out into the garden, which always helps me to think, hoping that what eluded us indoors would become obvious as we sauntered under the shady trees or sat on the large log

which had been conveniently placed near the rose
garden. Just behind that part of the garden we could see
the stone grey wall that enclosed the northern side of
the abbey. Eleanor, gesturing, made an obvious point.
'Abbeys are always surrounded by walls.'
'So are castles,' I replied.
'And so,' Heloise added, 'are prisons.'
Walls may enfold us, like a mother's womb, nourishing
the germ of spiritual life. They may also confine so
tightly we are prevented from flourishing. Instead we
become as a desperate vine sending out tendrils in all
sorts of places in the climb to freedom. Life in religion
should not countenance this, for the fruits of
desperation are immoderate behaviour, doubts and
heresy.

With this thought I stood up and walked over to the
wall and placed my hands on it. The stones were warm.
That much was a comfort. The stones were thick and
strong, too high even to see over. That was a problem.
Only after learning of Bernard's letter did I take much
notice of walls. Some are beautiful, with variegated
stone. Some have a formal, sculptured appearance,
shaped and fluted around the edges. Others are
uniformly grey and forbidding, cutting out light and air.
The walls that enclosed me at Disibodenberg, when I
was still young, were cold and restraining, until I
learned to pray through them.

St Benedict had wisely ruled that, once they had taken
their vows, monks and nuns should remain with their
monastery. No longer should bands of monks roam
about, singing their theologies, fighting with those who
chanted a different tune, creating mayhem and scandal
in God's name. That was a practice that had to be
curbed. It did not mean that all travel was forbidden.

Are monks and nuns to be totally segregated from
the rest of God's people? Where is the sense in that?
On the other side of the wall I saw trees, stretching back
to the hill behind. Forests encroach upon our villages
and abbeys. Wolves and other dangerous animals roam
amongst the dark shadows of those trees. Travellers talk
about monsters, fabulous animals, hairy wildmen and
women but I wonder what actually exists beyond our
imagination and fears. At dusk and dawn, when the
spirits are said to wander, the leaves and branches of
the trees form strange shapes and shadows. Even so the
forest may provide refuge and shelter, wood for
buildings, fuel for our fires. All things can be good if
used in the right way and for the right purpose. Even
walls.

*   *   *

Sometimes Heloise needed to be elsewhere,
administering the abbey and its priories, so we did not
meet every day. I had no difficulty in making good use
of my time. My concern was for Elizabeth. Adele, away
from her familiar surroundings and friends, had
attached herself to my young companion as a drowning
woman grasps at any solid object which floats. Would
Adele dangle the delights of the world before Elizabeth
like a delicious plum, tempting her to reach out and
taste, just as Eleanor attempted to tantalise Heloise and
me with her stories? We could smilingly refuse her
blandishments. Elizabeth, being younger and less
experienced, could well yearn for what appeared so
attractive.
My young companion proved to be solid, in the best
sense of the word. Adele spoke of the joys of music-
making in the court, and Elizabeth begged to be taught
to play the harp and flute, making wonderful progress

in a short time. Adele spoke of her hope that one day she would marry a fine nobleman who would endow her with prestige and privilege. Elizabeth cautioned her to choose a man who was honourable and who feared God, for riches and power can not compensate for a cruel husband. That, Elizabeth had told her, was one reason why she had chosen to become a nun, for then no man could hurt her. When she repeated that to me I said that I hoped there were other reasons. Elizabeth laughed, her freckles dancing across her cheeks, and assured me that God knew all that was in her heart.

Adele spoke of beautiful clothes, green and blue silks, wool as red as any blood, gold braiding and silver shoes. Elizabeth asked Adele to show her new embroidery stitches, and this is how I found them, heads bowed over a cloth of cream linen, which Eleanor was giving to the Paraclete for an altar cloth. Elizabeth's needle moved steadily, in and out, to produce a bunch of purple grapes. Adele, working the other corner, was creating a large bee, symbolising, she told me, the honey at the Paraclete and the industry of all the sisters there. I placed a kiss on the top of each head, so delighted to see them using their time and talents to good purpose.

*   *   *

Heloise's fear was not of physical walls as much as being silenced. She was a true scholar, superior to most of the men who would approve the suppression of her ideas and writing. She was preparing to write a Rule more adapted to the needs of women.

'The same yoke of monastic ordinance is laid on the weaker sex as on the stronger,' she explained, 'but it's only men who can obey it fully.'

'Are men and women so different that they cannot follow the same way of life?' asked Eleanor.

'Let me give just one example. How can women deal with tunics and woollen garments worn next to the skin during the monthly purging of the humours when they need to avoid such things?'

'Surely making suitable adjustments in such matters would not stop you from following the Rule. Isn't it just a matter of common sense?' said Eleanor.

'You don't understand,' I said, supporting Heloise. 'If individuals start to change this or that of the Rule as seems sensible to them, then they run the risk of being in error, although St. Benedict did allow for some flexibility at the discretion of the Abbot.'

'But not the abbess,' said Eleanor with a snort. 'Typical!'

We had decided once more to sit outside. It was one of those afternoons in which the sun wraps you in a warm blanket and the scent of jasmine inspires delight. How we would have looked to a stranger? Two women dressed in religious habit, sitting side by side on a large log, and a third woman in a gown of deep green, flowing hair, covered by a light veil, sitting opposite, on an old wooden chair. Would it be obvious that we were deep in discussion, turning to each other from time to time, leaning back, gesturing. Would that stranger have known that we were three women fighting for their freedom?

Eleanor, needing to rest her back, wriggled about claiming that sitting on a broken chair was neither seemly nor comfortable for royal persons. Restless as always, wanting to drive forward, push away opposition, she stood up and leaned against the tree and idly pulled at the leaves.

'Another thing that concerns me,' said Heloise, ignoring her, 'is the dictum that we are to test the constancy of the women we receive during the space of a single year, and only instructions we give them is three readings of the St Benedict's Rule. Who could be so foolish as to set out on an unknown path, not yet defined, or so presumptuous as to choose and profess a way of life of which she knows little or to take a vow she is not capable of keeping? It's contrary to reason and discretion to impose a burden upon those whose capacity to bear that burden has not been tested.'

'That is exactly why I would not allow young children to be given to the abbeys as oblates before the age when they are able to make such a decision for themselves,' I said. I walked over to the garden bed and began to tear at the petals of a deep red rose until Heloise asked me what it had ever done to offend me.

'Children are given in marriage to the highest bidder, with no thought as to how they can bear that burden. Would your Benedict agree to that?' Eleanor had sat down again and, as usual, brought the conversation back to her own situation, but in doing so she brought us back to the point of our meeting – the letter.

It was true that I was very concerned about the possible consequences if Bernard's letter met the approval of the Pope. In my heart I believed that if God wished me to establish a monastery that this would come to pass, although I did not think I could passively wait for it to be achieved.

Eleanor stood up again, this time saying that she was going to her room, to the chapel or to another part of the garden; anywhere but where she was, and how we could stand living in a monastery and never being able to travel about was more than she could understand.

'That's why I will retire to Fontevraud Abbey only when I'm quite old, ugly and infirm,' she said in conclusion as she hurried away.

Heloise watched her leave then turning to smile at me, she said, 'Does she regard us as old, ugly and infirm?' I made no answer, for what could one say to such a comment? I felt old and, at times, infirm, and I had no real idea if I was ugly, not having looked in a glass for many years. Certainly Heloise did not seem perturbed by Eleanor's remark. We were both well past the age of vanity.

There was no time to talk further then as the bell called us once more to chapel. It is a discipline to leave what is important to go to pray, but once on our knees, chanting the Office, that is what becomes really important. I always knelt opposite Elizabeth at the back of the chapel. We stood at times, knelt at others, eyes focussed on the altar. The seats in the choir stalls are built so that the old or infirm sisters can support themselves at the times they were expected to stand. Sometimes I was grateful to rest my poor knees in this way. Once our prayer was finished we walked in pairs to the altar, bowed or genuflected, then moved in silence back to our work. Could any life be more fitting, focussed as it was on the things of heaven and the needs of those on earth?

*   *   *

No matter how much others try to make you comfortable there comes a time when you yearn for your own place and familiar people. Volmar had travelled on to the abbey at Cluny, so I could not see or talk to him. Were those back at St Disibodenberg missing us? Elizabeth became especially dear to me over the time we were away, and she remained a faithful daughter. But on a chilly autumn evening it was Volmar, with his measured speech, calm demeanour and optimism that I missed.

Before we retired that night I asked Heloise to tell me more about Fontevraud Abbey.

'Robert of Abrissel founded it on land which was endowed by the Montmorency family.'

I had heard a great deal about this Robert. He was a monk who had attracted a huge following, especially of women, and he set up a monastery to serve not only the sons and daughters of noble families, but for reformed sinners and the poor and needy. Fontevraud allowed mothers to keep their babies with them, and had a hospital for lepers. I did not know anything of the Montmorency family.

'The Montmerencys were your family?'

Heloise nodded. 'Indirectly. My mother was married to William of Montsoreau, and it was his son, by an earlier marriage, who allowed Robert to establish the monastery on his land. Montmorency is an important family in the Loire valley.'

'And William was your father?' I asked.

'William died a long time before I was born.'

'More than nine months?' I asked.

'Much more. Nor can I can tell you a great deal about my father although the little I know of him suggests that he was a godly man. There's a rumour that Robert d'Abrissel is my father. It would be wonderful if that were true. Of my mother, I know that she was close to Robert, and that she strove, to very good effect, to place Fontevraud on a firm foundation. I have learned from studying her ideas and methods.'

'All I've heard about Robert d'Abrissel is to his good. He was a holy man, perhaps misjudged only because he chose to be near women. If you remember, our blessed Saviour had a close relationship with certain women. I've never heard that Robert was not chaste, so I doubt that he's your father,' I said.

'It is only a rumour. Robert and Hersinde may have loved each other in the same way as Abelard and I did, but I have no evidence of that; no letters, no family stories. Surely my Uncle Fulbert would have told me, or Abbot Peter from Cluny would have said something. His mother would have known. No, much as I would like to claim him, there is no proof that this is so. Even so, before he died Robert asked to be buried next to my mother,' said Heloise. 'I wish I had known more of her. She chose to dedicate her life to helping Robert in his work, so I was sent to Argenteuil as a very young child.'

How more easily we could talk when it was just the two of us. Eleanor, who had a personal interest in Fontevraud, would have laid claim on such a conversation.

'If Abelard had not agreed to be the abbot at St Gildas would he have established a double monastery with you, here at the Paraclete? Something like Fontevraud?' This idea had just occurred to me, but I could see that Heloise had considered it before. She shook her head. 'He'd already left the Paraclete and had been in Brittany for two years before we were expelled from Argenteuil. Had he been still here at that time he may have helped us but I'm not sure that he would have considered offering the Paraclete to us. He would have been afraid of the scandal. Even then people accused him of harbouring lustful thoughts towards me. How small are the minds of such people. What he initially established here was not exactly an abbey, more a hermitage, and then a place where he could teach the students who sought him out. Abelard did not believe in monasteries for both men and women. He most certainly would not have approved of women being in charge of men. In his opinion that would be against nature and all that God intended.'

'He had no regrets leaving what he had begun at the Paraclete?' I asked.

'It was one of the greatest regrets of his life. Agreeing to be abbot of St Gildas turned out to be a terrible mistake. A desolate place, he said, where the wind never stopped blowing over high, rocky cliffs, cold with the sea and spray. He could not speak the language, even though he had grown up in Brittany, nor could they understand his. No scholars there, only rough monks, corrupt and dissolute. They tried to kill him many times, even putting poison in the chalice that he used during Mass, which gives you some idea of their degraded natures. One attacked him with a knife. Another monk paid ruffians to set upon him on the road. It was not a happy time, although I think he did all that he could to reform them and bring them to holiness.'

'Maybe they needed a Bernard for that,' I said.

'If it were ever possible, it would be by someone like Bernard. Abelard was a brilliant teacher but he had no idea of how to deal with ordinary minds. He existed in a higher sphere.'

We left the subject there. When Heloise referred to Abelard she became thoughtful and withdrawn as if she, too, was in another sphere. I also had other things to concern me.

* * *

Heloise was free to develop the Paraclete from the
time Abelard offered the land and primitive buildings to
her. It was far more difficult for me when I wished to
do the same at Bingen. Whenever I had talked of my
plan to establish a monastery the monks asked why we
should want to leave the lush fields and vineyards of
Disibodenberg to go to such an arid place. I saw it
differently; we were leaving Egypt to travel to our
Promised Land. Abbot Kuno insisted that I was a
foolish and deluded woman. Being a stubborn man, he
put more and more obstacles in my path, refusing to
accept that God was directing me. The result was that I
became troubled to the point of being ill. This time my
affliction was particularly severe. My eyes clouded over
until I couldn't see any light, and my body felt so heavy
that I could not lift myself from my bed. Overwhelming
pain consumed me, so that I thought I must die if only
to gain some relief. When Abbot Kuno saw that I was
utterly paralysed and rigid as a rock, he finally
understood that he should not stand in my way. Once he
gave his permission I was able to rise from my bed, full
of life, ready to begin. God had restored my health for
his own purposes.

I know that Heloise and her sisters worked very hard in
the beginning. So did my sisters and I when we were
eventually permitted to go. Such a time it was, of
details and sorting out all the formalities. When the day
for us to leave Disibodenberg came we felt great
sadness. Some of the sisters were in tears. As we
approached Bingen people from nearby villages came
running to welcome us, singing, dancing and praising
God. It was as well that we had that beautiful welcome,
for the weeks and months that followed tested us. We
had left an established abbey, which comfortably

supplied all that we needed, to live in a place that consisted of a ruined chapel, some old farmhouses and makeshift buildings. To make matters worse it was a very difficult time for everyone in the area. First there was a famine, where people suffered greatly, even dying from hunger. Then the rains came in such abundance that there was a great flood. Those who would normally have helped us were too occupied ensuring their own survival.

Troubles followed trouble. Some of the families of my religious daughters were angry to see the privations that we suffered and spoke strongly against the venture. Some of these daughters left us. But we survived and triumphed, showing those who had put obstacles in our path that God is not to be disconcerted.

 The vision and direction came from God but he left the planning and importuning to me. It was some comfort to think that Heloise had endured similar difficulties, yet had succeeded in establishing a community of nuns within a fine abbey, and succeeded so well she then established priories attached to her abbey. Like her, I insisted on my sisters being educated, for in knowledge we find strength. To become wise we must be strong and then Wisdom is vindicated by her deeds.

*   *   *

Bernard's letter had brought us together. We found that we also shared a love of music. Heloise had introduced new hymns to the liturgy, as had I. How could Bernard believe that it was God's will that we no longer compose music? I would never accept that. Eleanor had less interest in sacred music, but told us about the songs of the troubadours. One evening she sang some of them for us, with her lady-in-waiting, Adele, playing either her small harp, or a flute. Adele also sang, and I noted

that she had a fine voice. One of the songs made me
think of travellers. Eleanor said that it was a lament by
a young man leaving his home because the woman he
loves does not return his feelings. Even though it was a
lover's lament there was something in this song that
made me think of the sacred, but isn't love a gift from
God? The love we feel for God or his Blessed Mother
will always be returned to us one hundred fold. I tried
to explain this to Eleanor, to show her that the
Benedictine life was not all privation and deficiencies.
She just laughed and said, again, that when she was old
and had lost her beauty she would retire to Fontevraud
to pray out her remaining years.

Heloise, exasperated, pointed out that an abbey is not
just an escape.

'Wasn't it for you?' asked Eleanor.

'In a certain sense you might say that,' replied Heloise,
'but to say that is to tell only a part of the story.'

'If I didn't have to be a queen I would be a troubadour,'
announced Eleanor. 'I'd travel about from place to
place, performing songs and composing new ones.
Music runs in my family.'

'You'd find that life quite unsupportable,' Heloise said,
her face lighting with amusement. Later she told me she
had a sudden mental image of Eleanor's entourage,
when she arrived, 'travelling simply, but with a few
necessities' as though life could not go on without an
ample supply of rosewater.

'You do not have to be a queen,' I reminded her. 'Life
gives us some choice.'

Even as I spoke a vision came to me, so vivid that my
breath quickened and I turned away to hide my fear. I
saw Eleanor confined more closely than ever she would
have been in any monastery; an older Eleanor, who

paced about in a small room lit only by grey light seeping through a high window, and a small candle. I could just discern her bed above the straw on the floor, and I knew that she would lie there listening to the rustle of rats in mould and damp.

'Eleanor,' I said. 'You must be very careful.'

'What a strange thing to say. You're so pale, Hildegard. Are you unwell? One minute you tell me my life is full of choices and then you warn me. Against what?'

I remained silent. Now was not the moment to tell her. When later I did try to warn her, she simply thought me fanciful. Did she remember that when, many years on, hearing that her husband Henry, King of England, had imprisoned her, I wrote:

Your mind is like a wall battered by a storm. You look all around, and you find no rest. Stay calm, and stand firm, relying on God and your fellow creatures, and God will aid you in all your tribulations. May God give you His blessing and His help in all your works.

I hope that my words gave her hope and strength, for I never forgot her and what we shared at the Paraclete.

*　　　*　　　*

Sister Agatha, being related to Abelard, should have been a comfort to Heloise and provided a link to her son. Heloise agreed that would be so if Agatha were not always so gloomy and negative, hardly allowing a smile to her face. That spoke to me of liver, a most important organ. The liver is like a bowl in a person, into which heart, lungs and stomach pour their juices. The liver allows these juices to flow to different parts of the body. Sometimes livers cannot function because people overload their bodies with rich food and drink. I wondered about this, as Agatha was in charge of the kitchen, but the food she came into contact with each day was nutritious and not overly rich. Nor did her shape suggest overeating. It was more likely that her liver was full of holes and fragile, unable to absorb the good juices so that they returned to the heart, stomach lungs, building up and causing pressure. Persons suffering in this way give in to excessive brooding and melancholy.

There are a number of remedies to heal the liver. Crushing chestnuts in honey, and eating them is one. I also recommended to Agatha that she take a hart's tongue fern, and boil it in wine, add pure honey and boil again. Add long pepper and twice as much cinnamon powder to the prepared wine and boil once again. Strain it through a clear cloth and drink the liquid both before and after meals. This strengthens the liver and takes away inner decay and slime.

Agatha looked glumly at me as I set out the details and said that she was far too busy to be concocting special drinks for herself. One of the problems in healing melancholics is they lack the energy to help themselves. Elizabeth, who was with me when I spoke to Agatha, offered to make the brew and she and Adele were soon at work, boiling and straining, crushing and mixing and insisting that Agatha at least try it.

*   *   *

I digress. I was telling of the time we talked of the different paths our lives had followed. We had relaxed into a friendly informality quite soon after that difficult first meeting.

'You had no choice,' said Heloise, turning to me. 'Your family offered you to God when you were still a young child.'

'I had no choice either,' said Eleanor. 'My father told me I was to marry Louis, and I had not so much as set

eyes on the fortunate man. But you,' as she turned
to Heloise, 'certainly had a choice. You chose to enter
an abbey.'

'I chose to enter Argentieul because Abelard asked it of
me. In that sense I had no choice, for had he asked me
to follow him through the portals of hell I would have
done so without hesitation. You're right in surmising
that I did not want to become a nun, and I can't claim
spiritual benefit from that choice, for I entered for
Abelard, not for God.'

Heloise spoke so calmly that the impact of her words
was delayed. Such a declaration from Eleanor would
have been accompanied by a flourish of trumpets.
Heloise, sitting, seemingly serene, looking at the view
outside the window as she spoke, was detached,
indifferent to our reaction. But then she turned to
Eleanor and said, 'Don't you always do what your
husband asks of you?'

'Certainly not,' then less firmly, 'I suppose you are
right, I have little choice, but I rarely obey him
willingly, and not without protest if I feel it helpful.
Although if I did do everything he asked of me I would
spend my days quietly, in prayer and meditation,
dressed in simple garments and taking no interest in the
affairs of state. There would be no time for troubadours
and music, laughing, tournaments, games or gossip.
Such a regime, according to Bernard, would give me
many children.'

'He would have you live as a nun,' said Heloise. 'We
are more alike than I realized.'

'Except for bearing children,' I added, remembering,
too late, that Heloise had a son.

Love between a man and a woman is complex. Volmar
loved me, but in a spiritual way, and our accord was

almost absolute. Even so we guarded against any
thoughts of physical love, as this would have been a
betrayal. I could never say, as had Heloise, that my life
in religion was chosen to please a man rather than God.
'Is our path in life mapped out for us, even before we
are born?' asked Eleanor.
'To a large extent, I think so,' replied Heloise,
'depending on where you are born, and the gifts you
possess. But life, or chance, may offer us some
opportunities.'
'If Abelard had not asked you to enter the abbey what
would you have done? What else was there for you to
do?' asked Eleanor, pursuing the subject.
'I could have lived in an abbey as a lay person, not
taking vows but pursuing my study and writing. Or I
could have gone to live with Abelard's family away
from Paris. I would have been without him for much of
the time but I would have been with our son. Maybe I
could have stayed in Paris, not with my uncle, but in
another household. But perhaps you are right. There
was no real choice.'
Eleanor, I think, was about to protest that life offered
many choices. Heloise, however, gestured farewell and
hurried out of the room. I later saw her sitting under the
tree where she told me she used to sit with Abelard. I
left her to her thoughts.

*   *   *

The gatehouse was Heloise's escape. After I had spent a
morning there I could see why. The window, looking
on to the road and the countryside beyond, framed the
life and work of the people who lived in the nearby
village, and of travellers moving about for a myriad of
reasons. Horses had always fascinated me; their nobility
and spirit, powerful arched necks, yet with dainty legs

placing hooves among the stones like dancers in a field of mushrooms. As a child I loved to run my hands under the mane of an old plough horse. Even on the coldest days his neck was warm. Knights and noble men and women rode by the abbey, their cloaks spread across their horse's rump, bridles and reins decorated with silver or coloured stones. Eleanor rides, and rides well, she said. I would love, just once, to gallop across a grassy meadow past forests and streams. That must feel as close to real freedom as is possible. The little bay horse, which had faithfully carried me on my journey, hardly qualified for more than a convenient way to travel. At a walk it was not even faster than my own two legs, had they not been stiffened with rheumatism. Hours spent kneeling on a cold stone floor had not helped those poor knees.

If I had remained in the world, instead of giving my life to God, there are some things I would have coveted. A beautiful horse, for one, books, maps, and tapestries. Jewels would not interest me, nor elaborate clothes, perhaps because I have neither the face nor the figure to do them justice. My life has been filled with riches of a different kind, but whenever I see a grey horse, silver tail swishing, neck arched and ears alertly pricked, I regret that I will never ride one.

Not all those who passed the abbey were riding horses. Families in groups, heading for the fair, travelled on foot. Big sisters helped smaller children; mothers chivvied them to hurry and fathers marched in front as though they had nothing to do with any of them. Where there were larger groups the men often walked together, the women bunched behind, carrying their goods wrapped in a large piece of material. There always seemed to be one child who ran ahead, or lagged behind, holding a stone, a flower, precious objects found along the way.

When the road was free of people it seemed like a white river leading to who knows where. The world, God's world, has so many treasures. We fail to appreciate them until it seems we might lose them.

On returning to the abbey I was struck, anew, by the silence. Quiet reflection allows our thoughts to be steeped in prayer. I wonder if constant silence is necessary, for I feel that in conversing with others we can gain wisdom. I learned much from my conversations with Heloise. We discussed poetry, prayers and suitable liturgical music for nuns. Her suggestions for my hymns and music were valuable. We touched on what is needed for an abbey to be successful, the strategies and manoeuverings between officials, noble families, bishops and the guilds. What she told me about their early days at the Paraclete later helped me through that difficult first year at Bingen.

Yet, fittingly, it was our discussion about love, a discussion to which Eleanor contributed, which most inspired and enriched. It all came about because Eleanor had attended mass that morning.

'The music was beautiful,' she said to me. 'I can love the God who gave us music and beauty in the world, but not the God who brought us sickness, cruelty and suffering.'

'They don't come from God,' I replied 'These occur because we've been given free will and there are men who choose evil.'

'Do you mean all humans, or just men?' asked Eleanor. Before I could answer she spoke again. 'Men, much more than women cause suffering in the world, although my mother-in-law caused me much grief until

I convinced her that one queen in the palace was enough.'

I feared another story. Heloise looked at me and raised an eyebrow before breaking in.

'God made both men and women and loves them equally. It's for us to find a way for men and women to love each other as equals. I searched to understand how love can be truly manifested between us.'

'By us, do you mean between a man and a woman?' I said.

'Of course,' Eleanor interrupted. 'But how can we ever understand love?'

'I once asked Abelard that,' said Heloise.

'How did he reply?' from Eleanor, but I was curious as well.

'In a wonderful letter. He wrote that although love may be a universal thing, it has nevertheless been condensed into so confined a place that it reigned in us alone.'

'Meaning what, exactly?' I asked more sharply than I intended. Abelard must have written that at the time they were offending against God. Genuine love should have no part in sin.

'Meaning,' said Heloise, very calmly, 'that love had made its home in us. The two of us had a love, which was pure and sincere. We nurtured each other. Nothing was sweet or carefree for one if it did not benefit the other.'

'Did you not regret the loss of your virginity?' I asked, while fearing that such a question might give offence. It was the answer that offended.

'Oh, no, not ever. I would not trade those few years with Abelard for all the treasure on earth.'

'Or the treasures to be found in heaven?' I asked quietly, that Eleanor might not hear.

Even more quietly, so I still doubt I heard her correctly, Heloise replied. 'Then I was in heaven.' I said no more but that evening, kneeling in the chapel, I reconsidered the nature of virginity and its effect on our relationship with God. Virginity is a sacred calling. I cannot doubt that. This is what I believed from the time I first had reason to think about it. But were we so different, Heloise and Eleanor and I? Heloise had suffered much, and had lived a chaste life for many years. I believed her to be pious, despite her denials. Eleanor was a married woman, pregnant, still subject to a man. She was unlike any woman I had known. She exuded worldliness, but not evil. In fact she was closer to God than she thought, in her love of beauty, music and poetry, her sensitivity and generosity. On the other hand she fussed about her apparel, was restless and distracted, dominating and sharp with her tongue. Had she dedicated both her virginity and her undoubted abilities to God would she be any different?

Was I mistaken in my reverence of virginity, my wish to celebrate it? As soon as we moved to Bingen I planned to dress my spiritual daughters in white on special feast days, with their hair, a sign of their vitality, loose about their shoulders. I could picture it: how beautiful they would be, their silk veils, embroidered with the symbol of the Lamb, a circlet representing the Holy Trinity. Could this be vain ornamentation? Some might claim so. I saw it differently. These garments and symbols are marks that bless God, for he once clothed the first man in the whiteness of light. The rules of propriety in dress apply only to married women. Virgins are like Eve was before she yielded to the blandishments of the evil one.

So my vision of these pure young women was clear
to me then. Now, many years later I still wonder if the
married state is lower? Heloise, sweet-faced and serious
was a woman who was sorrowed yet strengthened by
her contact with a man, rather than stained. Was I, as a
virgin, closer to God than she, who had suffered so
much through an excess of love for one of God's
creatures? In true wisdom God is known. And is not the
bringing forth of children part of God's plan for
humanity? So while I think that virginity does set one
apart for God, there are others who choose to cooperate
with Him in the creation of new life. They bring
different gifts to the world. There is no need to make
further judgements.

*   *   *

Next day the sun shone on the dew and the scent of the
last roses was all around us. Their perfume would fade
and the petals wither and die. Other colours: the scarlet
and blue berries shaking their happy heads in the wind;
the grey-blue of the rosemary bushes, the red of the
robin's breast, would take their place. Soon I would
have to leave and I hoped to return to my own
monastery with more than the memory of a beautiful
morning. Maybe that memory would be my only
comfort in a cold windowless cell. I felt despondent.
Heloise and Eleanor, on the other hand, were
animatedly continuing their discussion on the nature of
love. Their voices formed a gentle murmuring
background to my thoughts until the word 'soul' broke
my reverie.

'Love is a particular force of the soul, existing not for
itself nor content by itself, but always pouring itself into
another with a certain hunger and desire, wanting to
become one with the other, so that from two diverse

wills one is produced without difference,' Heloise was saying.

That is how I try to love God, I thought.

'There must be a difference,' objected Eleanor. 'A woman is to be revered and protected by the man who claims to love her. How is this possible if there is no difference between them?'

'May they not revere and honour each other as equals?' said Heloise.

'Most men are rough, arrogant beings. They must be taught to appreciate the beauty and refinement of women, so they become less like animals.'

'And more like God's creation?' I asked. 'You pass a harsh a judgment on men.'

'Had you seen them at war so would you. All Heloise knows are philosophers and scholars. All you know are monks, praying in their chapel. They are men who have withdrawn from the world, and who shun the company of women.'

This made me aware how different our experiences had been. Heloise, petted and praised as a child, had spent some years living in Paris, near Notre Dame, near the scholars and the canons, stretching her mind. She had been to Brittany, where she had experienced the pain of childbirth and the exultation of cradling her baby. How tragically it had all ended. From such pain strength had emerged.

For her part Eleanor had seen so much of life: marriage, royal status, death, war, intrigues, music and poetry. She too had known the joy of holding her child. I lacked their experiences. I had seen little beyond my home and my monastery. God had, however, shown me wonders and sights and revealed truths to me. I had to count myself the richest of all.

We did return to the subject of love, more than
once, I recall. Love permeates all that humans cherish.
There was another conversation I had with Heloise, the
day after she had shown me Abelard's letter of faith.
'I've thought of what you describe as a good and proper
love between men and women,' she said. 'I imagine
you think only in terms of love between a husband and
wife.'

I agreed that this was so.

'But, and this may not please you, I do not believe that
it is marriage that inspires and creates such a true, close
love. Marriage brings affection and respect, yes, and a
mutual love for their children, together with the caring
for their estate. But the uniting of bodies which follows
the uniting of minds – that has nothing to do with the
married state. To give oneself to another person, as I
gave myself to Abelard, and as he gave himself to me,
is to give expression to a love that could not offend
God. Neither should any of God's creatures find it
sinful. There's too much talk of lust in the writings of
holy men. They are mistaken.'

Heloise had never spoken to me before in such a way,
and she never did again. How I might have replied I do
not know, for Eleanor entered at that moment. Yet even
though I reflected on what Heloise had said I could
never feel that the union between a man and a woman,
no matter how much they loved each other could be as
noble as the love between a virgin and God. One was a
union of equals whereas the other was the lifting up of a
flawed creature to the perfect love of God. What
physical pleasure could match that? And how had their
love ended? In sorrow and mutilation. Such a
consequence did not speak of God's approval.

*   *   *

'Let me tell you a story. It's about a knight.'

Eleanor was in high spirits.

But both Heloise and I begged her for no more stories. We needed to deal with more important matters than Court gossip. To our surprise she agreed, and without umbrage. We turned our attention to the purpose of Bernard's letter, with the firm intention of devising a definite plan of action.

Eleanor insisted that we each look to our strengths. Heloise said that she was a scholar so she would write a letter. In fact she had the model for such a letter, written by Abelard, in support of women in religion.

'How can we succeed using such a letter? Didn't Bernard oppose Abelard?' objected Eleanor.

'Not in everything. There were many subjects on which they did agree. You knew that they were reconciled before Abelard died? I only regret that they had not sought to do so long before the tragedy at Soissons, when Abelard was accused of arrogance and heresy.'

'That is all in the past,' I said. 'If you write a letter to Bernard, that will be all to the good. For my part I will seek to reach his heart and mind through music. There's nothing more powerful and uplifting than music.'

'If it is power you want, I could use my small army. I couldn't tell Louis what it was for, as he would never agree, but I'm sure I could think of some story to tell him,' said Eleanor.

'What exactly would your small army be for?' asked Heloise.

'To defeat Bernard. If he were to be taken from the field of battle then victory would be ours.'

'You mean kill him?' I asked, thinking the question ridiculous even as I uttered it.

'If necessary. Don't you agree? If not, we could incapacitate him in some way. Bernard would then retire to his monastery, where he belongs, instead of charging about the country stirring up trouble, and wanting us to live on in silence. Remember that he often says he's yearning for heaven. He might prefer that.' Eleanor glowed with energy and conviction.

'That is not our way,' Heloise answered reprovingly. 'We must work within God's law if we are to succeed at all. May I suggest you rethink your strategy.'

'Neither of you seem to understand how dangerous an enemy he is or how much I fear the future if he succeeds. Maybe you are the ones who should rethink your plans of action. Hymns and letters! I expected greater things.' Eleanor glared at us both for a moment then turned her back and was out of the door in three quick steps. I may have been mistaken but I thought she was near to tears.

'Being pregnant can do strange things to a woman,' said Heloise. 'We can trust her, when calmer, to find her own strength.'

But, I doubted that. Eleanor could do nothing but hinder us. When I heard, some years later, that she was accused of inciting her sons to rebel against their father I thought back to that day in the Paraclete when she had sat, straight and tall, ready to command an army to achieve her desires. Had she learned nothing since then? Taking up weapons is seldom the answer to disputes.

Heloise set great store on the power of words. I believed in the power of prayer and music. Arrows may pierce the flesh, but words and music reach into the soul and change it forever. Finding the right words is difficult. Our language belongs more to men than to

women, so that powerful words reflect war,
conquest and revenge. The language of women should
reflect their strengths: love, compassion and wisdom. I
sought to invent a language, which could do that, but
time eluded me and it was never completed. Had we
three spoken together, using such a language, would we
have sought different solutions to our problem?
I remember my anger when Eleanor suggested that I
invent a message from God to further our cause. I
responded with holy wrath, believing that she was
mocking both God and me. Later I wondered if that
were such an impossible plan, if all else failed. God
could speak with an authority that I would never be
granted.

*　　　*　　　*

We sat in a semicircle, with our backs to the window.
So comforting to feel the warmth of the morning sun on
our neck and shoulders. Through the far windows we
could see the garden, moist and shadowy, waiting for
its share of the day's sunlight. We felt more at ease.
Heloise was planning her letter, I had thought about the
music I would use and Eleanor had relaxed like a sleepy
cat, having abandoned her battle strategy.
By the following morning all was changed. I was
walking back from the chapel, thinking how pleasant it
had been to see Agatha's friendly smile. Running feet
sounded behind me, and I turned to see Elizabeth, face
flushed and excited.
'Bernard of Clairvaux is coming to the Paraclete,' she
said. 'Adele told me. You'll get to meet him at last. Are
you not excited, dear Mother?'
Excited! There was no room for excitement; I was filled
with apprehension.

'How does Adele know these things?' I asked so crossly that Elizabeth's face crumbled and I feared she would burst into tears.

'I don't know, but she finds out everything.'

I took Elizabeth's hand and told her I was sorry that I had spoken so sharply. By then I had calmed down, and begun to reflect. What were our chances of success? While we three had sat and talked about the danger we were in it seemed as though there was some hope that we could succeed in convincing Bernard to change his mind about women being totally cloistered. Now that we were about to confront him, the idea that he would reconsider what he believed to be God's will seemed impossible. Bernard was certain that he was close to God, and understood how things ought to be. He had the ear of the Pope. We were weak and feeble women, to his mind at least, and there were few women and fewer men who would disagree with him.

Then my head began to throb and I felt the dreaded pains in my neck and shoulders begin to gather for a full attack on my body. Enough, I said to myself, and to God if he was listening. I have been directed to come here. Why did I feel that our plans were all doomed to failure? Was it possible that God would ask me to return to a space enclosed in four stone walls, which would become smaller and tighter over the years, until they were no wider than a tomb.

Heloise, on greeting me later that morning, looked at me closely for a few moments. 'Go out into the garden. You have need of fresh air and solitude.'

I had need of more than that, but time in the garden always calms me, so I took myself there. It was so important to hide my fears, especially from Eleanor, that I tried to always have a cheerful, confident countenance. Not understanding that I needed solitude she came to join me. Still, I talked to her of the power of music and my faith that God would guide us all through this difficult time. Eleanor had grown spiritually in the time she was at the Paraclete, no longer as restless or afraid to allow the stillness within, no longer daring to suggest that I claim to have heard from God things that Eleanor wanted to hear. That suggestion had made me very angry at the time, yet later I saw the irony, for in worldly terms this would seem the perfect solution. Who can argue with the direct commands of God? God cannot be mocked in this way, and I believe that Eleanor came to appreciate this. But she was sagacious not to underestimate the power of Bernard of Clairvaux.

'You will not think much of him when you first see him,' Eleanor told me,' but be on your guard. He could teach the serpent something about wiles.'

She was right. Bernard was not an imposing man. My first impression was that he was so frail that he, rather than we women, should be thought of as weak and feeble. Further acquaintance made me think quite differently. He carried himself with an air, not of authority, but of total confidence. Was he directed in the same way that I was? He had never made such a claim, although he spoke so movingly about the love of God and the peace that was to be obtained by those who surrendered to it, that I believe he may have had some type of mystical union.

*   *   *

When St Benedict had set out his Rule he was living in very different times to ours. He devised a way for monks and nuns to live which was moderate and flexible, balanced yet ordered, so that his Rule had served to guide during the centuries that followed. However he could never have envisaged the events which occurred while Bernard was at the Paraclete. We had been horrified to learn that the monks at St. Gildas had attempted to poison Abelard with tainted communion wine. Now we discovered that we had nearly poisoned Bernard with a fish. Bernard's suffering was severe. He moaned and cried out as each spasm of pain burned and tore at his entrails. The only time I had heard such sounds before was from the woman who was possessed by a devil.

Bernard of Clairvaux, as loud in his suffering, was certainly not possessed by any devil. We were terrified that he would die from the effects of the meal he had eaten. He might not have minded a rapid entry into heaven. He made much of longing for death, as Eleanor had reminded us. But what would happen to Heloise, Eleanor and me if we were accused of murdering him? That terrible night, back at the Paraclete, I had stood in the cold shadows listening to his sufferings. It was my entire fault, for I had provided the herbs for the fish, and the betony leaves for his pillow, never thinking that Elizabeth and Adele would mix them together. For a man with chronic digestive disorders this combination could be fatal. At each groan the rack turned. Each sigh brought me closer to the abyss.

I am not sure how long I stood shivering in the shadows almost too petrified to even pray when I was distracted by a flicker at the end of the long corridor, which led to the cloister. The flicker became a light from a candle. It shone and disappeared, flickered, then disappeared again, as the person holding it was shielded and then revealed by the pillars in the courtyard. Then a second light followed the first, and a third. In the doorway I saw Elizabeth walking towards me, her serene face saintly in that light. She had taken off her veil and her hair was free, with small curls around her ears and forehead. Adele came behind her, her fair hair half shielding her face. Finally there was Agatha. In the moonlight, which caught them as they moved closer to the window, Agatha's hair shone silver. Adele began to sing.

Therefore rejoice, daughter of Zion
in the noblest dawn

My hymn to St Ursula, chosen to remind the holy monk that women may love God as ardently as any man, and sacrifice their lives with as much courage. Adele's voice was strong and clear. She sang those lines again, this time joined by Elizabeth. Agatha then took up the melody.

Because, like a fruit-laden garden and splendour of
flowers
she gathered a throng of virgins about her.

Adele sang in harmony, her voice rising higher and higher, holding the note then gently descending to take up the melody as Elizabeth now harmonized with her pure sweet voice, clear as the white light which shone through the far window. Agatha, whose voice was deep and melodious, held the securing note. Once again they sang it from the beginning and my eyes filled with tears for the beauty of the sound, and to hear my music given life. I stood further back in the shadows, while the singers were shrouded in light. I prayed that the nourishing moon would lend glory to their voices. I

prayed that Adele would not sing out of tune. I
prayed the other two would let the harmonies float
along the corridor, echoing, rising, descending and
fading with the final syllable. A dripping honeycomb
was the virgin Ursula, and her sweetness must move the
heart of Bernard. They left as softly as they had come,
their voices echoing and reechoing as they retreated
until there was but a thin thread of gold woven through
the soft silver of the moon.

I turned back to listen at the door of Bernard's room.
From the sounds of restless turning and tossing,
moaning and distress Bernard seemed less than
receptive to my small choir. Should I enter and offer
him some remedy? As I hesitated I again saw another
light moving along the courtyard towards me and I
stepped back into the shadows. Who was it? Elizabeth,
returning to see how I was? Dear thoughtful girl. But
the figure was too tall for Elizabeth. Adele? Had
Eleanor sent her for some reason? As the figure came
closer I could see that it was not Adele, unless she had
quickly changed into a white dress, and blue cloak,
covering her head with a white veil and putting on
golden shoes. It was the image of Mary in the chapel
come to life. No, that Mary did not have golden shoes,
nor was she carrying a candle in one hand and a flask of
rosewater in the other. Eleanor! Before I could speak to
her she entered Bernard's room. No doubt she had
come to send his soul to heaven.

That, I thought, is that. We were doomed either to
eternal incarceration, or to follow Bernard into the next
world.

*   *   *

My role in this part of the story ends here. My Light
had left me, as I approached my Gethsemane.

Eleanor was the one who entered Bernard's room to try to ease his pain and suffering, while I remained outside, afraid for so many reasons. She is the only one who can tell what followed on that eventful night. When she does our story will be complete.

ELEANOR'S STORY

We each promised Heloise to write about our time together at the Paraclete. I always intended to keep my word, but when I returned to Paris my life went in a different direction. Such was the good influence of both Heloise and Hildegard I made every effort to be a good wife to Louis and a wise queen. The baby I was carrying was, as Hildegard predicted, a girl, and there were prune faces all around when this was announced. I thought she looked like a little angel with her long limbs and fluffed, reddish hair, but the sex was wrong, so I had failed again. Not Louis' failure, note. In these situations they always blame the woman. After that the walls of the palace pressed in on me. The sobriety of the court bored me and Louis irritated me beyond belief.

There was no Adele. After we returned she kept wittering about joining a monastery, the one in Germany, to be with 'dearest Sister Elizabeth.' To keep her quiet I found her a handsome man so that within a short time her religious vocation had melted and she began warbling about 'darling Alphonse' until I was glad to see her safely married and leave Paris to live near Poitiers, where she could use her talents in my service.

Then Henry of Anjou returned to the court, and we were able to escape the eager ears and prying eyes for long enough to seal our pact. All I had to do was wait until I was free of Louis. Abbot Suger was dead, no longer urging Louis to keep me in the fold because my lands came with me. Bernard of Clairvaux favoured an

annulment. He might have spoken gently to me at
the Paraclete, but when he saw me again, in Paris, he
bowed coldly then turned away, his face a mixture of
embarrassment and alarm. Our secret was safe, I could
have told him if I ever had the opportunity, but he saw
to it that I did not.

So, with the wooing by one man, and the disentangling
from another, the thought of writing anything was
furtherest from my mind. Leaving my two daughters
was hard, but within the year I had married Henry and
given him a son. Then we moved to London to be
crowned king and queen of England, and for many
years I was happy there.

Later, when Henry had imprisoned me, I thought again
about my promise to Heloise, but although I had the
means to write, I lacked the will. I wanted only to write
to my children and Adele. It was she who told me that
Heloise's account was in the Paraclete library, along
with the letters that Abelard had written to Heloise.
Hildegard's account was housed in the library at
Bingen. Not only did she tell me, but she also brought
copies of their stories when she visited me at Chinon,
the Christmas Henry allowed me some freedom, before
returning me to captivity.

Reading those accounts brought so much back to me. I
was right to believe that they had little respect for my
abilities at first; right to think that they went off on their
own at times, but they were of an age and both nuns, so
they had more in common. After so many years had
passed I was not concerned with holding resentment.
Instead I remembered the beautiful music, the mornings
in the garden and the stories and laughter we shared.

At last, when I retired to Fontevraud, I decided that I
must keep my promise to them both. Now, at the end of

a long and eventful life, I write my account of the
time three wise women fought for the freedom to use
their gifts and talents. There will be other accounts of
my life, but none, I think, will include this. In the future
they will write that I was Duchess of Aquitaine, Queen
of France and Queen of England: that I had two
husbands and bore ten children. Chroniclers may record
that I travelled to Jerusalem on a crusade when I was
still young and rode across Europe when I was eighty
years old. That story will finish at Fontevraud Abbey,
as will I.

Told like that my life can be seen as an extraordinary
list of achievements. It does not reveal in what ways
these events affected and changed me. One important
event will be omitted because few knew about it. I refer
to the time when I was at the Paraclete. Heloise and
Hildegard, who are undoubtedly learned or godly, have
already written about this time, but their stories belong
to them. For me to be there, so soon after I had returned
from the crusade, proved to be a turning point in my
life, and that is my story.

My first encounter with Heloise was not what I
expected. After all, I was her Queen. While she treated
me with courtesy there was no sense that I was an
exceptional visitor as she showed me to their second-
best guest room. A nun who had arrived earlier already
occupied the best room, Heloise explained. I assumed
this nun would be asked to relinquish the room of
honour. As Heloise and I approached the door we heard
an enthusiastic snore, the song of one in a sound sleep.
Even so, I stood my ground, but Heloise smiled,
shrugged her shoulders and beckoned me to follow her
further down the corridor. This sleeping nun is now

quite famous, but she was not so then, and even if
she had been, royalty takes precedence over religious.
You may think that queens can do as they like, but
really we are under more scrutiny and restrictions than
ordinary women, as I discovered when I was married to
Louis. One can't even relieve oneself without half the
palace learning about it. Ladies-in-waiting here, ladies-
in waiting there. Waiting for what? My sister Petronilla
said that they were waiting for me to do something
really bad, so they could report me to Abbot Suger, who
would then inform the King, who would consult on the
matter with Brother Bernard, and come back to me with
a further list of 'do and do nots'.

As the years of my first insufferable marriage continued
I had become more resigned to the sober atmosphere in
the Paris court, but at the beginning, when I was only
fifteen, I found it very difficult. In Aquitaine the lush
grasses and warmer climate encourage music, poetry,
laughter and freedom. Our dresses match the flowers in
colour, if not in variety and form. Music is part of our
daily life. Grandfather William was a poet and musician
as well as a great soldier. My father was musical as
well, and it was he who insisted that I be well educated.
Even though my mother died when we were quite
young my sister and I had a happy childhood, and I
often wished that my father had arranged for me to be
the wife of a man who would live with me in Poitiers.
Marrying the heir to the throne of France sounds all
very well, but if you ever look at a map and see how
much land I brought with me and how small his
kingdom was then, you would not need to wonder who
had really gained from that marriage contract. He
acquired a beautiful wife as well as a larger kingdom.
Louis was never my ideal of a gallant romantic lover,

but I accepted him as my father's choice. After a decade of a boring marriage from which there seemed no respite, I was less resigned, and yearned for my freedom. Then I discovered that worse was in store. I was in serious danger.

This, while I was still young, still beautiful and desperate to experience more from life than I had so far. I paced about the room, thinking, thinking what I could do. Then I hurried to Louis, not for advice, but with my plan, which involved travelling to the Paraclete to consult Abbess Heloise.

Predictably, he began by forbidding me to go, saying that in Paris there were abbeys, abbots or abbesses enough to provide me with spiritual guidance, without having to seek out Abelard's whore.

'That was many years ago,' I replied, 'and I might remind you that Abelard and Heloise were married.'

'Accepting that their marriage was valid. He was a cleric, as I recall,' Louis said with that grating whine in his voice.

'Can you be so sure that our marriage is valid?' I challenged him. 'Don't be too hasty in your judgement of others.' Then, realising that if we fought he would prance out of the room, with his head waggling as though he were balancing the royal crown, I continued more gently, 'Abelard is at peace in his grave and Heloise has lived as a religious for nearly thirty years. Does it not say in the Gospel that there's more joy in heaven over one sinner who repents than all the good people put together? Be charitable, dear husband!'

I always found it helped to refer to Scripture when arguing with Louis.

'*Dear husband*, is it now? Perhaps I may permit you to go but first I would like to consult Abbot Suger concerning this idea of yours,' he said, relenting a little but, as I knew he would, playing for time.

Abbot Suger had been a constant trial to me throughout my marriage to Louis. He had been part of the establishment for what seemed a hundred years, advising Louis' father when he was king, and then Louis. Even worse, he'd been Louis' mentor when he was in the abbey at St Denis, so he'd had plenty of time to coil his tentacles around the impressionable princely mind and soul. I knew he would oppose me for no other reason than that he neither liked nor respected me and took every opportunity to thwart my will. The only thing in my favour, according to Suger, was my endowment. No, Suger was not to be consulted.

'Would you forbid me seeking spiritual strength and solace from a wise and learned woman, one who is noted for her piety and scholarship? A woman who has sinned, suffered and been converted, devoting her life to the practice of prayer and reflection?' I said. My voice started to reveal my anger. Louis looked sharply at me, so I quickly re-formed my attack.

'My overwhelming desire is to provide France with an heir. Our failure to do so makes me wonder if our marriage is acceptable to God. I wish only to please him and you.'

Louis smiled then, and took my hand in his.

'If it will bring about such a joy then go with my blessing. The Holy Father is praying for this, you know. Have faith in the power of his intercession for he has the ear of God.'

He reached out and gently pushed a strand of hair away from my face. He would surprise me sometimes, with such a tender gesture. Then he would retreat and become reserved and inhibited.

'Take enough servants to protect you, but travel as inconspicuously as possible. We do not wish for any scandal. I will make a novena for your intentions while you're gone,' Louis said, capitulating. He kissed me gently on the cheek and left the room, no doubt heading for the chapel to pray for a son. Dear, deluded Louis, thinking that a novena on his knees was likely to produce a child.

If he had known the real reason I wished to speak with Abbess Heloise, Louis would have locked me in my room. Even more, if he'd suspected that I might, even then, be pregnant, permission would not have been forthcoming. I wasn't sure. My monthly bleeding had been delayed other times, then, just as hope was growing, it would gush forth, leaving me feeling bereft and barren. Was it my fault, as Bernard of Clairvaux had accused, for being too ready to take my part in the concerns of men? Was it Louis' fault, given his attendance in my bed was inspired more by the intention to do his duty than any loving or even lustful desire? Repression inhibited any expression of passion, if indeed he felt it. Maybe he was born that way, as Petronilla, giggling and totally unsympathetic, would say, but I always believed that the monks and clerics debased healthy male lust. If they had their way the human race would end within a few years. Louis had been an impressionable boy, raised in an abbey. Whatever the reason for his lack of desire it was not that he did not love me. Even so it made for a dull marriage.

*   *   *

'Do you want the blue or the red cloak?' Adele asked, as she was packing.

'The red, no, not the red, it's too ornate. The blue.'

On such small decisions hang great consequences.
The blue cloak meant the matching white dress, and a
white veil for my head because abbeys are invariably
chilly.

'Maybe the gold shoes as well. Otherwise just pack
plain clothes. We must travel simply.'

'You have no plain clothes,' Adele said, a little pertly,
but I was in no mood to reprimand her.

'Make sure that there's enough food among our
provisions. I may be going to pray, but not to fast. Tell
them to prepare a goose as well. On second thoughts,
we'd better take it live and let the nuns chop off its
head. Then we'll know it's our goose and it's fresh,' I
ordered, sending her out of my sight before I lost my
temper. I would need her to be in good humour during
our journey.

So we prepared, planning to travel as simply as I could
bear. Adele and I rode palfreys; six men rode in front of
us, six men behind, with their weapons ready. Then
there were three servants who walked with the pack
mules.

'Maybe you could speak to Brother Bernard,' Louis
finally suggested, just as I settled my foot in the stirrup,
ready to leave. 'Talking to him helped you once
before.'

'To bear a daughter,' I replied. 'We can do better than
that.'

Speaking to Brother Bernard of Clairvaux was most
certainly not a good idea, because he was the schemer
planning to keep me forever imprisoned in the palace or
in a monastery. It was just good fortune that I had
discovered this in time, through Adele. If you want to
know what is really going on, ask the servants. Well, I
could hardly demean myself by speaking directly to

underlings, but Adele could. She had been my lady-in-waiting for three years and had developed an instinct for discovering information, an instinct which I encouraged and guided. Her web of contacts spread through castles and abbeys, via travellers and merchants who came to the Royal Palace, pageboys, squires and the maids in the kitchen. The source of food was also the starting place for news, she told me. Being small and quite pretty – a shame about the squint – she could move about so unobtrusively that people forgot she was there, standing in the shadows. A cardinal's servant travelling home after some synod or other (they were always having these convocations where much food and wine was consumed, while obscure points of doctrine which interested no one but themselves, were considered) mentioned to her that Bernard had written a letter asking the Pope to decree that if any marriage were annulled the woman involved would have to enter an abbey, and forfeit all her possessions and her children. There was something about nuns as well, but this did not concern me until I realized that I could call on an abbess or two to support me in the battle against such a decree.

'That should make a few rebellious ladies think again,' he said. 'Some have more to lose than others,' and then he had fondled her bottom, enraging her.

'Has the Pope received this letter?' I asked, this to me being of far more import than her wounded dignity.

'Not as yet, according to that rogue. He should keep his arms folded,' she replied. 'He has a copy, though. He showed it to me.'

'You must arrange for that letter to be stolen.'

'Bernard would only write another.' she pointed out.

'We must at least see the copy. It may not be as bad
as you believe,' I suggested.

'That will take much trouble and some gold,' she
replied, 'I run the risk of being manhandled by that ass
again.'

She placed the coins that I gave her in a little silk purse.
Adele would not lose in the transaction, I understood,
but neither would the cardinal's servant. Within less
than half an hour she returned with a copy of the letter,
and it was only then I suspected that she had it all the
time.

How can I now describe my feelings when I first read
that letter? Fury? Red-hot anger? Fear? Despair? There
are no adequate words to encapsulate the myriad
emotions that engulfed me. I sat down suddenly, for my
legs could no longer support me. Adele rushed to help
me, but I had recovered enough to wave her away. I
can't stand people fussing all over me.

'We must take action,' I said, when Adele had returned
bearing sweet wine to soothe my nerves and rosewater
to cool my throbbing head. 'And we need help. There is
only one person I know who has the intellect, the
learning, and a good reason to oppose Bernard of
Clairvaux.'

'Peter Abelard! Oh, isn't he dead?'

'Not Abelard, you fool. We will visit the Abbess
Heloise.'

*   *   *

There were a number of reasons why I decided to visit
Heloise, but the location of her abbey was not one of
them. I wished that she had been the abbess at
Fontevraud, for this would have confirmed a close link
between us. Noble families of the Loire Valley,
including my own, had endowed Fontevraud when it

was first established by Robert d'Arbrissel. Two wives, discarded by my grandfather, William of Poitiers, had ended their days there, happily prophesising his downfall. I had always accepted that I would end my days there as well, although I did not intend this to be because I had been discarded and replaced.

There was a connection between Heloise and Fontevraud through her mother, Hersinde, who had been the first prioress there, after Heloise was born. Mystery shrouded the identity of Heloise's father. Some went as far as to say that Robert d'Arbrissel was her father, but that it is just rumour. I know how such stories can grow, encouraged by malice and jealousy, from a small spark to a raging bonfire. Yet I have sometimes wondered if there was some truth in it. Why had Robert, on his deathbed, asked to be buried next to Hersinde? He wasn't, of course. Others had different plans for his burial place, but it does make you wonder. Fontevraud is unusual in that it provides for the virginal daughters and sons of the nobility, but also for redeemed 'fallen women', widows, and lepers who are nursed there. While it is an abbey for men and women, its founder insisted that a woman would always lead it, for he believed that they were more capable than men. Hersinde had presided over this religious establishment, and through her efforts it expanded and acquired land and other property. Heloise, it was said, showed equal ability as an administrator, developing a dilapidated building to prosperity, while never losing her reputation for being gentle and discreet. Nevertheless, I hoped that she would think outside the Rule, and not just reassure me that God's will was being done whichever way things turned out. She must know, as I did, that while the Church had many holy and charitable men and women, it was top heavy with corrupt and venal prelates, abbots, abbesses and bishops. I'd seen enough of them hanging around Louis like jackals to know that they had little interest in following the Christ's teachings.

A voice in my head warned me that Heloise might envy me my youth, beauty and freedom. The years since she and Abelard had parted could have turned her into a sour grape, wrinkled with age, withering on the vine. I could do nothing about being young and beautiful, but I could assure her that freedom for me was a mirage. I was subject to a man, who although, in his inhibited way, was sick with love for me, yet could never satisfy me. His courtiers regarded me as a brood mare, an unsuccessful one at that, and the bringer of a dowry, which had enriched Louis' kingdom. They crowded me, spying, anxious to discover and report any peccadillo. Then there was Henry of Anjou who had come to my attention. We had circled each other, teased and taunted, suggested and denied. If he became King of England, as he intended, and my marriage to Louis was annulled, as I intended, he could wed and bed me as we both intended. His lands and mine, together, would form an empire. That, I believed, would be freedom!

*   *   *

The story of Heloise and Abelard is a great love story. I had reminded Louis that they were married, but that was almost at the end of the affair, not the beginning. When it happened it was the talk of Paris, and beyond, I believe. I can say, with no fear of contradiction, that many women envied Heloise her place in Abelard's bed. I could have been one of them but unfortunately by

the time I was old enough it would have afforded
little satisfaction to either of us.

Such songs he wrote for her: exotic, evocative,
passionate. You could still hear them being sung all
over the city when I first went to Paris. They must have
caused him much embarrassment, and reminded him of
what he had lost. While I rode along, remembering
their story, I thought of all the things I would ask
Heloise. Was he a wonderful lover? Did she and
Abelard ever quarrel?

'Often and often,' she told me, when I finally asked the
second question. She never did answer the first.

'Why did you quarrel?' I asked. 'Your love for each
other was so strong.'

'For that very reason. Deep emotions exclude
indifference. Perhaps the first serious quarrel we had
was when he apologized.'

'That should have led to forgiveness and
reconciliation.'

'Not in this instance. He had compelled me to many
things; loving him, passion, feasting on ideas and
learning, poetry, music. But then he wrote that he was
sorry that he had compelled me to sin. This outraged
me. I saw that he did not understand our love in the
same way I did. I felt deceived and wanted no more to
do with him, so I replied that I hoped he would be
brought back to the road of salvation and that all our
writing to each other should now finish. "Take your
complaints away from me," I said. "I will not hear them
any more." But we were soon reconciled.'

Heloise told me all this after we had been together for
two weeks, and she had come to trust me. But, as usual,
I have jumped ahead of my story. I was still jogging

along the road to the Paraclete, as now I, and I hope you, recall.

The day we set out was pleasant. We were soon free of the streets of Paris, where curious faces had looked down on us from high windows, past the market stalls, where traders called to us to buy their wares, to ride through the countryside beside the river as we moved towards Troyes. The warmth of the sun and my horse's smooth gait relaxed me so that my thoughts ambled along as well. Again I pondered Heloise. What did she look like? She had been the object of a great love. Abelard had word-painted her as brighter than anything that the earth had produced, although that was when she was young. Now she must now have been over forty. That thought led to a different picture, of her stooped and short-sighted due to long hours spent at her writing and studies. But would that image be worthy of a tragic heroine? I would have to wait and see.

My initial instincts were not wrong as I discovered on the morning we finally arrived at the gate of the Paraclete. The riders checked their horses with a great deal of noise and clatter, while I waited towards the back of the group, taking in the view. The Paraclete was not a large abbey, but of pleasing proportions, and all the surrounding buildings and land, as much as I could see over the wall, was orderly and cultivated. Across the top of the gateway was a small gatehouse, and I thought I saw some movement at the window there as Adele went forward, with two of the serving men, to announce that we were there. To my amazement, the nun who opened the gate turned out to be Heloise. This is not normally the duty of the abbess, but later I discovered that she liked to sit in the gatehouse and read or write as she watched the road outside.

A nun's habit does little for any woman unless her features are very regular and her cheekbones high. Heloise possessed both attributes, and despite the veil shielding much of her profile I detected a good complexion, eyes an unusual slate-grey colour, eyebrows defined without being bushy, a firm, well shaped chin, full, even sensuous, mouth; a face worthy of a thousand songs. Her manner was gracious and courteous, without any suggestion of servility, even though she had instantly recognised me.

On the other hand I could not imagine the Abbess Hildegard, whom I met the next morning, being the recipient of passionate love. She was shorter than Heloise, stocky in build, and while there were lines around her eyes, lines, which I later learned were caused by her constant headaches, she had an air of serenity, almost otherworldliness. At our initial meeting I judged her to be an ineffectual and self-effacing woman. First impressions can be deceptive. Her slightly distracted manner hid a mind that was sharp, and eyes that missed nothing.

It says something about Hildegard that she continued to sleep in the best room throughout our stay. Adele was shocked at what she judged as disrespect. For my part, I considered the privations and suffering of the men and women who had followed their king to the holy lands, and decided that in accepting a smaller room and thin mattress I was being truly gracious.

Nevertheless, Heloise did offer me the room where we came to meet, for my use at other times. She understood that I must have some space for myself if I was to endure the confines of an abbey. This room suited me, for it was roomy, and light, with windows at either end. Through them I could watch the play of the shadows on

the trees and garden beds as the sun passed
overhead. One door led straight into the garden and I
often walked about in the fresh air amongst the flowers
and herbs. Scent of rosemary always takes me back to
that time. The sisters who worked there would smile in
greeting, but rarely spoke. Their life was spent almost
entirely in silence, but amongst bird song and gentle
breezes this seemed a minor deprivation. Of course this
was still early autumn. In winter, when the birds have
all flown away to a warmer spot, and the trees and
plants are but bare sticks, the delights of nature would
have compensated less. Hildegard was sometimes in the
garden as well, not, I noted, keeping silence as she
questioned the gardeners about plant arrangements and
the properties of unfamiliar herbs.

The first meeting when we came together to discuss the
letter was a complete failure. We began in the room
where we ate our meals. My horse would have just
fitted there comfortably. Not being horses, and there
being three of us, we were most uncomfortable.
Hildegard and Heloise eyed each other like knights
about to joust. This I could understand. What I could
not understand is why neither needed to engage with
me. I may not have been a prophet whose revelations
were read aloud by the Pope to an assembly of bishops
and church dignitaries. Sadly, I had not been involved
in a passionate love affair with the most exciting and
charismatic man in Paris either. However I was the
equal of these women in other ways. They needed to
know that I was no simpleton. I had travelled through
foreign countries, ready to fight for Christianity until I
became sickened and disillusioned by the behaviour of
these Christians. I had looked death in the face more
than once. I had tended wounded soldiers, promising to

convey their last words to their wives, knowing that
I would never be able to find most of them. I had seen
my husband come to fear that he was a failure as a
commander, then turn to his inept advisers, rather than
his wife, for reassurance. When I sought freedom from
a marriage that was eroding my spirit the same Pope
who had approved of Hildegard's writings had
outmanoeuvred me. They needed to know me for what I
was. So I talked of my life and the crusade from which
I had so recently returned. They would see that I had
seen more of real life than they could ever imagine.
They would understand that humbler forces could
defeat great armies. No matter how powerful Bernard
of Clairvaux might be we could conquer.

They were very unresponsive. Days later Hildegard
asked me why I had spoken so urgently and at length of
my travels. If she could read thoughts she should have
known, as I pointed out to her. At the end of that first
meeting I returned to my cell, disgruntled, disillusioned
and ready to return to Paris immediately. Adele stopped
me. She had done her duty and found out all she could
about Mother Hildegard.

'My lady, I can tell you this much. Elizabeth thinks she
is very holy and wise. Mother Hildegard prophesises
and listens to God who talks to her directly, just like I
am talking to you. Sister Elizabeth says she's writing a
book about her visions and she knows all about herbs
and healing, and if she has time and God wills it, she'll
write about those as well. It will please you to know
that she composes music, which is quite beautiful. She
wrote to Bernard of Clairvaux and he spoke very highly
of her writing and visions, so Elizabeth said. But I
found out that she's not an abbess, only a magistra.'

A prophet and mystic she might be, but only a
magistra. This put her below Heloise who was an
abbess, and well below me as a queen. But a prophecy
or two might prove useful, especially from one who had
Bernard's approval. That didn't sit well with Bernard's
letter, however, and needed to be investigated. My
decision to return to Paris may have been too hasty. As
they prayed in the chapel I sat alone and thought.
It could be advantageous to nullify the difference
between us all and allow some informality for the
purpose of our meetings. I would suggest that Heloise
find us a better meeting place, which would allow us to
converse in comfort. So that our time was not wasted
on irrelevant talk I would direct the discussion,
although I accepted that we did need a little time to get
to know each other better. I had expected them to be
respectful, overawed even, by my title and position.
The look of surprise on Heloise's face when I spoke
Latin revealed much. Did she think I was one of those
women who simpered over her embroidery? I
reminded her that I was the granddaughter of William
of Poitiers, Duke, Crusader and Troubadour.
Then there was all the talk from Hildegard about
virginity being a state almost higher than the angels, à
la Louis, who had come with such reluctance to our
marriage bed the first time. Outrageous! Was it my fault
that he wanted to be a monk? Was it my fault that his
brother Philip went catapulting off his horse and died
the day after, which was probably a blessing as he had
broken almost every bone in his body? So, Louis was
obliged to be King of France instead of a monk
mouldering in an abbey. Any normal man would have
rejoiced at this change in his circumstances. Any full-

blooded man would have been delighted to share
my bed and body.

'It's our duty,' he sighed on our wedding night. 'We
must consummate this marriage and provide children. It
means we lose our virginity, but God will forgive us if,
throughout, we preserve our modesty of soul.'

He spoke as though it were a sacrifice! To couple with
me, Duchess of Aquitaine, beautiful and desirable, if I
could believe the compliments from ardent young
knights and older, rickety dukes. Even if they
exaggerated I had the evidence of my own reflection in
the mirror.

After that little loving speech he knelt and prayed for
such a long time that I, already weary from the wedding
festivities, found myself falling asleep. 'Come to bed,' I
urged, and he did, shivering, although I don't know if it
was fear or cold which gave him goose bumps and
caused him to breathe in uneven gasps. I was about to
lose my maidenhood, about to experience what I had
gleaned from songs and whispered gossip and jokes.
My grandfather's mistress, Dangereuse, had given me
certain instructions as to how to please. 'Keeping a man
happy in bed is your safeguard. Let me show you some
ways.' And she did.

Nothing she revealed prepared me for his shivery
reluctance. I put my arms around him to give him the
warmth of my body, and spoke soothingly to him as a
mother would to a frightened child. At first he lay quite
still, then he touched my breast; exploring the nipple,
first one then the other, then back to the first. I no
longer felt sleepy. In fact I was coming to warmth
which I hoped would grow into a fire to inspire and
match a corresponding passion. Suddenly he threw
himself upon me with a groan, poked and pushed about

until he was able to thrust himself inside me,
causing pain, not ecstasy, lunged about for a bit, then
withdrew and turned from me with a sigh. I think he
was saying an Act of Contrition. Thus was I
deflowered. I thought back to the way Dangereuse had
described her experiences with my grandfather, and
suddenly it seemed not tragic but funny. I started to
shake with laughter. Louis, believing me to be crying,
reached over to comfort me, until he realised his error.
He may have forgiven me the loss of his virginity, but
never that laughter.

'Let us take more time,' I suggested some weeks later.
'We can explore each other as though each is a new
land to be conquered by the other.'
He drew back as though I had branded him.
'Sensual pleasure is for animals and sinners,' he said.
'We must do only what is necessary to produce a child.'
'Any more would be a transgression!' I mocked him.
'Yes,' he said, quite seriously.
Why did I not take a lover? There were many
opportunities. You may not believe it if you saw me
today but I was a very beautiful woman. However, until
I had borne Louis at least two sons I felt it would be
more than foolish to look elsewhere for the pleasures I
craved. I could not risk a son of mine to be called a
bastard and be denied his right to the throne. They were
difficult and frustrating years. You can understand why
I reacted so strongly when I read that letter Bernard
wrote. If he had his way there was no escape possible. I
had only talked to Bernard once and despite my best
intentions found myself almost mesmerised by him.
That gave me less reason to trust or to like him. He was
too fond of interfering in my life, and it was he who
ensured that France would lead the army on a crusade.

What promised to be a pious pilgrimage for Louis
and an adventure for me turned out to be a time when
we both discovered even more things about each other
to dislike. Nor did it bring any glory to France.

*   *   *

Again I am far from the story I began. But at the time of
which I write I had just returned from the crusade, and
it was much on my mind. Now returning to that time
brings other memories back. Having lived such a long
and eventful life I have too much to tell. The twelfth
century has passed away to be reborn as the thirteenth.
In the same way I will pass away soon. With neither
impatience nor dread I wait for death, although I pray
fervently that the next world will be an improvement on
the one I presently inhabit. My last long journey,
travelling to Castile to select one of my granddaughters
to be a bride for the royal house of France, has made
me weary to my bones. Blanche was not at all fatigued
by the travel back to Paris. In her I found myself when
young. She will marry another Louis and become
Queen of France. The story has turned a full circle.
I have been queen of two countries, although the title
brings small power. We women fight and win our
battles in the bedroom, even if that proved a
disappointing arena of war where Louis was concerned.
With Henry it was quite a different tournament, except
that he was too often away, whoring and warring, after
first planting his seed within my womb. I proved to be a
fertile field, bearing him eight children in all, and have
outlived most of them. Both my husbands are dead. Of
my ten children only Eleanor and John are still here,
and I would willingly exchange both of them for my
beautiful Richard, the one they called the Lionheart.

As Duchess of Aquitaine I presided over a large
area of land, but women cannot rule duchies in their
own right. Presumably we cannot lead our knights into
battle, although this was precisely what I did in the
crusade, leading the Aquitaine knights, or what was left
of them, into Jerusalem.

How, you might ask, did a woman such as I find herself
entering the holy city as part of a raggle taggle army,
remnant of the proud force which left France one spring
day. It started with Louis, but Bernard of Clairvaux
must take full responsibility. Louis' dearest wish was
that he might command a crusade to free Edessa from
the Turks. The Pope warmly approved, but few of our
courtiers and advisers considered it a good idea. They
had memories of the thousands of good men who had
died during that first crusade, fifty years before. Abbot
Suger was especially opposed to the idea. The people of
France, he said, would be resentful of the taxes needed
to finance such a grand expedition.

Who changed their minds? Bernard of Clairvaux. At
Vézelay, Bernard preached the crusade; a day I
remember well. He stood there, such a frail figure (it
was said that he only ate enough to keep a kitten alive)
pleading with us all to offer our lives, our wealth,
everything, to free the holy lands from the scourge of
the Infidel. So I offered. You should have seen his face
when I knelt before him to receive the Red Cross, but
for once he was outmanoeuvred. If he refused me, the
knights of Aquitaine would not enlist. So I became a
crusader.

Bernard was noted as a great preacher. On that day I
doubt if many heard what he actually said, but the fact
that he was there, standing on a wooden platform, his
white robes blowing in the wind, his hair caught up like

a halo around his head, the aura of sanctity so strong that every demon for miles about cowered and retreated, was sufficient. Another monk with a bigger voice repeated his message and the whispered commentary circled and whirled about the crowd. No doubt it metamorphosed but the essence must have remained for knights ran forward, jostling each other in their efforts to be the first to make their vow and receive the cross. Bernard was obviously pleased with his success for he later reported that, 'I had opened my mouth, I spoke and at once the crusaders multiplied to infinity. Villages and towns became deserted, and women were widowed, although their husbands were still alive.'

'Why feign humility when you have that effect on people?' I asked Hildegard and Heloise. Hildegard looked affronted, but Heloise nodded and gave me her beautiful smile.

I determined not to be excluded. I knew of the legend that a woman in a white dress would lead the soldiers of France to victory, so I dressed in white that morning. Once I had my cross I rode about on a surly chestnut, encouraging others to follow my example, and the crusade was assured. Did Bernard tell the Pope about my contribution?

Now I wish to God that I had never been part of it, or that it had ever occurred, for it brought about so much destruction, uncontrolled greed and barbarity, all in the name of Christianity. How could I know that when, at the beginning, it seemed like a great quest and a chance to get away from the tedium of palace life? Not that it was only an adventure for many of the others. For Louis, I know that it was largely a chance to make reparation for what happened at Vitry-sur-Marne. It's

an old story now, and best forgotten. Because of the
battle Louis waged there hundreds of people were
burned do death. They were incinerated in the church,
which made it even worse. Where was God then?
Listening to their prayers and cries for help? The
soldiers had set fire to some of the houses and the
people were trying to escape. The flames, fanned by
strong winds, set the church alight, turning it from a
sanctuary to a fiery furnace. I tell you all of these
details so you can see that Louis was not responsible for
their deaths. He didn't order the houses to be burned,
and he didn't conjure up the wind, yet at the end of that
day he was overcome by horror and remorse.

Three years after that horrific event, Louis sought to
make reparation. They had been three years in which he
dreamt, night on night, about the people screaming in
their agony as the flames spread through the wooden
walls and roof of the church. The smell of burning flesh
stayed in his nostrils and the sense of guilt eroded his
spirit.

I told him, over and over, that it was not his fault. He
could not control the weather or the strength of the
wind. But when I tried to comfort him he replied that
but for Petronilla and me he would not have attacked
Vitry in the first place.

'It was your sister, so determined to marry Ralph of
Vermandois, even though he already had a wife. But for
that I would not have had to attack Count Theobold,' he
said.

I tried to make him forget the horror of it, and restore
his spirits, but it proved to be impossible. Soldiering
was not his craft, a fact I had learned early in our
marriage. In his first rush of love for me he was anxious
to do something gallant and heroic, so I asked him to

recapture Toulouse, which by rights belonged to my family. A simple enough task, I would have thought, a fitting gift for a new bride.

He set off willingly enough, while I waited at Poitiers, preparing to welcome him back as a hero. When he arrived at Toulouse, instead of attacking he retreated without so much as putting up a fight. He hadn't planned. He hadn't taken enough soldiers or siege equipment. He hadn't sent out scouts. Then Louis was amazed that Alphonse-Jourdain was waiting for him, fully prepared! I accepted then that Louis would not shine on the battlefield, so when he was chosen to lead the crusading army I felt apprehension, not pride. Armed conflict is, at times, necessary but not always successful. It was my encouragement that gave Henry's sons the courage to rise against him. Merlin, in the time of King Arthur had predicted it, saying that the cubs would awake and roar aloud. They roared, but Henry roared louder. Then, he forgave his sons and imprisoned their mother for fifteen long years, until my Richard ascended the throne of England and gave me my life back. Those years of confinement enabled me to fully understand Hildegard's fear of being similarly restricted.

It was during our third meeting together that Hildegard had talked about her fears of being forced to remain in a small room away from the earth, the sky, the sun and the sound of running water. Her love for God was contained within her love for his creation. Hearing her speak like that aroused my sympathy. She wasn't just an intruder on my time with Heloise, but a woman with fears and plans. I admired her facility for getting her own way. She must have persuaded her parents, by her tears and nightmares, not to send her to become a recluse at the age of eight. Just recently the abbot in her monastery had given her permission to travel the long distance to seek out Heloise. That could not have been easy, and no doubt she had called on her tears to persuade him. But tears or suffering would not sway Bernard. Nor were good intentions sufficient to defeat an enemy.

I was about to ask Hildegard what she believed would work with Bernard when a bell sounded. She and Heloise rose to go to the chapel. Heloise stood back to allow Hildegard to go through the door first. Hildegard demurred, and gestured Heloise to precede her. Hildegard won the battle and she followed Heloise, turning to smile at me as she went. Was there a display of pride in this battle for humility?

*   *   *

Was there spiritual pride when we set out, with our soldiers, to fight the Infidel? Equipping oneself for the crusade cost a great deal of money and sacrifice. A man would set out unsure if he would ever see his wife, his children or his home again. Perhaps worse, he might come home to find more children than he had left. Some may have had ideas of settling on the other side of the world, or bringing back spoils from the war, but I think that most would have wanted to earn the spiritual indulgences which would wipe out all their sins and gain them merit in heaven. But how little was gained. 'What were your intentions when you took the Red Cross?' Heloise had asked. 'Did you hope to save your soul?'

I was still young and healthy, and calculated that I had many years in which to repent my sins and ensure my soul's salvation. It was adventure that enticed me, not indulgences. Not that I told Heloise and Hildegard that.

I simply smiled and gestured. My humility prevented me from boasting of piety, or so I tried to suggest by lowering my eyes and remaining silent. Yet I wanted them to hear of all the things I had seen and learned as I travelled through foreign countries and faced death. At first it was exciting, I told them. I saw other countries with their quaint little villages, mountains and forests, lakes and beautiful cities. The greatest city of all was Constantinople.

I tried, also, to convey the duplicity of some of our religious leaders. For example, the Bishop of Langres urged Louis to attack the people of Constantinople although they had given us hospitality.

'These people are Christian only in name,' the Bishop insisted. 'Killing them, heretics in the main, is not sinful. They have joined forces with the infidel against the Christian soldiers in the past, and the father of the present ruler was an evil man. This city abounds in riches,' he concluded as though that clinched the argument.

Some of the other bishops and knights thought these words of great wisdom and prepared their weapons. Others said that we could not judge the disposition of the people of Constantinople.

'We have been commanded to visit the Holy Sepulchre in Jerusalem, so that our sins can be wiped out. We will not save our souls by killing Christians or fighting for money. Let us maintain our vow of obedience to the Pontiff,' Louis had argued, rejecting the idea that those who recited a slightly different creed were heretics.

'You must admit that the king's words were righteous,' said Hildegard. 'Did you support him in this matter?'

'He did not ask for my support, nor would he have welcomed it. But yes, I did agree with him.' I replied.

My advice, had I been asked, would have been not
to try to destroy a city of the strength and wealth of
Constantinople, but to make it an ally. That, I believe, is
what my grandfather William would have done. The
Turks were the enemy. They would have found the
combined strength of the Greeks, the Franks, and the
Germans invincible. The victors could have sorted out
the spoils later, instead of arguing about them before
they were even conquered. Afterwards, those who
wished could have made pilgrimages to every holy
shrine and place of blessed memory. Knights would
have shared the land amongst themselves. The weak
would have lost that battle, as is fitting. There is no
palm of victory for those who lack strength, courage
and initiative. But no one thought to ask me.

I wondered how much I could tell those two women,
both old enough to be my mother, both sitting encased
in their brown habits as though protected from
unpleasant thoughts or sinful people. I had not been
able to talk of it so freely to anyone before, because no
indiscretion went unnoticed or unreported in the palace.
Did Heloise and Hildegard need to know that Louis
proved, as I feared he would, to be a disastrous
commander? Too much praying, too much talking to
bishops and lackeys who hardly knew one end of a
sword from the other, and not enough seeking advice
from those who really knew what was needed to gain
victory. He didn't lack courage, but he had little sense
of military strategy. Thanks to his ineptitude and
prattling piety we came away at the end with nothing
but humiliating defeat for France and an unhappy,
doomed marriage. Perhaps they did not need to know,
but I needed to tell someone.

I tried to make them understand that what we
endured during the crusade caused Louis and I to be
totally estranged. That was why I had to protect myself
if our marriage were finally annulled. Louis had
forbidden me to travel with his entourage. He would not
claim his husbandly comforts when other men had to
sacrifice theirs. It seemed that he preferred the company
of the odiously pious Odo de Deuil and the eunuch
Thierry Galeran, neither of who had any love for me.
That arrangement suited me admirably. I travelled with
the knights of Aquitaine, my own ladies and our
musicians, troubadours and jongleurs. We did say our
prayers, as Louis had begged me to do, but did not tarry
over them. In the beginning there was time for music,
laughter, and storytelling in our party as well, but we
were not less sincere about the final goal for all that.
When we camped for the night the tents with their
colourful banners materialised as though we had
brought a small part of France with us. This, I thought
to myself, is partly my doing. We will show the world
that our knights are as brave and worthy as any others,
and we will safeguard the holy lands for the pilgrims
and Christians. History will sing our praises.
It took only a few weeks for the novelty of travel to
pall. Each day brought new problems, but it was not
until we were attacked at Mount Cadmos that things
became really desperate. There are many versions of
what happened, but I was there and witnessed it all.
We were ahead of the main army, making good
progress. Geoffrey de Rancon, leading our party,
wished to continue beyond the pass although this was
the place where Louis had ordered him to stay.
Geoffrey then consulted Louis' uncle, who agreed that
we could make further ground. No one had worried

before when Louis' orders were ignored, and we did not expect there to be any bother about it this time. We assumed the others would realise that we had continued, and would join us by nightfall.

Louis was with the main section of the army and with all the baggage, tagging along behind us. He did not have the perspicacity to realise that we had proceeded further than originally planned. His party stopped at the beginning of the pass, in a vulnerable position. The Turks, seeing their advantage, swept down the sides of the mountain. With cries of 'God is great' they attacked. The crusaders, blocked by the narrow pass, were an easy prey. They had been marching all day, over difficult country and were worn out and unable to fight back. Horses and baggage fell down the ravines. Louis' special soldiers were killed, and he only escaped the same fate through his own courage and good luck, because he was hidden from the Turks by a tree. We knew nothing of this. However, a few of the soldiers straggled through at midnight, with alarming reports about what had happened. A search party set out immediately to find any survivors. What they found was not an army camp but a slaughter field. So few of our men remained. It was a sorrowful and sombre camp as people went back to search for those who had been ambushed. Louis said that he was saved only by the intervention of God.

After such a tragic event someone had to be blamed. I became that someone, along with Geoffrey, who they said was following my orders. Then it was said that it would never have happened except for the excessive amount of baggage I and the other women had brought, which impeded the army. Women had no place in war, not even holy wars. No one seemed to think that Louis'

efforts at commanding his army had been so
slipshod and careless that such a disaster was bound to
happen sooner or later.

We could not retreat or regroup. We had to continue,
this time under constant attack and always fearful that
we would not survive to see the next day. The
adventure had turned into an ordeal. Finally our ragged
army reached Antioch, to the blissfully luxurious
hospitality supplied by my uncle. It was like going from
hell into heaven. For ten days I was able to enjoy such
necessities as a warm bath, clean clothes, delicious
food, cool gardens where I could sit with my uncle,
laughing and joking, reminiscing about childhood in
Aquitaine, and discussing war strategy. He valued my
opinion, and I supported his judgment that we should
attack and subjugate the neighbouring cities. Perhaps, I
thought, Louis will see that my uncle respects my
opinion, and he will listen to both of us.

Louis knew better, of course. After much discussion
with priests and hangers-on he decided that he would
not attack as Raymond advised. He had vowed to go to
Jerusalem, so we must go straight there. To his great
shame, Louis abused my uncle's hospitality by leaving
without farewell or explanation. He had allowed his
mind to be poisoned, so that he crept away from
Antioch like a guilty thief.

Armed knights snatched me from the palace in the
middle of the night, for he knew that I would not have
gone with him willingly. Some women might have
found such forceful action arousing, but after all the
years of seeing Louis make blunder after blunder,
creating a crisis where none was necessary, and then
hiding behind the robes of the monks and priests, I was

far from impressed. It was an action motivated by
spite and jealousy, not ardour.

'If you had wished for my services, my Lord, you had
simply to come to my bedroom,' I said when I
confronted him. 'There was no need to send knights and
that apology for a man you keep near you at all times.'
The last was a reference to the eunuch Galeran, whom I
knew to be within earshot.

'Had I been sure that you were alone, Madam,' replied
Louis, 'I may have come to you myself. I do not desire
your wifely comforts, but your loyalty. It would seem
that you value the company and opinion of your uncle,
over that of your own husband.'

I may have been able to talk him round, even then, but
Galeran came forward and said, in that sneering,
sycophantic way of his, 'The whole army talks of
nothing else but the queen's allegiance to her uncle.
Maybe France would be better served if the Queen
remained in Antioch, permanently.'

That treasonous remark should have been rewarded
with a separation of his head from his shoulders. I
waited for Louis to defend me, but he simply looked
sadly at Galeran and said something about how tragic it
was that we had come to this.

'I would remind you that we are related by the closest
bond, my Lord, so that family loyalty is an issue
between us as well. Perhaps our marriage is null and
void as Bernard of Clairvaux suggests. We'll petition
the Pope, and I'll return to Poitiers. I will not,' I added
looking through Galeran, rather than at him, 'be
remaining in Antioch; I will return to my lands in
Aquitaine. But will you not concede that my uncle, who
has lived here for a long time, and who is known to be a

brave and successful soldier, would have an
excellent idea as to how to go about a battle? '
'Better than I would?' asked Louis.
'You are a brave soldier,' I said to him.
'But not a successful one? I choose my advisers among
men who honour our Saviour. We'll go forward to
Jerusalem. You, my lady, will go with us.'
I had no choice but to go with them to Tripoli, and then
on to Jerusalem, the hated crown rammed on to my
head, like a crown of thorns.

The soldiers wept when, after much privation, they
finally reached Jerusalem, but whether from religious
fervour or sheer relief is open to conjecture. While they
trawled through the churches and holy sites I plotted
my escape. I could have returned to Antioch, and
Raymond would have given me sanctuary. If I could
ever talk to Louis alone I could persuade him that we
should apply to the Pope for an annulment. That is if I
could bring myself to ever speak to him again. But I
was closely watched and escape was not feasible at that
time.

The leaders of the Christian army in Jerusalem were not
united. They had brought their old quarrels and rivalries
with them. Despite their lack of unity they had to have
something to show for their campaign, some victory to
satisfy their people. So, in their blind ignorance, they
decided to attack Damascus.

Raymond had earlier pointed out that Unur of
Damascus was one of the few Muslim leaders who had
given any support to the Christians, so it was madness
to attack that city. The Crusaders were successfully
repelled by the Muslims. The Crusade ended in disaster
and Louis had to take much of the blame for that. He
wouldn't listen to the men with local knowledge and

experience. Instead he allowed himself to be swayed by pious predictions; a belief that God would reach down from Heaven and make it all happen for him. His brain was curdled by silly jealousy, turned by malicious gossip about me.

Raymond was my uncle, not my paramour, a good and brave man, and I loved and admired him. When I heard that he had been killed some time later in battle, exhausted in spirit, so it is said, by so much killing, I mourned him deeply. His head and arm were cut off and his skull sent to Baghdad as proof that he was finally defeated. Such was Raymond's reputation. The Caliph displayed his head at the city gate. Such was the Caliph's barbarity.

It is so hard to tell people how one really feels. Both Hildegard and Heloise listened to my stories with what appeared to be a mixture of impatience and interest, but could they really understand the sense of betrayal when a husband sides with his male companions against his wife? Hildegard understood evil but she wanted to believe that just being in the holy lands had transformed us. She would certainly have been content with Louis' attitude.

Louis, having arrived at the holy lands, was reluctant to leave. It suited his saintly predilections. He went from church to shrine to holy place, practically perambulating on his knees. Neither was there any danger of him returning in triumph to France. It took urgent letters from Abbot Suger to finally convince him that if he wanted to have a kingdom to return to he had better hasten back.

There were lessons to be learned, I said. Bernard, for all his good intentions, had brought about a great deal of suffering by preaching the Crusade. His letter was another example of how his zeal overcame a more realistic and measured approach to life. We cannot all be saints, living lives of extreme penance and deprivation. Even Hildegard was prepared to admit that the majority of people simply struggle as best they could, leaving the heroic spiritual life to a select few.

*   *   *

The nuns spent a great deal of time in the chapel. Adele decided to become prayerful and go there whenever she heard a bell ringing, although at night she became hard of hearing. I decided to attend there sometimes just for the company. It was a time when my faith in God was tested, for I could not see how a benevolent God could allow such suffering as I had witnessed. Hildegard said it was the result of Adam and Eve's sin. Was it justice for the rest of us to suffer for something we had not done? When I saw poor people, pale with hunger, I wondered why God did not send them manna from heaven. When I saw mothers clinging to scraps of babies, knowing that they would not survive the night, I wondered what they prayed for. When I saw a river red with the blood of slain men, and heard the cries of the unlucky ones who were not yet dead, calling out in their agony, I found it hard to see this as part of God's plan for his world. In the chapel, with its polished wooden choir stalls, pure white walls, silver crucifix above the altar and white cloth on the altar, I felt my faith renewed. Sometimes I looked at the mosaic of the Madonna, with her serene and compassionate face. Listening to the singing, praising and petitioning, I could believe that God was responsive. When my mind returned to things that I had seen in an ugly world, then it was not so simple.

*   *   *

But, let me finish the story of my journey, for my
own sufferings continued. It says something about our
campaign when I tell you we only needed two ships
when we departed for home. Louis sailed on one, I on
the other. Maybe it was a punishment from God for the
blood that had been shed and the indifference to the fate
of our own soldiers, abandoned along the way like so
much unwanted ballast, that our ships sailed into a
storm and were blown into different seas.

A storm at sea is both exhilarating and terrifying. A
small ship is a mere nutshell in a huge expanse of
water. Winds howl and shriek shredding the sails to
wisps, flailing ineffectually as the ship heels and bucks,
a plaything. But how exciting. If I am to die, I thought,
I am leaving the world in a magnificent pageant. As the
sailors rushed about in a frenzy I stood with my face to
the wind and rain, laughing. What could anyone do to
appease such a force? Then we were picked up by the
sea and thrown against the rocks. The last sound I
remembered was the splintering of wood and the last
sensation I felt was cold. My last thought was not to ask
pardon for my sins, or to regret all that I had missed,
but to be pleased that I had dressed myself earlier in my
red velvet dress. I would make a colourful corpse when
my body was finally washed up on some foreign shore.
Water engulfed me then, pulling me down to the bottom
of the ocean. Suddenly, totally, dark.

I do not know how much later it was that I became
aware that I was not dead, unless heaven was a sandy
stretch of beach between two large groups of rocks. I
was shivering despite the sunshine, thirsty, and hurting
in every part of my body. I had been spared, but for
what? There were three men looking at me, speaking a
language I had no hope of understanding. At first I

thought they had come to rescue me and I gestured
feebly that I was thirsty. They came closer. I looked at
them more carefully. Then I knew how the women had
felt as our soldiers entered their villages. The best I
could hope for was to be raped and left for some kinder
soul to find me. The worst was that they would kill me
there and then for my rich clothing. Perhaps they would
simply imprison me and ask for ransom. That suddenly
seemed the most likely, I thought, as I struggled to sit
up. One, a man with an ugly scar down his right cheek
came right up to me, leaned forward, felt my dress, then
my leg. His breath smelt horrible. I had not felt fear
during the storm at sea. Now I did, sickening and
debilitating. I hoped that whatever they were going to
do to me they would do it quickly. How detestable to be
left lying naked on a deserted beach. How terrible
would be the retribution when Louis came to hear of it.
I tried to stand up, ready to defend myself. Eleanor of
Aquitaine, Queen of France, would not be taken easily.
Suddenly the three looked over my shoulder, muttered a
curse and ran off. I turned to see if I had been saved or
faced an even fiercer foe. By good fortune (or perhaps
God thought that I had suffered enough) I had been
rescued by King Roger's soldiers. They found some
type of litter and carried me to his palace in Palermo.
My adventure was over.
Palermo is said to be a city of wonders, but at that time
I cared little if I lived or died. That brief feeling of
exultation I had felt at the height of the storm had
dissipated to a miserable numbness. Even when I heard
that Louis was believed to be dead I felt nothing,
neither grief nor a sense of release. Poor Louis. When I
found out later that he was not dead I still felt little,
unless it were a barely acknowledged disappointment.

When finally I was well enough I travelled from Palermo, and Louis from Brindisi, so that we were reunited at Potenza, where King Roger II of Sicily welcomed us both.

*   *   *

By the time we began our journey back to France together again neither the most romantic song nor the greatest heroic deed would have won me back to my husband. All I wanted was to be rid of him, of the interfering Suger, of the sanctimonious Bernard, in fact the whole ungracious, ungraceful lot. Louis, totally insensitive to my mood, babbled on about how relieved he was to see me; how he had worried about my fate, how we must renew our love and start afresh, do all we could to produce an heir. This pretty speech was no sooner completed than he headed off to his own bedroom.

'I see our futures separately,' I told him as he hurried down the corridor, prayer book in hand. He stopped and turned back towards me.

'You are distraught and worn out from all you have been through. Let's travel back through Rome and speak to the Pope. He, in his wisdom, will find the solution.'

I readily agreed because the Pope could grant us an annulment of our marriage. That idea turned out to be a total fiasco. The Pope was all for conciliation even after I spoke to him on my own, and told him that I was very unhappy and believed that it was God's will that the marriage should be annulled.

'Can you not, in the intimacy of your marital bed, renew your joy?' asked the Pope. I was surprised. I had expected that he, like Bernard, would tell me to pray more, or do penance, not indulge in sensual pleasure.

'There is no intimacy. There is no marital bed,' I
told him. If the Pope wanted to talk of such matters I
was happy to enlighten him. 'We no longer cohabit as
husband and wife.' And hardly ever have, I might have
added, but there are limits to a conversation of that kind
with a pope.

I imagine Louis had a longer list of complaints about
my suspected entanglements with every man who
crossed my path, including Raymond, my refusing to
even speak to him for weeks and my rejection of his
invitation to join him in the recitation of the Office. The
list would go on and on, until the Pope ran out of
patience, or died of boredom. At least he would see
what I had to put up with.

The Pope's solution to our problem, although it
disappointed me, revealed him to be a man of the
world. No annulment was on offer. Instead we were
ordered into the bedroom together, a room that he had
decorated himself in an effort to kindle passion.
Looking around at the ribbons, holy pictures and
candles, all I could say was that it was as well the Pope
was celibate. Louis saw that gaudy bed as a command
from God himself, and was quite keen. Maybe the
months of abstinence had had some effect. I will say
one thing for Louis; he was a faithful husband. I never
had to shoo a sloe-eyed beauty from his bed.

Despite Louis' best efforts in Rome and thereafter I still
did not experience any real passion. What Dangereuse
had told me about seemed like another country, which I
was yet to visit. My life had reached its nadir of
boredom, frustration and misery. Nothing could ever be
worse, I thought. Bernard's letter, which I read soon
after I had returned to Paris from Rome, showed that it
could. That letter, and meeting Henry, jolted me from

my lethargy. He was somewhat younger than I.
Such differences are of little consequence. I liked his
energy and confidence. A young man who would, I
decided, claim what he believed was his. My wealth
and experience would be no hindrance to his ambitions.
Until I was freed from my marriage to Louis such
thoughts were nothing more than idle distractions. Once
I was free, plans could be brought to fruition. Unless
Bernard, rather than Henry, had his way, in which case
I would be delivered to the Church as a worthy trophy
to the pious subjugation of women. Not if I had any say
at all in the matter!

Strangely enough, with Louis going on at me about
prayers and saving my soul and trying to live a life of
sanctity and self denial I used sometimes to wonder if I
would have been happier living as an abbess in great
monastery. At least it would have stopped his nagging.
Louis, who had been educated in an abbey, had told me
that the dedicated Benedictine aimed to attain true
humility. In this way he (always a he) would be open to
receive God's love and spiritual gifts. Since that early
but limited experience of the Benedictine life, I know
that I would not have wished to spend my entire life in
an abbey, although I am content to end my days at
Fontevraud.

During my time with them I must say that I saw little
evidence of this sought-after humility in Heloise and
Hildegard. The former was proud of her learning, proud
of her association with the famous Abelard, but at first
very distant, as though she had a secret, which she
refused to share with anybody else. Hildegard gave the
impression of being less sure of herself, until she began
on her music, which I am happy to acknowledge is
glorious, or her herbal remedies, or her direction from

this Light she said she experienced, and any one of those three subjects seemed to occupy most of her thoughts and conversation. Can one be truly humble and still claim direct contact with God? She was genuinely kind, like a stern but caring mother. I write of her now as though I did not like her. This is not true. At first I found her difficult, but came to love and admire her for her wisdom, kindness and strength of purpose.

'Dear Eleanor,' she once said, 'You have much to endure before you can claim to be truly wise.' Was that a prophecy or a reflection on my capabilities?

'I've lived in ways about which neither of you have any idea,' I replied.

'As you've told us,' responded Heloise.

And will continue to do so, until you understand I am not just a foolish woman, I thought, a thought which escaped Hildegard's insights, for she continued to nod and smile reassuringly at me.

They imagined that because I was younger I had little to offer them. The reality was that I had been the one to obtain a copy of Bernard's letter and bring it to them. Then I was the one who had the brilliant idea that Hildegard could report on a vision where God directed her that all women be given their due freedoms. This suggestion nearly produced apoplexy. Hildegard curled herself into a ball of dignity and rolled out the door, spluttering and choking on her outrage. Heloise could have supported me but she said nothing. The solution was so clear. Hildegard could simply have written that, as she sat praying in the chapel, she heard a voice speaking.

Write down, my daughter, all that I say to you. Men and women are equal in my sight and have an equal part to

play in this world. Men must not prevent women
bringing their gentle influence to all people. Women
must not be shut away behind walls. If their marriage is
annulled, women must have no blame attached to them,
nor must they be deprived of their possessions or their
children. Such women deserve special care and
protection. I have spoken.

No doubt Hildegard could have made it sound better.
She was more familiar with God's way of speaking. Of
course she didn't have to actually say the voice came
from God. In fact I could have whispered it to her in the
chapel, so she would not be telling any sort of lie. Her
conscience would have been quite clear. Bishops urged
the killing of men because they used different words in
the Creed, claiming that this made them heretics, when
what they wanted was their wealth. That was evil. A
small misrepresentation of the source of a message,
which was true and ethical, was not a grave sin. It was
common sense. Bernard would have had to rethink his
whole attitude to women, and much good may have
come from it. So easy it would have been, and they so
stubborn to refuse. These women believed that I could
teach them nothing, and I thought of them, in matters of
strategy, as babes in swaddling clothes. You can't beat
the evils of the world with any but worldly weapons, I
told them, but they were too stubborn to accept that I
could know better than they how to achieve victory.

*   *   *

Adele, as I had expected, had spread herself around the
abbey within a short time, and returned to me with her
booty. Did I know that Abelard's two nieces were here?
One was in charge of the infirmary. The other, Sister
Agatha, oversaw the work in the kitchen, and bossy she

was with it. And did I know that the abbess had a
son who had been brought up in the family of Denise,
Abelard's sister? And did I know that he had the
strangest name, Astralabe, as though he were a
scientific instrument? In any case they christened him
Peter as well, for what sort of saint's name is
Astralabe?

'Is he as brilliant as his parents?' I wondered.

'If he is it'll do him little good. Without a fortune or
property whom could he marry? I heard that he went
into the Church.'

'Where, with his breeding, there would be little future
for him,' I replied, with more malice than I intended. It
was chilly that day and I felt tired, queasy, and very out
of sorts. If Sister Agatha was in charge of the kitchen
she needed to put in more effort to improve the meals.
Surely I had provided her with enough fine food. Even
after all these years it is the memory of the small things
which remain with me, although food should not be
thought of as a 'small thing' considering that we would
die for the lack of it.

The soldiers and servants who had escorted us could
not stay at the Paraclete, so I had sent them to the
nearby village, with strict instructions not to divulge my
identity. Anyone who did would suffer a very painful
punishment. They were not to impose on any one, must
pay for their food and leave the women alone. One or
two would keep watch each day to warn me if any
messenger arrived from Paris. There was a bit of a
flurry on the first day, and a second summons, then
Louis either lost interest in my doings, or he was
convinced that I really was praying, for he did not
trouble me again.

'Fetch me a cloak,' I ordered Adele after she had
told me about Astralabe, 'and then play something.
Take my mind away from my concerns.'

We were sitting in the room where normally I met with
Heloise and Hildegard. Heloise had gone to visit one of
her priories, and a cold journey it would have been for
the day was bleak. Hildegard was somewhere behind
the infirmary, talking to the workmen about digging
drains and a system of cisterns. That woman had an
interest in everything! Because the day was overcast
this room seemed very austere and bare. I would have
loved to send Heloise some warm red rugs and
tapestries for the walls; polished wooden furniture and a
small support for her book. Then she could have sat
here instead of going out to the gatehouse, which also
lacked any real comfort. I knew, however, that such
gifts might not be appreciated, as Heloise seemed
determined to strict simplicity.

Adele was a neat musician who produced sweet sounds
from her flute without stirring the passions unduly. That
day she played a peaceful little air, one that my
grandfather had composed, if my memory is correct.
Whatever it was it soothed and charmed me enough to
feel at ease with the world again. I thought of asking
her to play the harp and sing for me as well, but
decided, instead, to garner more gossip.

'Tell me some more,' I asked her, when she put the
flute away.

'They're not supposed to talk at all, or only when it is
really necessary,' she reminded me.

'And how often is it really necessary?' I asked.

'More than you would imagine. They all want to know
who you are, my lady,' she said, hastening to add that
she had said nothing at all except to let them know that

I came from a very noble family. If only they knew how noble! Perhaps they would have been less impressed than I would have liked, for there was something about the simplicity and quiet of this life in the abbey which was far removed from the intrigues and striving for power and influence which permeated the court in Poitiers or Paris.

'There's another young nun from Germany, Sister Elizabeth. She travelled with the older nun, Mother Hildegard, and a monk called Volmar.'

'Do you think that Hildegard and Volmar are like Heloise and Abelard once were?' I mused. 'When Heloise fled Paris, when she was expecting her child, I hear that she travelled dressed as a nun. I wonder why she did not just dress as a man? Perhaps she was too far advanced. It would be only natural if a nun and a monk felt something more for each other than their vows permit, although I doubt the good Mother Hildegard is with child.'

'Elizabeth says not. Not about being pregnant, we didn't even mention that, but that there is nothing unchaste in their friendship. I had already asked her, very discreetly, and she was shocked and angry. She told me that Mother Hildegard is a saint who sees visions and can read your thoughts, so maybe you had better not think anything like that about the monk in front of her.' Adele put her hand over her mouth, trying unsuccessfully to hide her giggles.

'Enough disrespect, watch your tongue,' I chided, yet I wasn't too angry, for without her I could not have endured the place for more than a day or two. At least she had not taken a vow of silence.

*　　　*　　　*

This will show you what I mean about Heloise
being reserved, distant even. It was only at our meeting
when I showed her Bernard's letter that I suspected
that, for all her sagacity, she had not known about it
until Hildegard told her. It was obvious from the way
she read it to us, the sudden loss of colour in her face
and the growing anger in her voice. Hildegard and I had
both come to her for advice, and she knew nothing
about it. Was she, I wondered, the right person to
consult.

Hildegard had previously said that she only heard about
the letter from Volmar, who had earlier learned about it
from a monk travelling back from Mont St Michel who
had learned about it from a cardinal's secretary. I
imagine that it was the same one who fondled Adele's
bottom. Hildegard, as soon as she heard about it, was
anxious to know its full content. Even after the
compelling evidence, after hearing the actual words that
Bernard had written, she was reluctant to believe the
holy abbot was capable of any duplicity.

'Brother Bernard gave me such support,' she said,
'Bernard and the Pope. I was so afraid that they would
brand me a heretic or say I was in league with the devil.
I knew that I was not possessed but that must be small
consolation as the flames lick your ankles, and the
smoke clouds your lungs, no matter how strong your
faith in God.'

Mentioning flames always make me think of Vitry.
Talk of heretics is less disturbing, even though both
Bernard and Suger hinted to Louis that I was one. It's a
weapon Church people wield, but I could meet them
with weapons of my own.

Yet the most amazing thing was that Hildegard told me
I was pregnant and expecting a daughter. I wasn't even

sure that I had conceived, and although I should have been hoping for a son, a boy child would have made it more difficult to escape from Louis and the court of France. How could I argue that God did not bless our marriage with a lusty pair of male lungs ringing out cries to the contrary from the nursery? I worried that Hildegard could, as Adele warned, read thoughts as well as wombs. What if she divined that I not only wanted my marriage to Louis annulled but that I had chosen my next husband?

Henry, if he was anything like his father, was not a man to hover uncertainly outside my bedroom. He would storm the citadel and crow out his victory before seeking to conquer again. So I imagined, the first time I saw him. So he proved to be, in the beginning, and the later indifferent years did not entirely sour those first passionate ones. Was he faithful? Not ever. But I'd had 'faithful' with Louis and it did not satisfy.

*   *   *

After Hildegard had gone off in a bit of a sulk because I suggested that she assist us with a vision, I wondered if she would decide to go home. I thought it would be a relief if the next morning had seen her, Elizabeth and Volmar riding away, back to their own monastery. But there she was at breakfast, smiling in a friendly enough way, so I could do nothing but smile in return, while Heloise, looking very pale as though she had not slept well, put her head in her hands for a few moments, then said Grace. So it was still the three of us, but I had decided that I must take the initiative if we were to have any hope of success.

At the Paraclete we had spent time, wasted it in a sense, because we could not work out the best way to foil what Bernard may have thought of as God's will but which we regarded as Bernard's scheme. Heloise, being the scholar, looked to logic and reasoned argument to plead our cause. As Louis had explained to me, in the days when he still hoped for my conversion to a more religious frame of mind, Abelard was the one who believed that by reason alone we could find God, while Bernard believed in following our emotions and praying to excess (not Louis' words. He chose 'devoutly and frequently'), so that we learned to love God and accept the teachings of the Church. Louis might not have used the word 'excess' but if his life was any example, then excess it was. Louis agreed with Bernard that reason and study were impediments, not steps to gaining salvation. That was why Bernard and Abelard had clashed so often.

Therefore, I suggested to Heloise that her approach, based on Abelard's writing, seemed to be setting up another conflict of the same order, especially as, in Bernard's eyes, women were considered a significant obstacle for men who sought sanctity. Hildegard, when appealed to, demurred, seeming to have difficulty in agreeing to any plan that was not whispered to her from the sky. I refrained from offering her that remedy a second time. Not that she lacked motivation, but to her Bernard was a saintly man. She hadn't actually met him, and was guided by his reputation – always a mistake. Know thy enemy intimately.

So we began our council as usual by praying to the Spirit of Wisdom. Then Hildegard and Heloise talked about holy women and all the good things they had done, and couldn't have done if they had been totally cloistered, while I sat and cringed. When it became unbearable I leapt to my feet and strode back and forth.

'Forget about holy women. Find Bernard's weakness,' I insisted. 'Strike him where he can least protect himself.'

'He does have a very difficult digestion,' mused Hildegard. 'That's not a weakness we can exploit, but it would affect his humour. Such conditions can be eased with herbs and potions. I could suggest some for you, as well, dear Eleanor.'

At that point I felt nothing but despair. The future was hanging in the balance, and Hildegard wanted to tip it in our favour with a mortar and pestle. Was she planning to dose him from a distance, or just send recommendations?

The she announced that she would compose some music!

Heloise's plan was no better. She wanted to write a learned epistle, based on the ideas of Abelard! If Abelard hadn't managed to convince Bernard before, how were his arguments going to have any influence now? You can see why I felt discouraged, especially as just as we seemed to be making progress a bell would ring, Heloise and Hildegard would stop speaking and go to the chapel.

Louis had already warned me that monasteries were quiet places.

'You'll find that silence and reflection are difficult for you, Eleanor,' he had said. 'It will also be very good for your spiritual formation. There will be no allowing you to sit about in idle chatter.' Why I had never killed the man remains a mystery.

Hildegard and Heloise had enough common sense to relax the silence requirement when I was with them. Benedict, they said, allowed for some flexibility. The silence, which had greeted my suggestion that I arrange

for Bernard to meet with a fatal accident as he
travelled towards the Paraclete, was frightening.
Remove Bernard of Clairvaux and the problem simply
melted away, I told them. He had been responsible for
so many deaths in the Crusade. Would one more death
matter, especially if it were his own? That idea caused
Heloise to nearly faint. The plan was extreme. I was
prepared to admit that. It could be construed as murder
until our situation was considered. Was it not lawful
that we fight back?
To be honest, the plan had problems, including my own
scruples, so we did not pursue it. Ironically, what my
soldiers were forbidden was almost granted to
Hildegard's fish.

*   *   *

When I had first read Bernard's letter I saw within it
only a plan to ruin my life. I did not consider the first
part, the bit about religious women being vixens in the
vineyard, and needing to be confined behind walls, as
being such a problem. After all abbeys had walls and
nuns were not supposed to go travelling about the
towns and countryside, although I did know that some
were quite busy attending to the affairs of their
communities. Louis used to say that when an abbess
was involved in a lawsuit you could expect trouble, and
told me about one who threatened to march through the
town with a rotting corpse, in support of her claim for
some land, although how the corpse and the land were
connected was never explained.
I soon saw that the letter had serious implications for
religious women as well. Heloise had never had a
calling to the religious life, as she explained, but had
entered Argenteuil all those years ago at the request of
Abelard. Argenteuil was where she was raised and

educated, and it felt as near to home as anywhere could in her circumstances. Abelard decided to enter St Denis after he had been castrated. In my opinion this was more in an effort to resurrect his career than develop his spiritual self, so perhaps it could be said that he did not have a true calling to the life either. Heloise believed that he chose the abbey for its proximity to Argenteuil, and thus to her. On the other hand, I don't think that he made the short trip between the abbeys to visit her very often. To have done so would have drawn attention to his recent sinful activities, which sat uncomfortably with his efforts to be accepted by those who mattered. From the little she told me, and what I heard elsewhere, he did embrace a life of austerity and by the time of his death, became as humble as a man like Abelard can ever be. By then he had been humiliated by Bernard, the bishops and the Pope; but being humbled by others is not the same as growing in humility. Abelard never acquired the ability to bite his tongue until it was too late, and this was his downfall, so people said.

For myself, humility is for others to attain. Know your worth, and insist upon it, but also know when to remain silent. This maxim helped me endure Thomas Beckett when he came sniffing around Henry, looking for preferment and luxuries. He was able enough, I grant you, but too full of pride. Who would have expected him to become a saint? Poor martyred Saint Thomas, Archbishop of Canterbury! What a nuisance he proved to be either alive or dead.

But, back to Heloise. She asked me if I had seen Abelard when he was condemned as a heretic at the Council of Sens. How could I tell her that from my window I had seen him entering the main city square, riding with a group of his students. They had trotted confidently into the main square in front of the cathedral, only to be confronted by a mob that howled abuse and threw rocks. The sky was filled with shouts and threats to stone him to death for his heretical beliefs and only the action of a few brave knights saved him. Most of his followers, a totally useless bunch, deserted him when they saw his cause was lost. I couldn't tell her about the gloating and the bloating of self importance in all those who opposed him. In his prime and full strength Abelard had not been slow to belittle his enemies, and now it was their turn. As he rode away he looked more like an old, sick man than the greatest philosopher of our time.

'Did you see the trial in the cathedral?' she asked. 'Did you hear him speak?'

I did not. It was not the place for the Queen to preside. This was a battle to be fought between Bernard and Abelard in the presence of the bishops. Strangely, I had often thought that Abelard and Bernard were two of a kind, and that is why they were such enemies, although few would agree with me. I did hear that they were reconciled before Abelard died. By then Bernard had no need to fear him.

'Anyone who tries to explain the Blessed Trinity is in danger of being called a heretic,' I said, trying to comfort Heloise. 'Three Persons, distinct and equal, yet only one God; no one can make sense of that.'

'Of course it's a mystery, but that doesn't mean we shouldn't seek to understand it,' Heloise replied impatiently. 'Abelard gave each Person differing qualities, but said that together they made the divine substance. There was no heresy in that.' But for me this concept formed a jumble of confusion, which made my head ache, and I told her so. It was the relationship between people that interested me more than the relationship between a Father, Son and Holy Spirit who were three distinct persons in one being.

Heloise was not left in peace, even after she became a nun. Suger, the abbot who had valued me only for my lands, had no respect for the nuns at Argenteuil either. He expelled them from the abbey, claiming that it belonged to St Denis. This was on the evidence of some documents that he had forged, according to the rumours. To strengthen his case he also claimed that the nuns were living an immoral life. There was certainly something very unsatisfactory about the expulsion of those nuns. It was venal. The Abbey of St Denis acquired a valuable riverside property; the nuns lost everything.

The land, on which the Paraclete was situated, did not hold any tempting advantages, so there was no objection from Suger when Abelard offered it to Heloise and the other sisters. For Heloise it had the added advantage of creating a link between her and Abelard, so she blessed it, despite all the initial hardships, for that reason. The place grew from quite a primitive state to a worthy abbey with priories attached, thanks to her efforts. At the same time she continued writing poetry, letters and hymns. She certainly wouldn't, as I said to Hildegard, have managed all that caged behind stone walls.

Hildegard had a lovely way of really listening to you. With her round face and her deep brown eyes she looked like the raisin cakes I used to eat at Poitiers, soft and comforting. She was happy being a nun but she wanted to leave the abbey of St Disibodenberg, to found a separate monastery at Bingen, and take all her

nuns there. The land was on a river, two rivers in
fact, as well as having some buildings and a mill. As
she described it I could see that she could be instantly
aware of anyone who travelled between Mainz and
Disibodenberg. Was this simply coincidence, or part of
an overall strategy? She never really responded when I
asked her that question.

'I am directed there,' she had replied. 'We are to have
our own community.'

I know the Light directing her was what led her to be
so determined, but I think she was also entranced with
the idea that she could do things her way. She had ideas
about using gutters and pipes for running water to
achieve greater cleanliness. I heard her explaining the
system to Heloise who agreed that it would be a big
improvement, and they set about planning it for the
Paraclete. Less practically she had some idea of
dressing her young nuns in white cloaks with gold on
their veils on special feast days. I could see the point in
that, but I know of many who would not. They do take
on a life of poverty, after all. I am always happy to
organise festivities to allow the young ladies at the
Court to bedeck themselves as gaily as they like. It
helps them attract a husband. Why be gloomy when it's
May, the sun is shining and spring has brought the trees
to life?

'That,' said Hildegard, when I had agreed that dressing
up was a wonderful way to alleviate boredom and
monotony, 'is not the point. These young virgins, in
their white robes, symbolise the special place that they
hold in God's kingdom.'

Virginity is much overrated to my way of thinking.
These holy people tie themselves in a knot trying to
find new ways to deprive themselves of any of life's

pleasures, in the belief that this is what God wants. The question they never ask themselves is why God provided the pleasures in the first place, if they are not to be enjoyed. They hardly eat, they hardly sleep, they only perform or listen to solemn, religious music, they are told not to have paintings or decorations in their churches; they don't indulge in any sexual pleasure at all. Is it any wonder that they yearn for death? It must come as a welcome release. Louis, of course, admired such saintly people, and we know how that affected him. Hildegard was more robust, for all her glorying of virginity, and she certainly knew what was what in the business of men and women. To Hildegard all things in the natural world led to God.

'The Spirit is in the water and the wind. I see the love of God in the trees and the grasses and in all the beauty of nature,' she would say, looking around the garden. 'There is such healing in these plants. God has been good to us.'

She was curious about the life in Paris, how kings made decisions, whether they were prayerful or not. She did not shun the world, so it would be impossible for her to live totally shut away. But, as usual, I have wandered from the point. I think the real reason that Hildegard hated the thought of walls enclosing her was that, when she was a child, she had a fear of being shut in. It was a recurrent nightmare and the memory still troubled her. My own childhood had been such a happy one, and I took that for granted. When my brother was born, I was no longer the heir to Aquitaine, and the servants were not as fussy about me as they had been. After my brother died I became the centre of attention once more, which pleased me, although I never wished him harm. When I was just fourteen my father made his vassals

swear homage to me as heiress to Poitou, Aquitaine
and Gascony. I enjoyed that. Despite all his precautions
he knew that when he died I would be bait for fortune
hunters. My beauty was the additional prize. Even with
his care for my future I was nearly kidnapped and
forced into marriage more than once. My father was not
the cleverest ruler but he knew how to protect his own.
When he arranged for me to marry Louis he stipulated
that my lands should not be taken over by the French
crown, but be inherited by my heirs. Every day I
thanked my father for his foresight. Had I lost my
domains at marriage, I would have been fettered and
contained, like a beast in the barn.

*   *   *

The news of Bernard's impending visit acted like a full
call to arms, and set our energies racing. Heloise was
the first to know, when Volmar returned from Cluny,
and very shortly after the news reached me via Adele
who had already found a conduit of information all her
own through Elizabeth and Agatha. I rushed to the herb
garden where Hildegard was said to be settling the
plants for winter. I found her, not on her knees before
the comfrey, but sitting under the trees in the corner of
the garden, looking up at the sky as though she could
see someone or something.

'Are you talking to God?' I asked her.

Heloise would have disapproved of such a question, but
without asking, we never learn. When would I have
another opportunity to speak to a mystic so freely? Isn't
that what wisdom is all about, putting the question to
the person most able to answer it? When I had
reminded Heloise of this she said that some questions
are more apt than others and we should guard against
trying to impose upon another person's deepest being.

That is why I love poetry and music so much. The troubadours express the sorrows, the joys, the ecstasy of love and beauty through music. There is no plundering of one's own feelings. Heloise understood the importance of music in each person's life because she had gone to great lengths to have Abelard write hymns for their liturgy, and she had contributed to this as well. She was a woman of so many abilities and talents. There was more I would have loved to talk to Heloise about, so many things I wanted to ask her, but, without intruding into that inner self where she kept aloof, it was impossible.

Hildegard, sitting on her stone in the garden like a grounded gargoyle, answered that she knew Bernard was coming to the Paraclete, had known even before Volmar arrived, and that she was seeking guidance and direction.

'Music,' she said, 'music is the language which reaches all spirits. It is the breath of God expressed through the voices of his people. Our songs pluck at the wings of the angels, and all of heaven resonates. Yes, I know just the hymn for Brother Bernard.'

'He's been listening to hymns all his life,' I pointed out. 'He's even written one or two. He's not likely to change his mind because a few nuns sing. We can do better than that; something a little more spectacular.'

I was quite cross. It's fine enough to be a visionary and musician, and to write books about God and his Creation. If that were all that was needed why did she feel the need to consult Heloise? Saintly people are never practical. It may be possible to be practical and pious as well, but I have seen no evidence of it. I was sure that Bernard, being such a manipulator, wasn't saintly and he was the one we had to convince. When I said that to Hildegard, about Bernard, I mean, not about her being saintly yet having no understanding of how to control events, she just smiled at me with that maddeningly complacent look of hers, then said she was just a poor little feeble woman. She knew that made me so furious.

'Prudence is the mother of virtues, always maintaining the justice of God in all things. For in spiritual warfare and secular strife, within my conscience I always wait upon my God,' she added.

Then she got up and went about choosing some leaves from the herb garden, saying that it would make me happier to know that she was selecting a special bouquet to use in the preparation of the fish, for she knew that Bernard was partial to it. She assured me that such a dish would help him to sleep, and thus put him in a receptive humour when he read Heloise's letter. She had also prepared some special leaves to be placed in a pillow for his bed. I told her that lifted my spirits immensely. She looked at me, almost angrily, but then her face softened and she put her hand lightly on my arm as though to emphasize her words.

'Music is our celestial language. Before Adam sinned, his angelic voice had the sweetness of all music harmony. When the devil, the great deceiver, learned that men and women had begun to sing again through God's inspiration he was greatly tormented. Always remember that our body is the vestment of the spirit, which has a living voice, and so it is proper for the body, in harmony with the soul, to use its voice to sing praises to the Eternal One. If God can be reached through our singing, can Brother Bernard remain unmoved? At the same time that our music stirs his soul the food will nourish his body and the pillow will ensure a restful night, so I am not so impractical as you think, Your Majesty,' she said, and turned away as though she were dismissing me from an audience. Poor little humble woman!

Yet I felt calmer for having spoken to her, and went to tell Heloise about it, in the hope that it gave her more confidence.

*　　　*　　　*

We always had our meal in a separate room, not the refectory. I learned that Benedict's Rule stated that though any guest should be treated as though he were Christ, he should not mix with the monks or nuns. I wondered if Christ himself had come to their door would they hurry him away to the smaller traveller's quarters, then leave him while they went to the chapel to pray. The rule did make sense though. Monks and nuns mixing with ordinary people would grow restless and yearn for all that they were missing. Of course if the life in a monastery were all that wonderful perhaps it would work the other way, and lay people would be begging to join the monks or nuns. Who would be left to look after the kingdom? Best to keep them in isolation, I thought, and was shocked to see that I actually agreed with Brother Bernard on something. When the nuns ate they had someone read to them, undoubtedly to distract them from the food. Mealtimes were thus orderly and quiet. I had long thought that good manners at table were essential. Nothing is worse than seeing a man stuffing his mouth full of greasy meat, dribbling bits out as he chews, and even spraying his neighbour with lumps of food if he laughs or guffaws, except to see a woman do the same. I started to insist that people washed their hands and faces before coming to eat, even when we were on the march

to Jerusalem. It was a small thing, but civilizing.
Thinking on this gave me the idea of offering to read to
the nuns about the Crusade. If I dressed in a habit none
of them would know who I was. Heloise agreed to my
suggestion, although I think she was so distracted at the
time that she didn't take in the fact that I would read
only what I had written myself. It would give the nuns a
taste of reality; let them find out how their brothers and
husbands really behaved and died.

Adele came along to listen. She looked very fetching in
the habit, and the squint in her eye was now almost
negligible. I believe that Hildegard had treated it.
'Maybe you're meant for the religious life,' I said, more
to tease than advise, but she surprised me by saying that
she wondered the same thing herself.
'You, my lady, look beautiful in any clothing, but I
prefer you dressed for court, not monastery,' she then
remarked. Adele was adopting too free a tone for my
liking, something that I planned to nip in the bud as
soon as we returned to Paris.

My travels to Jerusalem were still fresh in my mind
when I came to the Paraclete, so much so that I decided
to write down my memories during the evenings, while
Heloise and Hildegard were praying or singing in the
chapel. There are those who are put in this world to
pray and meditate, and others who are needed for
action. I am one of the latter. So was Henry, which is
one of the things I most liked about him. He was
energetic – too much so, as he found it almost
impossible to sit still for a moment. Even when he
attended Mass he was bobbing about like an apple in a
tub of water. With all that practical ability he also had
an appreciation of music and storytelling. As I
considered the matter I could appreciate significant

advantages in our union, not the least being imagining the look on the faces of those sanctimonious scarecrows in Paris when they heard the news. But, I would never have married a man who wished to ban troubadours from my court.

Oddly enough I found a few pages from the odious Odo de Deuil who had written about the crusade as well. I think that it was with the letter from Bernard, and Adele picked them all up together. Thank God she did, for it saved me from a very difficult situation, although we should also be grateful for the fact that I could think quickly. Still can.

It was the first time that I had been in the refectory, a long room with two tables, benches on either side, with a table at the top where Heloise, the Bursar, the Choir Mistress and the Novice Mistress usually sat. There were a few spare seats at that table, sometimes used for visitors, although most visiting travellers ate in the other, smaller room. Although I was dressed as a nun I entered from a door towards the back of the room, away from the light, and went to the lectern, where the light was still behind me. Thus my face was always in shadow.

It was enjoyable to read to such an interested audience. Hearing of something real, and in their own time must have been a welcome change from all those desiccated Church Fathers, or the Old Testament, even though some of the stories there are somewhat salacious. I suspect that they never heard about Samson and Delilah, or the two sisters who tried to beget a child from their own father, as there were no other men around. Heloise would have chosen only edifying passages. Her nuns would have listened, for more times than you can imagine, to the interminable prophecies of

Isaiah, who must have lived to about two hundred if he wrote all that is attributed to him, or the dreary ranting of Jeremiah.

Instead, here was I, with a story they knew something about, which affected their villages, their families, and their king and queen. There is nothing quite like that feeling that people are really listening to you. I barely noticed Heloise enter and take her place, with a man who sat next to her. In fact I felt only irritation when I noted this man being brought a special plate with a fish on it. The rest of us had had only vegetables.

Then, from the corner of my eye, just as I was stressing how much the queen had supported the king in all his plans to free the holy lands, I saw Hildegard lift her arm as though to point heavenwards. Her uncharacteristic movements made me look across to Heloise. Then I recognized him. The man sitting next to her was Bernard. He must have arrived earlier than we expected.

So quickly that no one would have seen, I placed Odo's account of the crusade on top of my parchment, and began to read his sycophantic description of how Bernard had preached the crusade. But while I had him as a captive listener I mentioned something about the gentling influence of women, which inspires men to behave as God would wish. That was the point where I finished my reading, urging them to pray. That way, I thought, their eyes will be closed and I can leave the room unobtrusively. For one wicked moment I had thought of joining Heloise at the top table, but I knew that Bernard would recognize me, even dressed as a nun, and that all our plans would be for naught. This was an indulgence I did not allow myself, although I was sorely tempted.

Bernard seemed such an insignificant figure if you don't look beyond his slight frame. How could such a man yield so much influence, I often asked myself, but the answer came the first time I heard him preach. He spoke of love in such beautiful words. How should God be loved? This was the theme of his homily, and he spoke of a God who loved us so generously. We should return that love without measure. So immensity loves; eternity loves; the love, which passes knowledge, gives itself. While listening to him preach I felt that I could never love God enough, but I also wished that someone could love me with that intensity.

True love is content, Bernard said later in his sermon. True love does not ask for a reward, but deserves it. I sighed to think of how Louis claimed to love me but was never content and always wanted some reward. I was neither content nor selfless, but to see such an ideal presented to me made me hunger for such a love. These thoughts returned to me as I hurried away from the refectory. Without doubt I was influenced by the way Heloise spoke so longingly of Abelard. I know now that such a love, if it ever exists, is rare indeed. Certainly Abelard gave Heloise more sorrow than joy, as far as I could judge. Some said that Rosamund was the only woman that Henry had loved, but I doubt that. He loved me enough when we were first married. He loved her later, because she was young, beautiful and didn't argue. Henry never could stand being confronted by his own folly.

The memories of my travels helped me through a very difficult time later in my life, when Henry held me prisoner in dank, dark rooms, guarded by his lackeys. Hildegard had prophesied that it would happen, but I did not take her warnings seriously. She wrote me a

letter of hope and support during those dark years.
During those fifteen years I found great consolation and
distraction from four grey stone walls by closing my
eyes and conjuring up the colour, music, noise, even the
smells of all the busy streets and the market places.
Other times I thought myself back in rich palaces with
their fertile gardens, and wonderful food. On the days
when it seemed most drear and hopeless I would relive
the time I spent at the Paraclete. The world of the mind
can be a wonderful place, and at times it was all that
sustained me. I had a great deal of time to think and
reflect. Could I have lived my life differently?
Release came when Henry died. Regaining my freedom
was wonderful. His death was not. No one deserves to
die as Henry did, weak and ill, deserted by his soldiers
and servants, betrayed by the son whom he had
favoured above the others. I was told they stole his
rings from his fingers even before he had closed his
eyes, and left him to die in lonely squalour. He had
been such a magnificent young man, and I loved the
memory of him, as he was when we were first together.
 So much was prescribed for me, firstly by my father,
then by Louis and, finally, Henry and I wondered how
my life might have been if it were otherwise. Men
interfere even in something as important to a woman as
her children. When I saw my first daughter Marie I
thought she was lovely, perfect in every detail. Then I
saw the long faces around me. Louis and his entourage
were full of disappointment that I had given birth to a
girl. If he had listened to Hildegard he would have
known why I had not had a son. I felt some affection
for him, but not the true and proper love needed to
conceive a son. Marie was taken from me, to be fed by
a wet nurse, tended by servants, and returned for

inspection at infrequent intervals. Louis hardly
bothered with her at all. Then we were off to the
Crusade and it was years before I saw Marie again.
When I left Louis it was my two daughters, Marie and
Alix, who had to remain with their father, and while I
yearned for my new life I felt their loss more than I
expected.

The children I bore Henry were closer to me. William,
who was our first child, died when he was still very
young. Young Henry died before he could claim the
throne, but not before he had caused his father some
grief. Geoffrey was killed in a stupid accident, throwing
away his life while jousting. My beloved Richard did
live long enough to be crowned king of England, but
not long enough to exercise his power for he was
captured and held prisoner in Germany, returning from
fighting in Jerusalem. We paid his ransom, but it took
some time to raise it, so high was his price. Soon after
he returned he was killed in France, and I almost died
of grief. John, also crowned king, unfortunately did live
long enough to demonstrate his lacks.

My daughters, Matilda, Eleanor and Joanna were all
sent to prestigious and strategic unions. Nothing had
changed since I was a girl in that regard. I like to think
that, through Henry and me, Europe was enriched.
Would my own life have been more fulfilled had I been
able to keep my children with me always, watch them
grow, guide and advise them to use what chances life
provided? My sons were young lions. Should I have
encouraged them to rebel against their father? Possibly
not, for my Henry was the greatest soldier of them all.
But one thing I did learn during those fifteen restricted
years, punishment for my audacity – if we wait with
patience for what we desire we seldom gain it. The

prize is only for those who reach out and strive,
against all difficulties, to achieve their goal.
But, to return to that eventful time at the Paraclete.
Heloise, when I saw her later that evening, was quite
discountenanced by the whole business. What if
Bernard had recognized me? What if I had continued to
talk on in that ridiculous vein about the crusade? What
if...?

'You granted me permission to read to your sisters on
the subject,' I reminded her. 'As Queen of France I
have the right to speak in any abbey on any subject.'
I wasn't sure if that were true. In fact I was almost
certain it wasn't, for Louis often went on about how he
could never give an order to the most humble priest.
That seemed silly to me at the time, and still does. The
king must rule in all matters that affect his people. I felt
Henry was right when he ordered Thomas Beckett to
allow priests who broke the laws of the land to be tried
by the judges of the land. A murderer is no less a killer
if he has been ordained, and should pay the full penalty.
Hildegard came hurrying into the room then, all a
twitter about herbs and leaves and poisoning Bernard. I
had been about to go and change out of the nun's habit,
but decided to stay and hear what the fuss was all about.
It appeared that Hildegard, in her zeal, had arranged a
special meal for Bernard, but some silly person
(naturally they blamed Adele, but it was more likely
Sister Agatha) had put other ingredients into the
mixture, which meant that Bernard, given his delicate
digestion, might spend a very nasty night.
I, and my reading, were completely forgotten for the
moment, as the two nuns contemplated the seriousness
of Bernard accusing them of poisoning him. Much as I
sympathised with them in their dilemma I could not

help but smile to think that two such wise and learned women could find themselves in such a predicament. Clearly I was needed to extricate them. And I did.

*   *   *

It was the singing that attracted me to the corridor. There they stood, two nuns and Adele, creating beautiful music, enough to soften the heart of any man, even Bernard's. As I came a little closer, I heard another sound, less harmonious – the sound of a man groaning and giving out small moans of deep distress. Bernard was dying! The fish, I thought, and all those mixed up herbs and leaves. How could Hildegard have been so stupid? Was it possible to offer him some remedy? Bernard was dying here in this abbey, where the three of us had been meeting in secret for some days. This would lead others to only one conclusion. Louis would forgive me most things, but murdering Bernard of Clairvaux was not one of them.

 I hurried for a jug of rosewater and a small cloth, and then returned to Bernard's room. The night was chill. My dress was quite flimsy, although my blue cloak was warm, so I put the white veil over my head. Adele had not returned. I preferred not to call her in any case. The less people who knew what happened the better, and she was a terrible gossip.

There was a column of moonlight shining through the window of Bernard's room. As I entered, and stood there for a moment, he opened his eyes and murmured, 'I did not think to see you here in this world. Has my time come? I offer all my sufferings to atone for my sins and the sins of the world. Why has God forsaken me?'

He was not making a great deal of sense. Of course
he did not expect to see me here at the Paraclete, but
none of the rest followed. He must have recognized me,
probably knew I was the one reading about the crusade,
and I would be punished for my lack of womanly
modesty, or sacrilege, or some other charge he would
contrive for my downfall. This whole evening was
turning into a disaster. Perhaps, and now I am ashamed
to admit it, I thought it would be better if Bernard did
die. We could bury his body in the garden and pretend
he had left for wherever he was headed very early in the
morning. Then people would assume that he had been
attacked and killed by robbers. These were thoughts
born of desperation, and it took only a few minutes for
me to realise how futile it was to panic. Better to ease
the man's pain, and deal with the problems in the
morning.

I pushed my blue cloak back a little to free my arms,
and in the moonlight my white dress shone like a pearl.
My hair was loose under the veil; I imagine that I did
look quite ravishing at that moment. Not that Bernard
was in any state to ravish or be ravished. His forehead
was wet with sweat, and his face contorted in pain. I sat
beside his bed and bathed his face with the cloth that I
had soaked in the rosewater.

'You're not going to die,' I reassured him, 'not yet.
God still has work for you to do.'

His pain seemed to ease, for he stopped flailing about
and lay on his side, his knees slightly bent. I held his
hand and soothed him with gentle words, as a mother to
a fretful child. I reminded him that Jesus, as a baby, had
been fed, nurtured and cradled by Mary. She, with the
other holy women, had served him all her life, travelled

with him, saw to his needs, provided him with support and encouragement.

'You are a model to all mothers,' he said so quietly I had to bend my head to catch the words.

He must still be delirious, I thought. No one has ever considered me as a maternal person. I had left my little Marie to accompany Louis to Jerusalem, and she hardly recognized me when I returned. That hurt me more than you can imagine. Perhaps Bernard was thinking of his own mother.

'This is what women must do,' I whispered. 'Men fight and women heal, refine and comfort. Your own mother loved you, and tended you. The holy nuns help to heal all those who are ill or troubled. Their hands are gentle and their words bring solace. Women are necessary to refine men and turn their thoughts from war to love.'

I may have said more in the same vein. My actual words were not important. My first thought was to relieve his suffering, but it was a heaven-sent opportunity to argue my situation and that I did not intend to squander.

He spoke again. 'Hail Mary, full of grace. Why has the mother of my Lord come to visit me?' Then he began to breathe easily, and fell into a deep sleep. I had come to the Paraclete as the Queen of France. Now I was viewed as the Queen of Heaven. Poor Bernard would not have slept so soundly had he realized his mistake.

Hildegard was waiting for me.

'Is he still alive?' she asked.

'Is that a question a prophet needs to ask?' I said, then realising that I was being flippant, small minded and unkind even, I smiled and reassured her that Bernard, far from being dead, was in a deep, restful sleep.

'Thank God,' she said. 'We must both go to sleep now as well, for tomorrow may be an important day for us. Do you think he has already read Heloise's letter?'

'I have no idea.' Suddenly I was out of patience, and very, very weary. Without any further talk I hurried to my bed, but sleep eluded me. There was too much to think about. Whatever happened the following morning would affect the rest of my life.

BERNARD'S DECISION

I, Bernard of Clairvaux, Abbot and humble servant of the Lord, wish to recount my role in what became known, in the monastic world, as the Paraclete conundrum. Truth must be defended.

While still a young man I entered a monastery to free myself from worldly distractions. My path to find God has twisted and turned, and the world still intrudes. My prayer is a constant battle as my mind wishes to flit like a butterfly among gaudy flowers. Temptations are usually sent by the devil, but at the time of which I write the distractions came from a different source – rumours. Disturbing stories were filtering through the walls of Clairvaux concerning happenings at the Paraclete. These accounts were so extraordinary that they just might have been true. Initially it was the rumour that Eleanor, Queen of France was there. The favoured version was that she was pregnant, hiding from the wrath of Louis, because the child was not his. That story had grown offshoots. The father was her uncle, Count Raymond of Antioch. Most unlikely. No gestation period could be so long. The father was Pope Eugenius III. That rumour did not even deserve acknowledgement. Everyone knew that the Pope's chastity was a shining jewel in the Church's tiara. This left the third suggestion as being a very real possibility – some troubadour who had plucked the strings of his lyre and then... but it is too terrible to put into words. Still, just what one would expect from Queen Eleanor. Almost equally disconcerting was the news that Brother Volmar had been at the Paraclete and was now at Cluny. The monk should have been spiritually guiding Mother Hildegard at St Disibodenberg in Germany, yet other sources told me that Hildegard was also at the Paraclete. What were they planning? Could this mean that I had been wrong to approve her writings? Her letter to me had given every indication that she was a humble and holy woman. In my opinion she had been singled out by God to help in the fight against corruption and heresy. I might have been mistaken. What was the connection between Hildegard and Eleanor? And why meet at the Paraclete? Abbess Heloise, since her conversion, had become an exemplar of all that women religious should be. Would she allow any irregularity? These stories were too bizarre, too distasteful. I closed my prayer book. I would have to go and see for myself.

God had called me to spread his word, establish more and more abbeys and guide young men towards the appreciation of God's love. Almost a thousand monks had been, by this time, under my care at Clairvaux. Kings, popes and bishops were constantly calling on me to sort out their problems, problems which were nearly always of their own making, although they could not seem to see that. I was growing weary of all the dissension and strife. Because I believed that my time on earth would soon be over I wanted to prepare for my final judgement. Instead of which I found myself riding a bony horse toward Troyes, on the road to the Paraclete, feeling distinctly queasy. The two brothers who travelled with me seemed perfectly happy as they sang psalms and soaked up the late autumn sun. Would they never be quiet!

As I jolted and jogged along my thoughts returned to Heloise, dearest sister in Christ, gifted by the Spirit with a mind the equal of many men. As my horse stumbled on a stone, clumsy creature, I thought again of

Heloise who had stumbled but righted herself, with
God's grace. Heloise had a beautiful smile, which
welcomed and warmed. I was sure that she harboured
no animosity against me because of the actions I had
been forced to take against Abelard. Had she not, as
Abelard reported in a letter, seen my first visit to the
Paraclete as 'long awaited'. Had I not been received
there as though I were an angel? Such a reception is
gratifying even if I know that I am far below the angels
in splendour and virtue. I had expected that Heloise
would appoint me as the spiritual guide to her abbey,
but she chose Abelard. Was this wise, given their
earlier history? Heloise, when I asked her that question,
replied that it was Abelard's right and obligation.
There have been times when I wondered if I had not
been too harsh in my judgement of him. So bombastic,
so full of pride, so bumptious when vanquishing his
adversaries in debate. His triumphs were not as myriad
as he claimed, for he could never admit that he might be
wrong. Take, for example, when I had questioned his
use of the term *panem supersubstantialem*, instead of
the normal phrase *pane quotidianum* in the Lord's
Prayer. He had retaliated with a long justificatory
epistle on a point of semantics and translations,
claiming he was following Hebrew truth. Why couldn't
he have admitted that he was wrong and it would be
better to stay with the more accepted wording? Abelard
had his strengths, I admit. He had his weaknesses as
well. He failed to understand that once you allowed
people to think for themselves there was no way to
control those thoughts, so heresy and unorthodoxy
became rife. God is served by men learning to grow in
love through gratitude for all his blessings and gifts.
Then one could, as John the Evangelist directs, love

God and do whatever one liked, desiring only what pleased God. Abelard's pride, obstinacy and lustful thoughts led him to desire Heloise, for which he was suitably punished.

I had gone to be reconciled with Abelard, just before he died. Seeing him, sitting near the window of the small monk's cell, my first thought was that he had grown smaller. The lines of age and constant pain had written their story on his face, his habit was none too clean and he had the look of the old men who hang around the churches, begging for alms. Clearly Abelard's thoughts were no longer lustful or fixed on earthly things. Perhaps he had acquired humility. Abelard looked up from his book, greeting me as a welcome friend rather than a hated foe.

'Welcome, Brother, I am gratified to see you. I do not wish to go before my God without being reconciled with those who have shown me enmity, and misjudged my beliefs,' he said.

That man would have to live a lot longer to make peace with all his enemies.

'We have had our differences,' I replied, feeling I could afford to be generous, 'but perhaps our disagreements have stemmed as much from failing to appreciate each other's position as from dissension.'

'A philosopher searches for the truth, but that truth is necessarily expressed in words, which may result in misunderstanding, distortion even.' This was the closest Abelard would ever come to saying that he might be wrong about anything.

He had placed his table in the corner to take advantage of the light. There were books and parchment to hand, but the only book that was open was the Bible. I craned my neck and saw that Abelard had been reading the psalms.

'Words are imperfect advocates for ideas,' I replied, after a short pause. 'You speak of finding truth, but how do you differentiate between truth, knowledge and opinion?'

'What are your distinctions?' Abelard had replied, looking like a tired warhorse sniffing one last battle.

'My journey to God has been through learning, reasoning and using those gifts which God has given to me. How, Brother Bernard, for example, would you define faith?'

I had helped many men to die, and knew the signs. No doubt Abelard was also aware that he would not live to see the end of the year. There was nothing that I could say which would bring any comfort so I simply answered the question.

'Faith is a certain voluntary and confident foretaste of the truth not yet apparent.'

'You hold many articles of faith as truths. How do these articles of faith differ from knowledge?' continued Abelard, now looking less like a man wearying for release from this world and more like one preparing for a lengthy debate.

'Knowledge is a clear and certain grasp of things unseen. Opinion is holding as true something you do not know to be false.' I wondered if I should have added that knowledge included a grasp of things that could be seen. This was why I distrusted such arguments. Words escaped from my mouth and then my thoughts followed, and it was on these thoughts that a mind like Abelard's might engage.

'If both faith and knowledge grasp at things which
are unseen how do we distinguish faith from
knowledge?' Abelard had replied.

'We hold what we believe in faith as a mystery. We
hold knowledge as fact. When you know something
you do not seek further. In faith we have hope that what
is certain to us will become plain, as it is sure,' I
replied, feeling pleased with my response. Christ said
one should not worry about what one should say, as the
Holy Spirit would provide the words. Nevertheless I
waited, wary.

Abelard smiled then, as though to indicate that he no
longer wished to dispute with me, and slumped in his
chair. The old Abelard would have argued the matter
until he was satisfied that his arrows had reached their
target, as he attempted to establish that we only come to
faith through knowledge.

'I have written of the beliefs I hold to be true in a letter
to Heloise, my sister in religion, which will be sent to
her at the right time. I have no fear of death. It's this
world which disturbs me, but God, not men, will be my
judge.'

I refrained from reminding him that he had been
condemned at both Soissons and Sens by distinguished
bishops. There was no need to inflict further wounds.
Abelard was old, tired and ill. Perhaps he had really
come to understand that God is sought more worthily in
prayer than in debate. Had David finally vanquished
Goliath, I wondered, or had we both been warriors in
the same army, and I had not recognized it?

These thoughts distracted me enough to make the
second day of travel tolerable. My two companions had
sung themselves out and kept a merciful silence. The
only sounds were the warbling of birds in the trees and

the hoof beats on the road. Sometimes we passed
groups of farmers going to their labours. The warmth of
the sun relaxed me. It was not until we reached the gate
of the Paraclete that I realized how tired I was, and
hungry. We had arrived unannounced, so I could
scarcely hope for something beyond the usual boiled
vegetables and watery wine. I prayed that God would
forgive such thoughts. Gluttony is to be condemned.
The pleasures of the throat, which are so highly
regarded, take up scarcely two fingers' breadth; and the
small enjoyment of that little fragment is prepared with
such trouble and gives rise to such anxiety. My stomach
rumbled, but had I any idea of the degree of anxiety the
preparation of my meal would cause, and the effect it
would have, it would have protested far louder.
Now that I had reached my destination I wondered what
I would find. My first impressions disquieted and
puzzled me. Heloise's eyes seemed anxious even while
she smiled, gracious and courteous as always. There
was no lack of warmth in her greeting, or her concern
for my comfort, but the alacrity with which she tried to
steer me from the chapel to the small guest room, to eat
the evening meal alone with my companions, signalled
to me that she was agitated and ill at ease. Or did she
have something to hide?
'We'll eat with the sisters this evening,' I said. 'We've
no wish to place extra burdens upon you.' No
reassurances or blandishments on her part could
dissuade me. Clearly she had something to hide.
The Paraclete had become a religious establishment that
could serve as a model to all others. The fact that
Abelard was buried in the chapel at the Paraclete,
instead of Cluny, where he had died, was an irregularity

I decided to ignore for the moment, hoping that this was the only one I would discover.

With these thoughts, which fortunately the Abbess Heloise could not divine, I entered the refectory. I observed the sisters, sitting in neat rows on either side of a long table. I noted the main table, set aside for senior nuns, with a place that had been quickly prepared for me, next to where Heloise always sat. I noted that the customary reading was underway, no doubt something of scripture, the lives of one of the saints, or a reading from the Church Fathers. The reader continued, her only reaction to my arrival being to slightly raise her voice. I strained to identify the text. 'The crusade brought much suffering to the soldiers, as it did to the villagers and worthy people who offered the soldiers sustenance and shelter as they journeyed forth. If these humble villagers did not offer enough food, it was taken in a totally un-Christlike manner and no woman, be she old or young, virtuous or wanton, was safe.'

Crusade. Not a word I liked to hear. The recent crusade was a dark shadow, cast by my quest to restore the holy lands to Christians and gain Louis VII a position of supremacy amongst European leaders; plans that had gone very wrong. I constantly strive for humility, but I have not been so victorious that I relish being reminded of the greatest failure in my life. Then I heard my name, and expected condemnation. My fears were allayed.

' ...an angel, an emissary from God with the voice of silver, Brother Bernard called them all to arms, and they responded. Even your queen rallied to the cause, inspired by the fervour and virtue of the saintly Bernard of Clairvaux. Had he accompanied the crusading army he would have turned all from the path of sin to virtue.

Fortunately the presence of women, especially your queen, softened the hard hearts of the soldiers and reminded them of the gentle admonitions to be virtuous and chivalrous, teaching which they had received from their own mothers.'

This part of the story I was happy for them to hear, although I wished that people would not refer to me as saintly. Not before my death, at any rate. And too much credit was being given to the women who had accompanied the crusade. I had never intended women to be part of the army. From all that I had heard the women had been nothing but a nuisance, with their baggage, and the Queen, rather than being an influence for good had encouraged her own knights to sing secular songs and play at cards in the evenings. Why was this being read to the sisters? Was it spiritual? No. Was it likely to lead their thoughts to higher matters? Impossible! This was a most unorthodox spiritual reading. I turned to ask Heloise for some explanation, but at that moment my meal was placed on the table. A small fish, gently poached, I imagined, in spring water, and with a delicious aroma of herbs, invited. The bright eye confirmed that the fish's demise had been recent. Surely this was not the work of Sister Agatha, who on my previous visit had rendered the freshest of ingredients to an amorphous pulp? I hesitated for a moment, fearing that such a delectable meal would be against the spirit of self-denial, but my stomach disagreed and my bones felt weary, so I thanked God for all his gifts, for a safe journey, for the warm welcome that I had received, and for the safe return of the royal couple from the crusade. No other urgent message sprang to mind, so I made the sign of the cross and began to eat.

It was even before the Grace after meals was said
that I began to feel discomfort, which rapidly turned
into severe pain. Heloise, conducting me to my room,
could not have known of the shooting pains that burned
and tore at my entrails. If she had she would not have
talked of her letter, women in the Church, and humble
requests that I consider her arguments and reconsider
my advice to the Pope. So great was my pain that I
could scarcely prevent myself from calling out. All I
could do was grimace, hoping it resembled a smile, and
promise to talk seriously about all her concerns in the
morning. If I am still alive, I might have added, but had
no wish to alarm the wise and pious abbess.

It is my practice to examine my conscience each night
before I go to sleep. I reflect on all that I have done and
said that day, all that I have omitted to do or say that I
should have said or done, any distraction during times
devoted to prayer and meditation, any lapse at all. This
might take some few minutes, after which I would beg
God's forgiveness for my sins in a fervent act of
contrition. My mind and soul thus settled I would
mentally conjure up the picture of a beautiful garden
with pomegranate fruits, picked from the Tree of Life,
which the Bride brings into her Beloved's garden. With
spiritual fruits and flowers my soul would be nourished,
and grow in the love of God. If the pain in my stomach
would ease for just a few moments my vision of this
celestial garden could hopefully induce sleep.

As if in answer to prayer the pain abated slightly. My
candle was still alight so I decided to read Heloise's
letter, the better to be prepared for our talk in the
morning.

*To the illustrious abbot Bernard, spiritual father
and brother in Christ, guide to popes and bishops,
Heloise, called abbess of the Paraclete, wishes that he
may live for the Lord and die in the Lord.*

To live in the Lord was my desire. To die in the Lord
might be my fate that very night unless my stomach
stayed calm. Suddenly my head whirred about, and the
letters blurred. Increasingly I felt hot and clammy, only
able to read the letter with difficulty, although I could
see that it set out, with skill and erudition, the virtues of
women in the Church and in God's kingdom on earth.
Had I ever suggested otherwise? Mary, the mother of
our Saviour, was a woman. But then, so was Eve.
Draughts blew through the window and under the door.
The candle was extinguished. Moonlight, casting a
beam of light amongst the shadows of the room only
added to the chill. I tried to join my sufferings with
those of Jesus on the cross. I reproached myself for
being so concerned about my own wellbeing. Did not
Christ suffer from much more than indigestion and a
body that ranged from feverishly hot to shiveringly
cold? I closed my eyes and tried to place myself back
in the imaginary garden but my pain overwhelmed me.
I could not tell if I were alive or dead, awake or asleep.
My body, curled up in agony, belonged elsewhere.
Silence. Chill. How could all those nuns, and my
brother monks sleep so soundly as I suffered? Then the
silence was disturbed. Was someone coming to help
me? There were birds. No, there were angels singing. A
melody I had never heard before, solemn, sacred,
soaring to the heights. Clear, virginal voices as one
would expect from angels who had no bodies and were
constantly in the presence of God. They had come to

escort my soul to face its final judgement. I felt no
fear at first, then a great fear, for who does not dread
the unknown.

'Mary, Queen of Heaven, I place my trust in you.
Intercede for me before the throne of God.'

Renewed spasms of pain. I moaned aloud, trying to
stifle the sound. Were these my death throes? Should I
fall on my knees, or call for a rush mat to be placed on
the floor of the chapel, where I would wait for my end
with Heloise and her sisters praying around me,
Hildegard too, if she really were here. Eleanor, even if
she were here, need not be disturbed. I tried to raise
myself, but fell back against the pillow and closed my
eyes, attempting to gather more strength. The angelic
voices reached out to me, surrounded me, soothed me,
tapered to a thin thread of sound, and then increased
again in strength and beauty. Prelude to my death, or
balm to my spirit? I tried once more to pray but could
not.

The door opened. Soft footsteps. The angel of Death?
Heloise? A figure, wearing a white dress and blue
cloak, stood lit by the moon's rays. On her feet were
golden slippers. The feet of the Virgin Mary should be
clad in gold. She should have a crown of gold as well,
with precious gems, but in her humility she had chosen
to wear a simple white veil. Her face, glorious in the
clear light, contained more beauty than I had ever
encountered.

'If you've come to take me to my eternal rest I am
ready,' I whispered, 'but I feel that your Son has more
for me to do on earth. Not my will, but his be done.'

The vision approached and sat by the bed. She carried a
small jug and a white piece of material, and she began
to bathe my face and hands while murmuring

comforting words such as a mother would use to her child who is ill. The voices of the angels continued to sing, but gradually faded as though they were floating away and I could not follow.

Slowly the pain eased. My face felt refreshed and breathing became easier. As I drifted into gentle slumber I looked once more at the figure beside me. Mary had come to me in my hour of need. Her face; her face reminded him of another woman, although surely no earthly woman could ever approach this ethereal beauty. I dreamed of rose-petals and songbirds flitting about the apple trees, chirping and chirruping.

It was the song of birds, not angels' voices that woke me. I remembered all that had happened during the night, and the beauty of the heavenly visitor. I also remembered the vision's loving gentleness and soothing voice.

Next morning I felt drained but free of pain, well enough to say mass for the sisters, as I had promised. As I stood at the altar I strove to keep my mind firmly fixed on the prayers and words of the liturgy, although the temptation to turn and peruse the kneeling figures, to see if either a nun from Germany or a queen from Paris were there was compelling.

Heloise's Story

I am no stranger to distractions during mass, but that morning, as Bernard presided at the altar, I was tormented. Thank God the greatest of my fears had not come to pass. Bernard was alive, and seemed in reasonable health, if a little paler than usual, if that were possible. What must he have made of a night in my abbey, with nuns singing outside his door, and a woman coming into his cell to splash rosewater all over his face and subject him to a monologue, for how could Eleanor have resisted such a captive audience? Was it the tale of her grandfather eloping with the woman with a ridiculous name, her father brought to an early grave, or her miserable marriage to the King? Then I felt ashamed for my lack of charity, but the whole experience had been totally demoralising. What hope was there despite all my efforts to save us? None at all. In despair I prayed for immediate death so that I could join Abelard in heaven and leave the other two to deal with the problem.

Of course that prayer was not answered. God does not let us go so lightly. Bernard had summoned me and with a sinking heart I sat in the small meeting room to wait for him. When he did arrive he immediately began to talk about the love of God, a worthy subject but not my most pressing concern at that particular time.

'You and I, dear sister in Christ, do not doubt that God deserves our love.'

I had doubted this, more than once, when thinking of the way Abelard had been punished. Bernard would not have understood, so I simply nodded.

'Man's dignity is in his free will, a gift also bestowed on women. How else could Mary have consented to be

the Mother of God? It is God's will, never the less,
that women must be subject to men as the church is
subject to Christ.'

'Do you not acknowledge the dignity of women?' I
asked, fearing at the same time that I might anger him if
I appeared to disagree in any way with his opinion.

'Dignity is nothing without knowledge, and you are a
shining example of how even a woman may attain
knowledge. In knowledge we find virtue. Through
virtue we seek God and cling to him once we have
found him. There are few women your equal in wisdom
and it is for Godly men to protect the virtue of women
and prevent them from being led astray.'

Desperation suddenly overcome caution but although I
wished to argue, cajole and insist that he was mistaken,
just as I drew a deep breath ready to put the arguments,
my mouth dried up and I could not utter a word. It was
left to Bernard to the ensuing silence.

'Forgive my asking this question but at the Paraclete
have you, or any of your sisters been blessed with a
vision of the Mother of God?

I shook my head assuring him that I knew of no such
event. What could he be talking about? Was this to a
ploy to distract me? All was lost. I was coming to
accept that. In one final attempt to breach the walls of
his condescension and prejudice I decided to broach the
subject of my letter.

'Forgive me for presuming to trouble you. Dear Abbot
Bernard, you who have so honoured us by visiting our
humble abbey; you who spend your energies in great
works and advising kings and bishops, did you, in your
generosity of spirit, find time to read my letter?'

'Are we speaking of any other subject than the love
God has for women and the need to ensure that they can
fulfil God's plan?'

'Permit me to ask if you consider it suitable, as some
have suggested, that all women religious should be
strictly enclosed?' I probed.

'Enclosure would certainly protect women from
themselves and from the world. The devil sets as many
traps for women as he does for men. But do I consider
total enclosure for all religious women necessary? That
is a difficult question. Examples of great and holy
women, such as you have written in your excellent
letter, show that women, as well as men, may be
capable of knowing, loving and serving God in many
capacities. This is his gift to all people. Yet these
women are rare and too many of the weaker sex
succumb to the blandishments of the evil one. More
easily than do men, I believe. We have the example of
our first parents always before us.'

I was unsure about where this conversation was leading
us. He seemed to be saying, on the one hand, that God
gives gifts to both men and women, so there is no
justification for restricting and restraining all women.
At least I hoped that I had understood him correctly. On
the other hand, he suggested that women are not the
same as men because Eve was the first one to eat the
apple from the Tree of Knowledge. Eve had to answer
not just for taking a bite, but the first bite. Couldn't it be
argued that she had a stronger desire for knowledge
than Adam, and hence was seeking more closely to
attain virtue? I considered arguing this, before realising
that Bernard would not be sympathetic to that point of
view.

Was I foolish to cling to the hope, still, that Bernard
had understood the import of my letter? Our letter,
rather, although when I thought of the over-seasoned
fish, midnight serenades by Hildegard's 'angels',
Eleanor's attempt to render the crusade unto Bernard,
and her indiscreet nocturnal intervention I found it
difficult to apportion them much credit. I sought to
clarify the matter.

'Most gracious Father Bernard,' I said. 'I'm willing to
concede that women lack the physical strength of men,
but they are man's equal in wishing to love and serve
God. The gifts of the Holy Spirit, as St Paul points out,
are given to us all, in different ways, but it is still the
same Spirit.' It was my last throw of the dice. Time
would tell if the numbers favoured us.

'That is so, dear Sister in Christ, but there is another
matter which now concerns me. You know that
Benedict, in his Rule wisely directs that newcomers to
the monastery must not be given an easy entry. As I
recall, he has written: *If someone comes and keeps
knocking on the door, and if at the end of four or five
days he has shown himself patient in bearing his harsh
treatment and difficulty of entry, and has persisted in
his request then he should be allowed to enter and stay
in the guest quarters for a few days.* I believe that you
have guests here at present, women of some note. Are
any of them, perhaps, wishing to enter this monastery?'
How much did he know?

'We would never treat any person with discourtesy.
This would not be in the spirit of St Benedict's Rule,' I
replied. 'While it may necessary to be assured of the
sincerity of any woman who wishes to visit this
monastery, I do not do so by forcing her to stand

outside the gate for several days. Such treatment
would expose her to danger and cold.'
The room, always too small, became claustrophobic. I
longed to be rid of the man, rid of my worries, left in
peace with my writing and study. Bernard wriggled
about as though he, too, felt uncomfortable. He spoke
again.

'Benedict also rules that visiting monks and nuns
should be allowed to stay as guests in the monastery for
as long as they wish, as long as they do not make
demands which upset the monastery. It is even possible
that such persons are guided there for a special purpose.
You have guests, I am told and they have been here for
some weeks now. Has any such special purpose become
evident?'
Who had been telling him, and what had they reported?
As I expected he had not been satisfied with my earlier
answer. I decided that admitting to Hildegard should
not ruin our cause. She was a Benedictine nun after all.
'We have been honoured to welcome Mother Hildegard
and Sister Elizabeth from St Disibodenberg. I have
gained much from discourse with Hildegard. Such a
pious woman, close to God, gifted in music and the
knowledge of medicine; she has brought her own
wisdom to us. We have been blessed by her time here,
soon to draw to a close.' Had I said too much? Would
he want to know the nature of our discourse and
whether it justified breaking our rule of silence?
'She travelled far. Her abbot agreed to this journey?'
'Assuredly,' I said, thinking to myself of Hildegard's
account of the struggle that she had undergone to obtain
that permission.

'I would like to speak to her, as she is here. The revelations she receives from God are great gifts, not only to her but the entire Church.'

It was as though I was negotiating a tightrope, afraid to look down, yet conscious of the chasm beneath me. Should I offer him Eleanor? Did he know already? If I said something about Eleanor and he had not known, what then? Silence seemed the wiser option.

'Last night I was afflicted with some small discomfort, caused, no doubt, by fatigue from my journey and unfamiliar food,' said Bernard, standing up and looking up towards the tiny window. 'This is no criticism of your excellent hospitality, but to try to explain an extraordinary event. I had, what appeared to me in my pain and fever, a vision of the Mother of God. She ministered to me, as angels sang. Truly I thought she had come to take me to heaven. But, as I finally drifted into a peaceful sleep, I found myself thinking, for what reason I cannot imagine, of Eleanor, Queen of France. She's not been seen at court for some time. Is it possible, I ask myself, that she's here, at the Paraclete?'

He did know! Of course he knew. Bernard knew everything. But why should I be fearful of his anger? Queen Eleanor had every right to retire to a monastery for a time, to meditate, pray, reflect on her spiritual progress.

'It is true that the Queen is here. We all need time to retreat from the world, but none more than members of the royal family,' I said firmly.

'Then I would also wish to speak with her, if she can spare the time from her prayers. But first, I'll speak with our dear sister Hildegard.' Bernard had the look of a cat that has cornered its mice, played with them for long enough, and was about to move to the kill, one by

one, slowly. How foolish I had been to imagine that
there would be no retribution after so many flagrant
breaches of the Rule. Silence had gone out the window.
We had laughed and told stories and shared memories
and experiences of childhood, friendship and love. In
retelling Abelard I had him with me again. Such
activities, which had lightened and enlightened me, did
not lead to detachment from the world and enrichment
of the inner life. Happiness commanded its price.
Despondently I left the room and intending to send
Hildegard. Sister Elizabeth waited nearby as though
anticipating the summons. I asked her to let Mother
Hildegard know that Abbot Bernard wished to speak to
her. Then, with the forces of a beesting I was struck by
a sudden realisation. Trying to sound calm I called
Elizabeth back.

'Quickly,' I said, 'Go and find the lady Eleanor. Tell
her, no, warn her...' How could I word this message?
'Tell her,' I said again, 'that last night the Abbot
Bernard was visited by a woman called Mary.'
'Sister Mary?'' asked Elizabeth, looking puzzled. ' Do
you have a Sister Mary? Or is it some other lady?
Should I ask Adele to deliver your message?'
'No! Say nothing to Adele. Nothing. Is that clear? Say
nothing to anyone but the lady Eleanor. Mary to whom
I refer is very special. Be sure that the lady Eleanor
understands that clearly. It is a matter of great urgency.
Run, dear child, hurry. Everything depends upon it.'
Eleanor must understand that Bernard believed he had
a vision of Mary the mother of God before she had her
interview with him. Otherwise she would babble on
about herself, her rosewater and her maternal and
healing touch, all the while expecting him to thank her.
Bernard would take a very ungrateful view of a Queen

whom he regarded as ungodly masquerading as the Queen of heaven.

Was I doing wrong in allowing, encouraging even, Bernard to believe that Mary, the mother of Jesus, was happy to manifest herself in our abbey? Such a visitation must speak of heavenly approval. What was approved should not be changed.

Hildegard's Story

Heloise, with guarded face, had told me only that
Bernard now knew I was at the Paraclete and wished to
speak with me. 'Don't mention Eleanor,' she said.
Nothing in her tone or expression gave me reason to
hope. I reminded myself that God was directing me; I
must have faith even when obstacles seemed
insurmountable. God and I could deal with Brother
Bernard. With this thought I entered the room and knelt
holding my hands out in supplication for his blessing.
The floor was cold on my knees, and the early morning
sunshine filtering through the window provided no
comfort. Nor was there warmth or any hint of comfort
in Bernard's greeting. How could a holy man have such
cold eyes?

'God's peace be with you, Sister Hildegard. I was
surprised to learn that you had travelled here. No doubt
it is at the behest of Abbot Kuno that you have
journeyed so far from your own abbey?' as he gestured
me to the chair opposite his own. His tone suggested
that he had doubts aplenty.

'It is God's work which brings me here,' I replied, 'and
most surely in a spirit of obedience. I am but a frail
vessel, the least of God's creatures. As Mary was
directed to visit her cousin Elizabeth, I have followed
the living Light. It led me here, to the Abbess Heloise
who is both pious and wise.'

'Should you not speak rather of the Christmas star
which led the Magi to find Christ in the manger at
Bethlehem?' It was hard to tell from Bernard's voice
whether he was annoyed or amused. There was no sign
yet of the sudden rages to which Eleanor referred. Was
this the moment to express my thanks to him for his

gracious letter and his approval of my writings? To remind him that I was no ordinary nun? It might lead him, instead, to the conclusion that I lacked humility. I yearned to speak openly to Bernard about his letter to the Pope and how it would affect my plan to build my abbey at Bingen; my sense that as long as God was guiding me in wisdom and understanding, I was doing his will. Instead I held my tongue. Bernard, the most powerful man in the Church had opened a door for me. He could, just as easily, close it.

'I too, am just a humble conduit of the Lord, striving to bring the message of his love to his creatures on this earth. My fight against the devil and the world is relentless. It is not my belief that you are the devil's dupe, Mother Hildegard.' Bernard smiled then and I gained courage.

'Father Bernard, your words are wise, pearls beyond price. It is the breath of God that places wisdom in our heart and soul,' I answered.

His face relaxed completely and he turned the full force of his gaze on me, as though suddenly really seeing me for the first time. He was an angel.

'My dear Sister, you speak well. Does not Wisdom call, and does not understanding raise her voice? Good men and women take her instruction instead of silver, and her knowledge rather than fine gold,' he said.

'When the Lord established the heavens and the earth, Wisdom was there beside him, like a master worker,' I continued.

'And was daily his delight,' responded Bernard, completing the quotation. 'Mother Hildegard, I had been concerned that you may have been led into pride and ambition. God bestows his gifts on the humblest of creatures, but even they must pay a price for those gifts.

Now that we have had this opportunity to meet I no longer believe that there is any conflict between us.' As he spoke he stood and took a step towards the door. I followed, and was ushered back into the corridor even before I realised that I had been dismissed. I had no chance to ask him about Heloise's letter, or his plans to place me behind four strong walls and silence my writing and music.

In reporting later to Heloise, I feared that we had no real reason to hope.

'But he did not actually mention his advice to the Pope, did he?' Heloise asked. 'Did he speak of my letter? Did he compliment you on your beautiful hymn?'

'Not as you express it. Am I reading too much into his words? If my head would stop pounding I could think with clarity. As it is I'm buffeted about by doubts, worries, fears for the future, yet still I do not want to lose all hope. He did not talk of the fish, or having spent the night in pain. Nor did he refer to the beautiful singing of my three angels or heavenly visions. Heloise, let's go to the chapel and pray.'

'He did speak to me of hearing angels singing and the visitation from a celestial creature who gave him comfort,' Heloise whispered as we walked towards the chapel. 'I do wish Eleanor hadn't come here.'

'Bernard is speaking with Eleanor now. I think that prayer is all we can do at this moment.'

We walked to the chapel, glancing at the door of the meeting room as we went. What was Eleanor saying to Bernard? What was he saying to her? If the walls and door had not been so thick the temptation to stay there and eavesdrop would have been almost impossible to resist.

In the chapel I pleaded with God to listen to my prayer. Then I looked at the picture of Mary, which hung on the wall near the altar. Was it a trick of the light, a flickering candle, or did she begin to smile?

Eleanor's Story

Bernard has such an obsession about being humble, so I
wore the dark blue woollen dress, a simple dark veil
and no jewellery. Not a glint of gold about me. My
pregnancy showed in that dress, and I hoped this would
also show that I had God's approval. Even Bernard
would respect that. Adele tied my hair back, and tried to
subdue the curls. Otherwise Bernard would forget my
baby bulge and be confirmed again in his opinion that I
was frivolous and vain. A few ringlets can do untold
damage. In the end I hoped that the woman who
presented herself to Bernard was the personification of
a sober, pious matron. Oddly enough I was no longer
afraid of him.

Bernard, standing away from the window and shaded
from the light, seemed almost embarrassed to see me.
Did he really believe that it was Mary and not I who
had bathed his face in cool rose water and offered him
words of consolation in his distress? Heloise had
warned me that this was so, and urged that I say nothing
to change that belief. Was that honest? Was it not better
to let him know that it had been his earthly Queen who
had eased his discomfort? This was no more than I had
done to wounded soldiers during the crusade, although
Odo de Deuil had not seen fit to report on that amidst
the criticisms of my entourage and baggage. I had many
reasons to feel resentment but such an emotion would
be unproductive. Better to take opportunities when they
are offered, and not burden myself with umbrage. Louis
never forgot a slight, and this had so often worked to
his detriment.

 I knew that Bernard of Clairvaux had criticised me,
claiming that I was a bad influence on Louis. My critic

having returned to his chair, sat with a straight back and stern expression, hands folded in the sleeves of his habit and faced me. I waited for him to speak. After a long silence, he did.

'I was surprised, at first, to learn that you were here, my lady, but on reflection it occurred to me that the Holy Father had recommended a time of prayer and penance as well as wise guidance which the Abbess Heloise could offer.'

'The Holy Father gave me much good advice,' I agreed.

'And you are with child, I see,' Bernard continued.

'God has granted this blessing to you and the King. Perhaps I was hasty in my judgement, deciding that your influence on him was not for the good. Now I think that your gentle compassion, that which a mother shows her child, or a wife to her spouse, may have saved him from even greater indiscretions and excesses than his majesty has already demonstrated.'

'The King wishes only to please God and to rule his people wisely, but, at times, he shows an excess of zeal,' I said, thinking to myself that it would be so much easier if I could simply say that the King, while far from stupid, was not fitted to be the leader of an army or the ruler of a kingdom. He would have made a capable abbot. I, on the other hand, born to a line of dukes and soldiers, could have extended the lands ruled from Paris threefold by now had anyone listened to my advice. Would explaining this to Bernard spare me incarceration? I thought not. I tried a different approach.

'I have long feared that our marriage was not pleasing to God. Louis and I are closely related, perhaps too closely connected, and have unwittingly offended both the Church and God.'

'I, too, have thought that possible,' replied Bernard.
'By your fruits shall ye know them – and if the fruit of
your union is a son and heir, then we may see that as
God's love and acceptance.'

I sat as far away from Bernard as was possible in that
small room, hoping that he might not connect me with
his midnight visitor. Could he still believe that it had
been a vision from heaven?

'God sends us messages in many ways,' I probed.
'Mary was told by an angel that she was to be the
mother of the Messiah.'

'Mary was asked if she would accept this honour,'
corrected Bernard. 'At times God asks something of us
which might seem very difficult, impossible almost, but
we must agree, out of our love for him, and he will give
us strength to bear any burden. Have you ever thought
of retiring to an abbey, my lady, if this was for the good
of the kingdom? And your soul,' he added.

'I would follow any course of action that God desired
of me,' I replied, 'but how can we know his will? My
father entrusted Aquitaine to me. The inhabitants of
those lands have sworn their allegiance, and until I have
a male heir I could never desert my people. Didn't they
support me during the crusade, and fight valiantly? My
place, alas, is in the world, just as Louis was called
from St Denis at his father's behest, to rule France.
There are times when our duties and our desires do not
coincide.'

'So you do not intend to retire to this abbey?'

'One day I will retire to an abbey, not here, but in
Fontevraud, where Abbess Heloise's mother was the
first prioress. May I ask for your prayers, Father
Bernard, to give me strength to meet all that life offers
with courage and integrity.'

Bernard acceded to my request gladly, saying again that he had indeed misjudged me, and in doing so may have misjudged all women. God, he said, had created both men and women and each had a place in his kingdom.

'I came to the Paraclete because I was concerned at the stories I had heard. I find three wise and reflective women, and my fears have been allayed. When two or three are gathered in God's name then the Lord is present also. It's now time to take my leave and continue his work.'

I burned to ask him what he saw as his work for the Lord. Did he intend to travel to Rome to deliver the accursed letter to the Pope? I also wished to ask his opinion on the status of women whose marriages were annulled, to clarify the position, but to do so was to admit too much knowledge. It was better to cease negotiations while in a neutral position. Besides, who knew what Bernard was really thinking? Was all this talk of God's plans and women's part in it just a blind to deceive us until he had achieved his *fait accompli*? Through our smiles and farewells I reserved the right to distrust the man.

Heloise and Hildegard were in the chapel, singing psalms and responses. I felt too tired to either join them or speak with them. Instead I returned to my cell, took off my shoes, curled up on the tiny bed and covered myself with the rough woollen blanket. All so different to the palace to which I must return tomorrow. Would I rather stay here, and spend the rest of my days in prayer? I knew enough of abbey life to realise that our free congress would not be able to continue indefinitely. This meant that I would not be given the consolation and stimulation of Heloise's conversation and Hildegard's guidance. Hildegard and Elizabeth were also leaving on the morrow, with Volmar, so life at the Paraclete would drift back to the normal activities, muffled in silence. St Benedict saw no end of evil in idle chatter and laughter, and who knows, maybe he was right. Put a group of people, all of the same gender, in a restricted environment, deny them the normal pleasures of life such as sexual passion, an appetising meal or merry music and who knows what irritations might lead to violent disputes. I knew that if I were forced to embrace the monastic life it would be a living death. Heloise had learned to cope through her writing and study. The pleasure that I, Eleanor, Queen of France, had derived from my visit to the Paraclete and Bernard's apparent newly acquired respect for me was no more than a temporary reprieve, insufficient to deflect me from my purpose. That purpose was to improve my life and might well include a vigorous young man with laughing eyes.

Heloise has the last word

Hildegard and Eleanor were in the gatehouse, where it had all begun. I could sense rather than see their anxious faces as they watched me farewell our illustrious guest, the Abbot of Clairvaux. No matter how they strained they could never hear what he was saying to me, and that was a shame for his last words gave me hope.

'I have always believed that women represented a danger to the immortal souls of men and as a consequence the souls of women were also in danger. The story of Adam and Eve is always before us. Your letter, however, has given me cause for thought. As I read it I heard the voices of angels, voices resembling the sweet sounds of young women. And what of those women who remain in the world? May they not wield a softening influence on their husbands? Could it have been spiritual pride that led me to believe that women lack the same moral strength and intellectual integrity which has been granted by Almighty God to men? I asked myself this question. I trust in God that I have found the correct answer.'

I stood outside the abbey gate as he and his brother companions rode away. When they reached the fork in the road I held my breath. Which way would they turn? Would they go south towards Rome, or to the east, to Clairvaux? The three figures paused, appeared to confer, then they turned east. I had an almost uncontrollable urge to sit by the side of the road and cry or laugh with relief. Instead I hurried back to the others.

'The problem,' Eleanor was saying as I joined them 'is that we couldn't ask about his letter in case he asked us how we knew about it. He wouldn't refer to the letter in case we knew nothing about it. We have hope, not certainty.'

'How much certainty can we ever have in this transient life? Didn't he say anything at all to you about the letter he has written?' replied Hildegard.

'Nothing. What did he say to you?' replied Eleanor.

'Nothing specific, although he did seem to hint. My fear is that I'm being too confident, but I do have some hope we've succeeded.' Hildegard sat with her hands clasped before her, fingers tensed. Yet her face was serene.

Eleanor moved across to the window as though she could find the answer outside.

'If we didn't think like that, we would build our houses on a foundation of sand,' continued Hildegard.

Eleanor's response was an impatient hmmph.

'Let us not disagree with each other on our last day together. Heloise may have good news for us,' Hildegard persisted.

'Bernard's last words to me were that he had come to believe that women could be a good influence in the world. He had taken notice of my letter, he said.'

'No mention of Eve leading mankind to original sin?' said Eleanor.

'Eve was not forgotten in the approbation and euphoria, but she did not dominate. He made mention also of angels who sang with the voices of young women and wives who have a gentling influence on their husbands Much can be said for a well-prepared meal of fresh fish and beautiful music,' I said.

'And an inspired and inspirational letter,' said Hildegard.

'To say nothing of the soothing effect of rosewater and a heavenly vision,' added Eleanor.

'Can you tell us, Heloise, what did Bernard say to you about his letter?'

'Nothing. But he must surely have understood what had prompted my letter. He would have guessed that I had heard of what he was proposing, at least. More likely he believed that somehow I had seen a copy of what he had written. He, more than anyone, understands how letters and news are passed along. So the subject of his letter was not broached directly. Despite this,' and I paused, enjoying the effect, 'we may say we have been victorious.'

Suddenly we were quiet, full of joy, while still shaken by the thought of what might have been. Hildegard closed her eyes for a moment and her lips moved in silent thanks. Then she said aloud, 'I was lacking in faith to have doubted. Yet, how hard it is to maintain trust in God when the powerful men of the Church seem against us. I will treasure the memory of our time together. Perhaps you could both visit me at Bingen, when the new abbey is established.'

'Would that it were possible,' I said, 'but I don't have your energy to travel along rivers and over mountains. Once I did, when I was with child, but that was a lifetime ago. Be content with knowing that you are both in my thoughts and prayers. As it is, I can scarcely believe that we've been rescued from the chains of suppression and constant surveillance.'

'We were not rescued. We saved ourselves. Never forget that, ladies. I should be totally elated but the way I feel now,' said Eleanor 'puts me in mind of soldiers after a battle, even when they are victorious. All their energies subside and they sit drinking by the fire, checking their booty and remembering the dead.'

Hildegard, ever practical, explained that it was the humours regrouping after such a concentration of emotion. Now they were freed from one fear, but had other battles to consider.

'Do you, a holy woman who is close to God, think in terms of battle?' asked Eleanor.

'The devil is never quiescent. There are enemies within and without the Church, and I need constantly to put God's word before them.'

Eleanor smiled at me, murmuring something about Hildegard being a poor humble weak female, but I frowned and shook my head. On this final day there was to be no dissension between us.

Eleanor suddenly stood up. 'There is another explanation. That letter I brought to you; the letter which caused us so much heartache and distress, was not written by Bernard. He made no reference to its contents to any of us. Did he even indicate that he believed all religious women should be strictly enclosed, or that women whose marriages were annulled should enter an abbey? I really believe that his purpose in visiting the Paraclete was to find out why I was here,' she said.

'What are you saying? That is such nonsense. Bernard wrote that letter. We saw it with our own eyes. Or, if he didn't write it, tell me who did?' asked Hildegard.

'How do I know! How will we ever know?' replied Eleanor.

'Of course he wrote the letter,' I said. 'This is the premise upon which we acted. We could not have been so wrong. Or could we? The letter read as Bernard would write, but his name was not on it. It's possible could have been written by another monk, or by the cardinal whose servant sold the letter to Adele. Was he the same secretary who whispered about it to Volmar? Eleanor and Hildegard, think about it. Is it possible we were afraid for nothing?' I said this in a rush, then I sat down, as my legs no longer wished to support me.

Hildegard, in reply gesticulated, unable to form any words. She was incapable of responding because she was doubled up, tears pouring down her cheeks.

Eleanor and I infected by her laughter, began to laugh aloud with unholy glee, until I waved at them to stop, fearing that our amusement would be heard even in as far away as the abbey. What would the holy Benedict make of that!

'We can thank Bernard, or whoever it was who wrote the letter because it brought us together for a time. God does work in very mysterious ways,' said Eleanor. More subdued, we talked of where we might be in a year's time. That was easy for me to answer, as I had no intention of going anywhere. My life was at the Paraclete continuing what Abelard and I had begun. 'When I die I shall be buried with him, and we shall be reunited in heaven. Until that blessed day I continue my work here, never forgetting my love for Abelard, but loving and serving God as best I can.'

'It is strange, and wonderful, to hear an abbess speak of a great love for a man. Your story will be immortal, Heloise, told whenever stories of lovers are recounted,' said Eleanor. 'Louis and I will never be remembered as great lovers. My future with him is uncertain. A girl child will not quell the discontent of those who have influence at court. I don't intend to spend the rest of my life being tolerated at best, or totally shunned. As for where I'll be next year, nothing would please me more

than to return to Poitiers, and rule Aquitaine with
the help of a lusty husband.'
She looked at us both, with mischief in her smile. 'Does
this shock you, Abbess Hildegard?'
Hildegard said that, far from shocked, she approved. If
two people chose to marry before God they were
permitted to enjoy the pleasures of the marriage bed for
the purposes of procreation. She had her plans and she
expected within the year to be presiding over her own
abbey at Bingen, with her beloved sisters, especially
Richardis and with Volmar as their spiritual guide.
'Then, my dear Abbess Heloise and your Majesty, I
will follow whatever path God, through the living
Light, directs.'
Although we had begun the process of distancing
ourselves from each other it was with a genuine sense
of loss that we finally said goodbye. Hildegard,
Elizabeth and Volmar, a humble trio, travelling steadily
until there was no sign of them at all.
Eleanor, no longer needing to hide her identity, left in
style, dressed regally, attended by knights and servants.
Adele wept as she mounted her horse, until Eleanor
sharply told her to stop snivelling.
From the gatehouse I watched until Eleanor, turning
towards the road for Paris, had disappeared from view.
I would never forget our time together. We had all
promised to record in writing all that had happened, and
it would make interesting reading.
I returned to the chapel, knelt by the tomb of Abelard,
and offered thanks to God for the gifts of love, of
friendship and of wisdom.
Since his death my conversations with Abelard usually
took place sitting under our tree, but special topics were
reserved for the shelter of his tomb.

'Hildegard's returning to found a new abbey.

Eleanor's returning to have a baby and then arrange for a new husband. I remain here with much still to do. My most noble and dearly beloved teacher, did we outmanoeuvre the holy Abbot of Clairvaux? I whispered. 'There was a letter. That is knowledge. We believed it was by Bernard. That is an opinion. That we succeeded is our confident hope.'

I knelt back on my heels for some minutes, considering the problem.

'Perhaps Bernard did write the letter, but confronted by my arguments, Hildegard's heavenly music, and Eleanor wearing the Virgin's apparel, down to golden slippers and soothing rosewater, he had a change of heart. Did the vixens outwit the fox?' I whispered, 'Or were we fighting against spectres which had no substance?'

Silence covered the chapel like a cloak. The sisters were about their tasks, in the garden, the scriptorium, or the infirmary. I placed my head against the cool stone, closing my eyes, feeling simultaneously serene, and lacerated with longing to see him again.

'Then again, it could have been the fish,' I said as I stood up, ready to go and attend to my duties.

From somewhere behind me came a familiar sound. Was it his laughter, sonorous, spontaneous, delighted merriment? Was it the wind curling and coiling through pillars? No matter. I made reply to my one and only love.

'Well may you laugh,' I said. 'If it hadn't been for you I wouldn't have had a problem in the first place. Do you agree? If not, then we will dispute it when next we meet!'

END

CPSIA information can be obtained at www.ICGtesting.com
Printed in the USA
BVOW03s0458080813

328043BV00001BA/4/P